ACADEMY X

ACADEMY X

A Novel by

Andrew Trees

BLOOMSBURY

Published by Bloomsbury Publishing, New York and London
Distributed to the trade by Holtzbrinck Publishers

All papers used by Bloomsbury Publishing are natural, recyclable products made from wood grown in well-managed forests. The manufacturing processes conform to the environmental regulations of the country of origin.

Library of Congress Cataloging-in-Publication Data

Trees, Andrew S.
    Academy X : a novel / Andrew S. Trees.—1st U.S. ed.
        p. cm.
    ISBN-13: 978-1-59691-177-2 (hardcover)
    ISBN-10: 1-59691-177-8 (hardcover)
    1. English teachers—Fiction. 2. High school teachers—Fiction. 3. Private schools—Fiction. 4. Rich people—Fiction. 5. New York (N.Y.)—Fiction.
I. Title.

PS3620.R444A65 2006
813'.6—dc22

                                                              2005032384

First U.S. Edition 2006

1 3 5 7 9 10 8 6 4 2

Typeset by Westchester Book Group
Printed in the United States of America by Quebecor World Fairfield

For Heesun

BRAVE NEW WORLD

Whether I shall turn out to be the hero of this story, these pages must show. Well, actually, I think it is safe to say that I'm no hero. Not that I aspire to rescue kittens from burning buildings or anything like that. I want to be the kind of hero Jane Austen would create—a gentleman, in possession of a good fortune, handsome, in need of a wife, and with lots of lovely young ladies offering to roast my chestnuts. I am in need of a wife, particularly if you ask my mother, but it is hard to make that into a heroic virtue. And when people see me, I don't remind them of Colin Firth or Ewan McGregor or even Hugh Grant.

I wish I could tell you that I lived in a world like Austen's, a world of winsome ladies in low-cut bodices attending balls at elegant country estates or taking the waters at Bath and talking of, I don't know, Michelangelo. But Austen's world and my world, the world of Academy X, don't share much in common. To mix literary allusions, my world is a place through the looking glass, an ethical wonderland in which up is down, and right is wrong. Where it is not who you are but who you know, not what you do but what you have. It is a place where a powerful Wall Street broker is willing to manipulate the stock market on behalf of people still using sippy cups, so I think it is safe to say that it is a world where things have gone awry.

I am part of an elaborate system designed to ensure that children end up in the right nursery school so that they can attend the right elementary school so that they can gain entrance to the high school Ivy League so that they can win admission to the actual Ivy League. What happens after that seems to be superfluous. And the pressure only grows as the children get older, until you find yourself face to face with a student or, worse, a parent who believes that changing the B+ you have just given to an A— will somehow be the difference between Harvard and South Dakota Community College. People kill over such things. Well, maybe I'm exaggerating. I don't really know anyone who was killed over it (although there are rumors that Hoffa's disappearance was related to a botched preschool assignment). And this book isn't a murder mystery, just a tale of sex and deceit and betrayal on a scale so vast that it changed the lives of millions. Okay, to be completely truthful, there isn't that much sex. And it didn't change the lives of very many people. But it did threaten the well-being of someone particularly near and dear to me—namely, myself.

I taught English at Academy X for several years. I guess I still do, although my position has been a little precarious lately. You are probably wondering about Academy X—where it is located, what sort of school it is, all that sort of thing. As for appearance, the school's only distinguishing architectural feature is a monstrous Gothic bell tower that has never been opened during my years there as a teacher. And as for location, let's just say that it's in New York City to avoid adding further complications to my life. I apologize for being vague. Specificity, I'm always telling my students. Don't tell me Jay Gatsby is a little weird. Show me precisely where his weirdness lies. As for general reputations, Academy X is for brains. Dalton is for jocks. Brearley is for artsy types. And so on. But those differences are merely for the uninitiated. If you have to ask what sort of a school Academy X is, that question already reveals you as an outsider. You may be rich enough. Or your child may be smart enough to gain admittance. But you will be marked.

You see, there are a dizzying array of sociological and cultural considerations that determine which children end up at which schools. The choices were pretty simple where I grew up. If you were what used to be known as gifted before that term became problematic (these days every child is supposed to be gifted in some way), you took calculus. If you were slow, you took shop. But things are not so simple here for children—or for parents, many of whom treat the education of their children as a competitive sport. There are wheels within wheels, options, variations, subdivisions, niches, exceptions, and countless nuances.

I can only tell you the basics. For example, are you from the Upper East Side or the Upper West Side?—although the division marked by the green expanse of Central Park matters less than it used to since the children of the sixties became Wall Street types and decided that they could sacrifice a little propriety on the east side for a little more funk on the west side. Religion still counts here, although not in the mushy way of Protestant denominationalism. Harder, deeper divisions. Jew or Gentile. The problem is that these categories quickly subdivide, creating added complexities. Are you a practicing Jew, proud of your cultural heritage, perhaps even Orthodox? Or a self-hating Jew who does everything but hide the menorah behind the couch?

Most important, of course, is the question of money. How much you have. And how old it is. Love may make the world go round, but in New York the axis it turns on is money. Obviously, it is great if your money is old enough that various cultural institutions around the city have a painting, a room, or perhaps even an entire building named after one of your forefathers. A family portrait from last Christmas will impress only your aunt Millie. But a family portrait from at least three generations back shows an admirable grip on the top rung of society. A home in the Hamptons is good. A compound on Martha's Vineyard is better. However old your money is, though, try to make sure that it looks old. I once had an extremely rich and obnoxious student who liked to rant against the gilt-edged, faux patina of Louis XIV furniture as revealing the gauche pretensions of the bourgeoisie. He also didn't shower very often, which I took as an aristocratic disdain for that other bourgeois concern, cleanliness. He ended up going to Harvard, where his family already had their names on a number of buildings, including at least one, I hoped, with good bathing facilities.

There are schools that specialize in old money Wasps and others for new money Wasps who would like to appear to be old money Wasps and schools for assimilated Jews and others for nonassimilated Jews. And even a subset of unbearably polished all-girls schools, such as Spence (think Gwyneth Paltrow, an alumna, in *Emma*), places of such refinement that only the oldest money goes there, so old that the Jewish and Wasp divide no longer seems to apply, as if all rich families from far enough back come from a kind of monetary Adam and Eve. And for those who can't fight their way into one of the top schools, there are schools like—well, in the words of my nonshowering student, the schools that are not quite the right schools are legion.

At Academy X, Jews and Gentiles break bread together—new money Jews and Gentiles, that is. Money that is a little brasher, a little showier, a little louder. Bling bling, rather than Brahmin. Parents stand a little too close and speak a little too loudly. That is, in part, what Academy X is for, to smooth off the rough edges until the children have the well-modulated tones that will raise no eyebrows in the boardrooms and clubhouses of the city. But if you don't know that already, that says everything about you, at least as far as certain people are concerned.

This is a story about those few who don't have to ask. It is a peculiarly New York sort of story in that it takes a common problem—getting into college—and manages to throw vastly more money, more attention, and more worry at it than most people spend on actually going to college. Needless to say, a somewhat painful process is transformed into a complete train wreck, which can be fun to watch—unless, of course, you happen to be on the train.

4

GREAT EXPECTATIONS

We had reached the final few weeks of the year when everyone, even the most die-hard teacher, was ready to call it quits. I am not the most die-hard of teachers, so I was especially ready. Which is not to say that I don't love to teach. In fact, I am still surprised each year by how much affection I develop for many of my students and how sad I feel when they graduate. But it was tough to sustain much enthusiasm in the melting heat of this particular May.

All four of my classes were hopelessly adrift. My ninth grade class on world literature had become stranded in the land of the lotus-eaters. One of my tenth grade sections begged me daily to spend the final weeks studying the cultural significance of *American Idol*—"cultural significance" apparently revolving mainly around which contestant was the hottest with an active side discussion about just how much junk in the trunk qualified as too much. My other tenth grade section was still slogging through *Huck Finn*. If the pace of our progress was any indication, Huck and Jim were paddling up the Mississippi, rather than down it.

The class that really broke my heart, though, was my senior spring elective on the novels of Jane Austen. Given teenagers' hyperactive interest in the other sex, I had thought Austen's world, although a bit quaint, would be familiar and interesting. But the class had not worked out as planned, since nearly every senior was mired in a profound senior slump.

I should have known better. Teaching seniors in the spring was always a dicey proposition, and most teachers planned accordingly. My fellow English teachers were finishing the year with hard-hitting courses like "Teen Romance and the Films of the '50s: Beyond Heavy Petting," "Guys and Guns," and "The Culture of Comic Books." Suggesting that seniors read not just one novel but several was spectacularly stupid, although it did mean that my class consisted of a very manageable seven students.

Two of the four girls, Rebecca and Ally, were obsessed with Colin Firth. I had to keep reminding them to use the names of the characters in the books, not the names of the actors who played them.

There were three boys, all of whom took the class in order to stare at the girls for forty-five minutes. Marcus Lipschitz was the biggest nerd in the school, an undersized senior with an overdeveloped fondness for computers and Dungeons & Dragons—even the nerds thought he was a nerd. His presence incited the most mild students to elaborate classroom pranks. It was a little like having a class hamster who kept escaping his cage. His questions were usually thinly veiled attempts to understand the high school dating scene, which remained terra incognita for him. He somehow had become convinced that Austen would show him how to get a girlfriend. Like Moses, he seemed likely to wander in the desert for a long, long time. It would have helped if his Dungeons & Dragons wizard name—Goldorf—hadn't been sewn in bright red letters on his backpack. He explained to me one time how this name was based on Old English and was a sign of respect from his fellow players. Unfortunately, he did this in front of other students who have since shown great ingenuity in coming up with various nicknames based on Goldorf, nicknames that did not owe much to Old English but that did show a detailed knowledge of male and female anatomy. I took solace from the fact that

Marcus was off to MIT in the fall, where he could at last nest safely among his own kind.

I had come to think of the two other boys, David and Jacob, as the two dwarves Sleepy and Grumpy. Both were part of a growing trend at Academy X, the learning disabled. The big advantage of being LD was extra time—twice the time to take all of your tests, including, most importantly, the SATs. The Educational Testing Service, gatekeeper to the promised land, had decided to stop reporting which students received extra time, setting off a mad rush by students to have themselves classified as learning disabled. All it took was several thousand dollars and compliant testers. In the past few years, almost one third of the school had developed some sort of learning disability. Considering that roughly half the students at Academy X went to an Ivy League school, one way of looking at it was as an inspiring story of kids overcoming their handicap to achieve success. I myself wouldn't have minded being designated learning disabled if that allowed me to take twice as long to return papers.

Even students who weren't labeled learning disabled were usually working some angle. So many parents were willing to let their children call in sick on days when they were supposed to take tests or hand in papers that it often seemed as if the plague swept the school at the end of each trimester. And it was an open secret that, in addition to the usual recreational drug use, many students took drugs to boost their academic performance. The lucky ones had Ritalin prescriptions, but it wasn't too difficult to find a friend who could provide one of the variety of pills that helped you to concentrate better for a test or stay up all night to finish a paper. If you thought ahead, you could even buy them at a discounted rate at the end of the school year when many students sold off their stash. And for many of the girls, the pills had the added benefit of acting as an appetite suppressant, thus killing two birds with one stone. Given the almost crushing pressure that most of them felt to get into an elite college, I felt more sympathy than indignation and considered myself lucky that Jolt soda (all the sugar and twice the caffeine of ordinary soda!) was the only performance-enhancing drug that people turned to when I was in high school.

David sat as far away from me as possible with a baseball cap pulled down on his forehead. He had a vacant stare that was almost Zenlike, the result of an apparently bottomless supply of high-quality marijuana. When I worriedly mentioned this to one of the guidance counselors, he laughed and told me about a poll in the student newspaper in which more than half of the students admitted getting stoned on a regular basis (many of those doing it frequently at school). He added that the numbers were probably a little low because most of the heavy stoners never realized that a poll was being taken. On the plus side, students smoking a lot of pot generally drank less liquor, resulting in fewer emergency room visits because of alcohol poisoning.

Even with the most charitable grading, Jacob should have been flunking the class. He didn't read the novels. He didn't watch the films. Generally, he didn't even know the characters' names. In one essay about Bath, he misunderstood and wrote a long essay about personal hygiene and the superiority of a shower to a bath. In another essay, he seemed to be under the impression that Elizabeth's parents had died in a car crash, despite the fact that the horseless carriage would not be invented for several decades. Although he had a similarly undistinguished record in his other classes, he was on his way to Duke in the fall—thanks to a large donation from his parents—at least as long as he passed all of his senior classes. I kept threatening to fail him, but he and I both knew that it was an empty threat. His mother was on the Board of Trustees and was notorious for waylaying Jacob's teachers to impress upon them just how hard Jacob was working.

There were two students, though, who still made me look forward to the class, Caitlyn Brie and Laura Sturding. They had a similar look, and once I made the mistake of saying so. After that, Caitlyn began finding ways to drop casual remarks about their differences. Caitlyn purchased her items from stores in NoLita and paid at least fifty times what Laura paid from her careful weekend perusals at the outlet malls in New Jersey. Both were attractive and slim, although Caitlyn's six-hundred-dollar haircut and three-hundred-dollar high-lights from Sally Hershberger's salon gave her a glamorous, tousled look. They represented the two poles of the school, the difference between those who had to ask and those who didn't. No matter how hard Laura tried, she could never quite move from the outside to the inside. Her effort alone disqualified her.

Their manners could not have been more different. Caitlyn glided effortlessly through school, an easy grace infusing all that she did, while Laura tackled everything from clothing to a test with the same determined, relentless approach. And Laura's reward was to live perma-nently on the outskirts. She generated no great warmth, no immod-erate affection, although I was something of an exception. I had feelings for her that bordered on idolatrous because she had proven to be the only one who could be counted on to do all of her reading on time. To her credit, Laura accepted her fate without a murmur. Her only response was to continue to pursue her goals with even more determination like some modern-day Jane Eyre—serious, resource-ful, and indomitable.

Caitlyn Brie was supposed to be my Emma. She was handsome, clever, and rich, with a comfortable home and happy disposition. She seemed to unite some of the best blessings of existence; and had lived eighteen years in the world with very little to distress or vex her. I liked to imagine her as Emma to my Knightley—not as some dirty old man lusting after one of his students, as some of you are probably thinking. As a kind of mentor, someone who would teach her to be a little less haughty and a little more humane. I have to admit that she was incredibly attractive. In my defense, though, it was difficult not to notice her appearance since her outfits generally fell somewhere between skimpy and obscene.

I had instituted severe measures to keep my libido firmly on the straight and narrow. I usually walked around the class during discussions, but I had stopped doing that because each day I was confronted with another of Caitlyn's wispy thongs—at least on the days that she decided to wear any underwear at all. And whenever she spoke in class, I directed my gaze a foot above her head, which happened to be where I had hung a poster of Freud, a useful visual chastisement for any wayward impulses. In my own mind, I had a chaste and high-minded view of the relationship. I believed that I, like Knightley, could transform Caitlyn into the person she was supposed to be. If the hint of an untoward thought crept out of the shadows, I boxed its ears and sent it scurrying back to the dark recesses of my mind. As it turned out, I was watching the wrong shadows entirely, but that's a later part of the story.

Caitlyn wasn't the smartest student I had ever had, although she was clever and sophisticated beyond her years. But when she smiled at me, I felt bathed in a warm radiance. Like Laura, I had always been one of those on the outside, someone who had to ask. And when someone like Caitlyn chose to smile at you, it was as if you had magically been transformed into one of those who didn't have to ask. Of course, I also had an uneasy suspicion that the warm radiance might turn fatally hot if I ever gave her any reason to lose that smile.

As I walked to the classroom on a muggy May day with a dog-eared copy of *Emma* under my arm, I made a silent vow that we would end the trimester on a high note. We were reading my favorite novel, and with a little luck, it was not too late to kindle a love of Austen in some of them. Do not go gentle into that good night, I thought.

When I entered, the students were already glassy-eyed. For some mysterious reason, the air-conditioning had stopped working in my classroom that week, and the room had the hot, languid air of a Graham Greene novel. The school was newly renovated—adding value to the customer's experience, according to the words of our esteemed Head—but the air-conditioning apparently only had two settings, arctic and tropical. Everyone was already slumped in his or her chair in various states of undress. Ally had rolled the sleeves of her shirt up and rolled her shorts down well below her navel. Rebecca was slowly rubbing herself, as if she was applying suntan lotion. I felt a spiky, prickly sensation across my neck and started sweating. Only David was oblivious, sitting with the same blank expression that he had on every other occasion. A slightly fetid smell pervaded the room because Jacob, along with all of his lacrosse teammates, had decided to express team solidarity today by wearing his lacrosse gloves and cradling his stick as he went from class to class. Unfortunately, a season's worth of sweat had been stored in those gloves, which were filling the room with their invisible miasma, an apt symbol for what Jacob generally did to my class.

I slammed my book loudly on the seminar table and was pleased to see everyone stir in their seats. Even David's eyes flickered briefly.

"Today, we are going to begin reading one of the great works of English literature," I said.

A couple of students groaned.

"And we are privileged to be reading it!" I continued. "That's right. Privileged. I know we are near the end of the year. I know you are tired. But this is a chance to learn something not just about an important book but about yourselves. To learn how to be a good person, how to lead a good life. Important lessons. Real life lessons. So, let's not throw away this opportunity. Let's make these last few weeks of school meaningful."

I gave them what I hoped was a confident, invigorating look, and I was pleased to note that only a couple of students rolled their eyes.

"I can't believe the school year isn't over." Rebecca yawned. After Rebecca had been accepted at Smith College, she had disappeared with a mysterious illness for a week and had come back looking suspiciously tan.

"Let's try to see that as an opportunity, not as a burden," I said.

"Green Mountain School got out last week," chimed in Ally. She was going to Wesleyan on the strength of her aptitude for the arts. When she had landed the lead in the school musical this past year, her parents had hired a voice coach, a dance coach, and an acting coach. Then, they had hired a professional filmmaker to put together a video package, which they distributed to various colleges. When Wesleyan showed interest, her parents signed on as donors to the school's new arts building, and the admissions committee decided that Ally was a very promising student.

"Green Mountain School—I had a friend who went there one year," Jacob said wistfully.

"Yeah, me too," said Ally.

I sat down and waited. I had learned long ago that it was impossible to dispel the mystique of Green Mountain with its short school year, no grades, and "self-directed" study—a utopian paradise, according to all of the students. Of course, it was also the resting place for wealthy New York students who had succumbed to stress, the current euphemism for an out-of-control drug problem. And as none of my students ever actually admitted, students at the Green Mountain School had already resigned themselves to the very great tragedy of not attending an Ivy League school or even one of the Seven Sisters. I was snapped out of my reverie when I noticed a bare foot with exquisite toenails parked in the lap of Jacob.

A MasterCard commercial formed in my mind:

Pedicure at Bliss Spa: $90

Gucci flip-flops: $135

Chance to show off your feet by sticking your toes into your
classmate's crotch: priceless

"Ally, please take your foot out of Jacob's lap," I said.

Ally was infamous for being caught in compromising positions in various spots all over campus. Her nickname among her fellow students was Always Available Ally, although some senior boys knew her affectionately as All Too Easy Ally. But her parents were as generous with the school as they were with Wesleyan, so the deans continued to classify her various escapades as "growing pains," although growing pleasures seemed like a more apt description.

"Ally, please give me both of your flip-flops," I said.

"But, Mr. Spencer, I was just showing Jacob my new toe ring."

"Ally, your flip-flops."

Grudgingly, she handed them over. I placed them on a bookshelf by the door. Ally looked at me sullenly.

"For each intelligent comment you make in this class, you can have one flip-flop back. So, you need to come up with two things in the next forty-five minutes if you want to have your shoes for the rest of the day."

"But, Mr. Spencer, I just had a pedicure."

"Well, I suggest you start thinking about what you are going to say," I said.

"It was only my foot," she protested.

"Actually many cultures make a fetish out of women's feet and think they are highly erotic," said Marcus. The fact that Marcus said this made Ally immediately feel intense revulsion for all things involving feet, and she curled up in her chair with a look of disgust.

"All right, back to *Emma*," I said hopefully.

Jacob began an elaborate routine with his lacrosse stick.

"Jacob." I sighed.

"What? I wasn't doing anything."

"How about leaving the lacrosse stick alone for the rest of class?" I asked.

He gave me a defiant look. The last time we had had a test of wills like this, I had thrown him out of class, only to be called into one of the dean's offices later to be berated for "stifling the creativity" of the little blighter and, in case I had missed the point, reminded that his mother served on the Board of Trustees' faculty compensation committee.

"You know why he wants to hold on to his stick," said Caitlyn.

Everyone stared at her, hanging on her next word. Jacob had already been the victim of more than one of Caitlyn's observations and looked nervous.

"Freud would say that it stemmed from a feeling of inadequacy. You know," she said, looking innocently at Jacob, "wanting to hold a big stick because you don't quite measure up."

A couple of students giggled. Jacob stared uncomprehendingly for a few seconds and then blushed. He placed the stick quietly under the table and looked at me with hatred.

"I'm sorry to interrupt," Caitlyn said, bestowing one of her radiant smiles on me.

"Okay, let's get started," I said.

Caitlyn stretched her arms above her head and managed to make her top, which was already verging on the theoretical, nearly disappear altogether. I pretended to have something caught in my eye, while the students looked at me expectantly.

"Um, right, right, Austen, let's see," I said. "Before we begin anything new today, why don't we clear up some lingering confusion over *Pride and Prejudice*? One of you wrote an essay suggesting that Elizabeth's problems were due to the death of her parents."

"Her parents weren't dead," said Ally, laughing.

Jacob turned a deeper shade of red.

"Very good, Ally," I said. "You have already earned back one flip-flop."

"Her problem was that Colin Firth was a stuck-up jerk," she continued.

It was going to be a long class.

14

THE ART OF WAR

As I left the classroom, the bounce in my step was somewhat deflated by the parent-teacher conference that awaited me, a meeting that usually fell under the heading, "Why isn't my child getting a better grade?" Nothing stirred my heart more than some good give-and-take between parents and myself to improve the lot of their child. And there were some wonderful parents who somehow remained immune to the insanity of the college process. Unfortunately, those were almost never the parents who came in for a meeting. Adding to my difficulty, all the simplest and most honest answers to the problems students generally had—things like, your child isn't very bright and doesn't work hard—were strictly off-limits. The result was a sickly specimen of conversation in which subtext had rudely shoved text into detention.

Most parents at a place like Academy X were, to put it bluntly, a high maintenance bunch. Many of them went on an annual safari bagging and tagging their children's teachers, until they had pried the last home phone number, the last cell phone number, and the last get-away-from-it-all vacation number from the damp and quivering fingertips of their prey. And if all else failed, a parent could always stalk the teacher on the school grounds. When parents ended their meetings by asking teachers to make sure that their children were doing their homework at night, it hardly seemed worth the trouble to point out that the parents were the ones in charge of their children's lives at home.

My spirits sank at the thought of another meeting with Bart Vern about his daughter, Andrea. In previous meetings, he had questioned my intelligence, my competence as a teacher, and my masculinity all in the service of moving his daughter from a B+ to an A−.

By this point in my teaching career, I graded by a few set principles: Reward the virtuous (students who worked hard got a little boost). Do not punish the wicked (any negative variance with the actual grades caused far too many problems). And never give a trustee's child a grade lower than a B− (a policy that I had instituted after a minor disaster my first year).

The same grades always caused problems. Not failing grades because even the parents recognized that a failing grade could hardly be attributed to the teacher, especially when the student had three, four, or even five failing grades to match it. C+ students sometimes raised a fuss, although usually those students had such obvious problems that it made it difficult for parents to mount a credible attack. By far the most troublesome grade was a B+. Because B+ students were close to the promised land. A steady diet of As and A−s at Academy X was generally enough to get you into an Ivy. Maybe not one of the big three but somewhere. The difficulty with the B+ student was that he offered none of the obvious flaws that allowed me to defend myself. A B+ student was a pretty good student. The differences between a B+ and an A− were subtle distinctions—the quality of writing, the sophistication of the analysis—and angry parents were rarely interested in subtle distinctions. Worst of all, the most obnoxious behaviors of B+ students were considered virtues by their parents. What I thought of as grade grubbing, the parents saw as ambition. What I saw as a lack of intellectual curiosity, the parents saw as efficiency.

What Vern was doing was all too common. Symptomatic, I believe doctors would call it. If you listened carefully, you could hear a

slight whooshing sound throughout Academy X—the sound generated by thousands upon thousands of tiny inflations going on during
any particular week in the school year. It began before students were
even accepted. With far too many students applying for far too few
spaces, parents and highly paid parental advisers made the rounds to
various nursery school admissions offices, Gullivers in the Land of
Lilliputians, visiting classrooms and sitting in chairs that caused severe
cramping in anyone more than four feet tall. They were there to
convince an admission's officer that their child's finger painting displayed a color sensibility reminiscent of Rothko or that their child's
tantrum was a sign of leadership qualities. Once this pattern was es-
tablished, it was difficult to break. By the time the students reached
high school, everyone was well trained.

Many teachers at Academy X played the game. Some recommended poorly performing students to their colleagues for tutoring
at one hundred dollars or more an hour and then found remarkable
levels of improvement in their work. Others gave all As, unless a student was really awful and insulted the teacher, in which case he or
she was punished with an A–. These teachers were then rewarded
with awards, endowed chairs, yearbook dedications, not to mention a
whole array of end-of-the-year "gifts" from grateful parents—box
seats to ball games, weekends in the Hamptons—the list was limited
only by the ethical code of the teacher, which is to say that it was
hardly limited at all. Those who did not play the game were warned
or threatened in a variety of ways—perhaps a meeting with a dean to
remind the teacher of a student's "special needs" or a letter from a
parent on the legal stationery of the parent's firm warning vaguely of
"further action." And if a student found himself with a poor grade
and an unsympathetic teacher, he or she could always turn to a dean
or even the Head. In one case, a teacher accused a student of having
a paper written by a tutor, only to find that the Dean of Students
himself had done the writing.

The whole system was geared toward a constant adjustment

upward, a New York version of Garrison Keillor's Lake Woebegone where all children were above average. When the school gave out prizes at the end of the year, a virtual army of students stood in line to receive them. It took the sort of persistent lack of effort that was itself an achievement to stay off the awards platform.

As I left my classroom and walked toward my office, I saw Vern or, as I thought of him, the Verninator. Vern was a short, heavyset man with a pinched face and greasy black hair, which gave him an unfortunate resemblance to a rat. His hair swirled around the top of his head in an elaborate comb-over. He wore a double-breasted suit that made him look like a double-wide in lamb's wool. I forced my face into a position approximating a grin.

"Mr. Vern, so good to see you," I said, offering my hand.

Subtext: I loathe you with a passion I usually reserve for people who molest children.

"Hello, John," replied Vern coolly.

Subtext: I can call you by your first name because you are the hired help. You make about as much as my cleaning woman.

"Why don't you wait in the conference room? I'll be right in."

Subtext: Are you ever forced to wait for your cleaning woman?

I showed him into the conference room—to be more accurate, it was the James Dixon Conference Room according to the plaque by the door. And my classroom was actually the Grimes and Philbrick Classroom. And my office, all fifty-four square feet of it, was the Paul Pennyfeather Room. Corporate and parental largesse had helped fund the building program (as had the evisceration of the faculty medical plan), and donor plaques dotted the buildings like a commemorative plague. Even stairwells had been named after someone or something. It was only a matter of time before some poor donor agreed to place his name above a urinal.

In fact, the development office put out a packet listing the various "naming" opportunities still available. For only one million dollars you could slap your John Hancock on the "history complex." I knew a number of history teachers who had complexes—one refused to teach on days when it rained, and another only bathed on a seasonal schedule—but it was difficult to imagine how a few offices and classrooms at one end of the hallway constituted a "complex." For those looking for immortality on a budget, there was the possibility of naming a seat in the auditorium for one thousand dollars, no extra charge for the gum that came with the seat.

While Vern waited, I went to my office. It was so narrow that I could touch both walls at the same time, but it did have a thin sliver of window that overlooked the street. I checked my voicemail. The only message was from weeks ago when Amy had called about an overdue book. She had a breathy, sexy voice, and I listened to the message when I needed to relax. I found it had a soothing effect.

I entered the conference room feeling a good deal calmer. I sat down without saying anything. I had read somewhere that it was a sign of weakness to make the first move. Vern must have read something similar, so we sat in silence for an uncomfortably long time. I began to feel a little hot, then very hot.

"So, what can I do for you?" I blurted out.

Subtext: I am so pathetic.

Vern allowed another uncomfortable silence to develop.

"I think you know why I am here. Andrea is not entirely happy with how the class is going."

Subtext: Andrea wants a higher grade.

"Shouldn't Andrea be the one to discuss that with me?"

Subtext: Your overinvolved parenting is going to put Andrea in therapy for years.

Vern glanced at me contemptuously.

"The grade you have given her is simply unacceptable," Vern said.

Subtext: The grade I had given her was unacceptable.

I wasn't sure how to respond to that last remark, so I said nothing. Unfortunately, Vern saw this as indifference.

"Do you know how much I give to this school?"

Subtext: I have paid far more than just tuition, and that buys me special consideration.

"Mr. Vern, tuition payments aren't really a relevant—"

Subtext: I'm going to pretend I don't understand you because to do otherwise would be intolerable.

"Not tuition, you fool. Last year alone, I gave one hundred thousand dollars to the capital campaign drive, and I expect some . . . return on my investment."

Subtext: I expect some return on my investment.

It was always a bad sign when the subtext became the text. I was somewhat appalled that his daughter had been redefined as an appreciating asset and also unhappy to learn that Vern was a major donor. I heard the Head's voice in the back of my head: the customer is king.

"Mr. Vern, that still does not have any bearing on Andrea's grade," I said weakly.

Subtext: If only I had known earlier . . .

"I've looked over her grades from the last trimester, and it is clear to me that you are not being fair to Andrea," said Vern.

Subtext: Fairness=A/A−=Ivy League. Unfairness=B+=University of Wisconsin.

I was, let us face facts, a trifle cavalier about my grading, perhaps at times even a touch whimsical. In my defense, I would like to point out that if you had read forty-five straight essays on Huck's moral progress or Macbeth's character flaw, your attention might wander as well. So, the idea that the grade I had given was somewhat shy of a bull's eye was an unfortunate possibility, enough so that most students knew how to ply my softer side and get me to reconsider a grade. To cave into parental bullying was an entirely different matter, though, so I tried to work up some self-righteous anger.

"Mr. Vern, I have been a teacher here for many years. I think I am a better judge than you or your daughter about how to grade her assignments," I said in a tone that I hoped at least approximated indignation.

Subtext: I don't have a clue. Grading is largely subjective. In this postmodern age, who can say where the truth lies?

"Well, her tutor has been a teacher for twenty years, and he agrees with me!"

Subtext: Why can't you behave like the other people I pay and give me the answers that I want?

St. Jude had at last decided to answer my prayers, even though my only association with Catholicism was dating Mary O'Malley in high school, a relationship that had not once necessitated the slightest need for confession. Andrea's last paper had been far too well written, and when I had asked her if she had received any outside help, she had smiled the smile of the pure of heart and said no.

"How long has Andrea been working with this tutor?" I asked.

"What the hell does that have to do with anything," demanded Vern.

"Perhaps he does not have a sense of the standards I have been applying all year."

"That's ridiculous. He has been working with her since October."

I had to stifle a smile.

"Mr. Vern, in the first place, I hardly think that someone who is paid more than one hundred dollars an hour to tutor your daughter is an objective judge. More importantly, I am afraid that what you have said raises a far more serious issue."

"What are you talking about?"

"I questioned your daughter earlier this trimester about whether she received any outside help, and she denied it. Now, I find out that she has a tutor. As you can imagine, this is a very serious matter."

Vern shifted uncomfortably in his chair.

"I have to consider whether to bring this matter before the disciplinary committee," I continued. "Offenses of this sort are taken very seriously and become part of a student's permanent record."

"But tutors are allowed! Everyone uses them," pleaded Vern.

"Yes, tutors are allowed, but lying about tutors is not allowed. It shows an intent to deceive."

"I'm sure Andrea didn't lie to you."

"I find it hard to believe that she could forget she has been working with a tutor since October."

"But, Mr. Spencer, I don't see . . ."

"Mr. Vern, I think we need to end this meeting while I consider what to do."

I stood up. Vern followed unsteadily.

"I'll be in touch," I said.

I left the room and walked to the faculty bathroom. After locking the door, I enjoyed a silent Indian warrior dance that only ended after I nearly fell in the toilet. I would never bring this matter before the deans, a group who scarcely had a full spine to share among them. Only recently, a student had copied most of his paper from the Internet, a second offense, and had received an "in school" suspension, a punishment that consisted solely of not being able to leave school grounds for lunch.

Through the years, students had developed a variety of excuses for academic dishonesty that the deans were happy to accept. In this case, the student had said that he hadn't known that the same rules about plagiarism applied to the Internet—or what I liked to call the technology defense. Learning disabled students had it even easier. They simply claimed that plagiarism was too abstract a concept for them to understand. And if standard defenses weren't available, there were always personalized options. In one case, parents defended their child by arguing that he suffered brain damage when he fell out of a jungle gym as a child and that his sense of right and wrong was impaired. Leniency was in keeping with the philosophy of the school— let no revenue stream be interrupted. I didn't care, though. I would never contact Vern about the matter, and Vern would be too cowed to contact me. Hasta la vista to the Verninator.

I walked back to my office triumphant and found Günter Rottingham waiting for me. He was one of the stars of the school—editor of the student paper, class officer, all-around brilliant student, and former boyfriend of Caitlyn. He was off to Harvard in the fall. He followed me nonchalantly into the room and lounged in a chair. Günter and I were supposedly doing an independent study on Victorian literature. Both of Günter's parents were professors of literature (his mother, or *mater* as he liked to call her, was a great fan of Günter Grass, hence the name), and Günter knew more about the books we were reading than I did. Günter was too refined to allude to that fact, and he spent the tutorials teaching me a good deal about how things at Academy X actually worked. He found my innocence amusing and had taken to calling me Candide when we were alone.

"I see you had a little chat with the Verninator," he said, smiling.

I reminded myself for the countless time to stop discussing private matters with Günter. After each slip, I always vowed to be more discreet in the future, but he offered me such good advice that it was difficult not to tell him about my problems.

"I don't know why you don't just give her the A−," he said. "You know, it doesn't really hurt anyone. At worst, it is a victimless crime. And if there is a victim in all of this, it is not Andrea."

He gave me a knowing look.

"Am I right, Candide?"

I sighed.

"Besides, at some point, this quaint moral rectitude is going to get you into trouble."

"But if I just give a student whatever he or she wants, it undermines the whole system. What about those students who actually deserve an A−?"

Günter snorted.

"Besides, she probably cheated on her last paper," I said.

"Are you kidding me?"

I felt vindicated by his reaction, even as I cursed myself for yet again breaking my vow about discretion.

"Cheating? You are worried about cheating?"

I felt a little less vindicated.

"Oh, my *pauvre* Candide," he continued. "You are sweet, but you are being even more quixotic than usual. Do you realize how rampant cheating is here? Don't take my word for it. The school newspaper ran a poll that is coming out next week. More than half the class admitted cheating—and we are talking about a group of people who have shown a willingness to deceive, so the actual number is probably higher. You are like the Dutch boy with his finger in the dike."

"Have you ever cheated?" I asked.

"Please, as if I need to cheat," he said contemptuously.

"So, why would you assume that everyone else is cheating?" I asked.

"It's the whole culture," replied Günter. "Everyone games the system. You have to admit that it is hard to resist with the Internet putting it all at your fingertips. And don't think it's just papers written at home. Students use their cell phones to instant message notes to each other during tests. And we haven't even talked about the economic element."

I groaned—Günter never tired of his hobbyhorse, Marxist theory. One time, he spent an hour trying to convince me that Austen could be explained entirely by dialectical materialism.

"It's true," he said. "Wealthy children avoid all the messy problems of the usual forms of cheating and hire tutors, who are certainly not going to become witnesses for the prosecution."

I knew all of this, of course, but it was far easier to pretend that I didn't. And if that made me Candide, so be it, because a certain cultivated naïveté made my job much easier. I had decided early on that I would be a better teacher if I assumed that all of my students were still innocent children, despite ample evidence to the contrary. What good would it do me or them if I became some crabbed, bitter

24

disciplinarian constantly trying to trip them up? And on the matter of childhood innocence, I had no less an authority than Rousseau on my side. Of course, his ideas helped contribute to the slaughter of the French Revolution, but I tried not to think about that. Even if they weren't as innocent as I liked to pretend, I saw them more as victims than victimizers, products of a system that fostered a ruthless pursuit of success. Günter knew how I felt and delighted in confronting me with precisely those things that I tried to ignore. And as it turned out, my willful ignorance would come with a cost, but I didn't know that then.

"You can hardly blame the students, though," he continued, smiling at my discomfort. "Most high school students cheat on a regular basis. And you can't expect our students to give up that kind of competitive advantage to other students, especially when there is a high correlation between wealth and cheating, a kind of *droit du seigneur*. The fact that only half our students admitted to cheating, well below the national average, is a moral victory of sorts."

I should have responded with some feigned outrage, but I was too impressed that an eighteen-year-old could use *droit du seigneur* in an ordinary sentence. Günter smiled at me.

"Now, can we talk about how Dickens's *Hard Times* actually reinforces the industrial system that it claims to be criticizing?"

"Only if you promise that nothing you say came from the Internet."

"No, my parents were arguing about it at dinner."

We ended the conversation amicably after I accused Günter of approaching the novel with all of the humanity of Gradgrind, and he described my teaching methods as worthy of M'Choakumchild.

THE RAW AND THE COOKED

After my meeting with Günter, I strolled down to the faculty dining room ready to take a good whack at the feeding trough only to find myself faced with the prospect of "Tacos Supreme!!!" The three exclamation points were a depressing attempt to supply grammatically what the food lacked in the more crucial area of taste. As I liked to tell my students, anything of superior quality in their writing should be apparent without a !!! to tip me off. The "Tacos Supreme!!!" inverted the usual meat-to-grease ratio, so that the shells turned a luminous red and went from crispy to soggy before they reached my plate. The toppings did provide some excitement for the adventurous. Browning lettuce and limp green peppers were the usual fare, but anything left over from the week before was fair game, including one notable occasion when beets and rhubarb had somehow been salsafied.

To add insult to injury, we had to walk past the students eating their meals before reaching the faculty dining room. To increase "customer satisfaction," the school had turned the student cafeteria into a food court that included sushi and a pizza oven. Since teachers were not revenue enhancers, we were confined to the faculty side and what was known as the hot lunch option, a choice that had been known to make even stout-hearted men tremble.

After receiving a particularly oleaginous plateful, I reached for the picante sauce, which looked suspiciously like doctored ketchup, when my hand collided with another hand, a soft, creamy, well-moisturized, manicured hand that sent a tingle down my spine. The hand was attached to an equally soft and creamy Amy Grancourt, a long-legged, blond-haired gazelle recently hired to work in the library. She had all the qualities that I looked for in a woman. Her hygiene was exemplary. She shaved her legs and her armpits. And she did not have a mustache (which distinguished her from more female teachers than you would think). I had, as my students would have said, a mad crush on her.

Truth be told, my efforts to woo her had not been crowned with much success. I would have compared her smile to a summer's day, only she had yet to bestow said smile on me. Not that I felt at all put out by this. Any ordinary woman could say hello and be polite. To keep up her reserve, despite my charm juggernaut, revealed her to be a woman of taste and distinction.

"Hello," I said, rather pleased with my opening gambit—polite, articulate, and even somewhat alluring, given the throaty quality I managed to give it because a carrot that I had shoved into my mouth had become lodged in my throat.

"Hello," she replied coldly. But not, I thought, quite as coldly as usual. Almost an imperceptible warming. I smiled inwardly.

"I see you stayed away from the Tacos Supreme!!!" I said in a strained voice—it was difficult to know what tone would imply three exclamation points.

"I don't eat meat."

I didn't really eat many vegetables, and I had a momentary pang that this was a sign of incompatibility. But when I stopped to consider that my last girlfriend had initially claimed that she didn't date men who earned less than six figures, the meat/vegetable divide seemed like a minor obstacle.

"Well, nothing to stop you there," said I, "there's really very little meat in it. More like meat by-product."

I smiled warmly. I had already blurred the dividing line between us. The neutral look on her face curdled into disgust, and I worried that her dislike of meat extended to meat-related humor.

"Not that there is anything wrong with meat by-product," I babbled. "Some of my favorite snacks are meat by-products. Take a Slim Jim, for example. Looks like meat. Tastes like meat. And almost no meat in it. You can actually buy them in the hardware store."

A slight quiver shook her frame.

"Yes," I said, desperately trying to find a way out, "as far from a cow as . . . as . . ."

I searched for the mot juste to rescue the situation.

"As you."

Had I just complimented her? Insulted her? Both?

"You're getting slime on yourself," said Amy, turning away.

I looked down and saw that the grease had spilled over the edge of the plate and the tray to trickle down my pants. After a frantic and ineffectual cleanup, I joined my friends Ron, a science teacher, and Kate, an art teacher, at their table.

Ron hadn't had a relationship with a woman since Watson and Crick had discovered the double helix. He had all sorts of evolutionary theories about why this was the case, but the simple truth was that he always smelled faintly of formaldehyde, lived with his mother, and tended to wear the clothes that you would imagine a high school science teacher wearing. He was a large, somewhat hairy man with a mustache, which he mistakenly believed made him look like Tom Selleck.

Kate, on the other hand, was long and slender. Sadly, she believed that any effort to enhance her beauty was allowing herself to be, as she put it, "colonized by the male gaze." Her own art tended toward the vaginal in a vague way. She and I had had a fling during our first year, which had ended disastrously owing to my somewhat complicated romantic entanglements at the time. Both of us pretended that it had never happened for the sake of our friendship.

Kate smiled wryly at my sodden arrival.

"Ron, you see what happens when you talk to strange women," Kate said.

Ron emitted something between a grunt and a groan.

"She's not strange," I said.

"To resist your charms for so long, I call that strange, unbelievable even," said Kate.

"At least he has a woman that he is pursuing," Ron said. "The last woman that I had a year-long relationship of any sort with was my dry cleaner. And I haven't been able to go back there since I asked her out."

"Ron, when are you going to realize that a good dry cleaner is more valuable than a girlfriend?" Kate asked.

"You should never have offered to martinize her pillows," I said.

"It's not funny," said Ron.

"And John isn't pursuing. He is being rejected," Kate said.

"I am not being rejected," I said. "I am simply laying the foundation."

Kate looked at me as if I was insane.

"You know, according to studies, men have sexual thoughts every seven point five seconds," said Ron.

"Not me," I said defensively. "I'm a mature adult. I think about literature and politics and things."

Actually, I thought about sex all the time, although most of my sexual thoughts tended to be of the despairing kind, generally about how I was possibly never going to have sex again. Sometimes I even fantasized about a mail-order bride from Asia. But then I worried that she would learn the language, think I was a schmuck, and run off with the mailman. Perhaps a Russian bride? But did I really want to marry a woman named Olga who could drink me under the table and beat me at arm wrestling? No, it showed more dignity simply to cling to my despairing thoughts every 7.5 seconds, thank you very much.

Ron began playing with an empty Gatorade bottle.

"Need to rehydrate after full-contact biology today?" I asked.

He placed the bottle in front of me.

"Look at it."

I glanced at it.

"Yes?"

"No, really look."

I leaned over to give it a closer inspection, and after a few moments I saw what he was talking about. The inside of the label, the part glued to the bottle, was covered with notes about biology.

"You can't be serious."

Ron nodded glumly.

"And the worst part is, I don't think he was the only one. There were a bunch of other students who brought drinks to an earlier class. The only reason I caught him was that he was dumb enough to finish the drink and keep staring at the bottle."

THROUGH THE LOOKING GLASS

The three exclamation points on my day were whittled down after lunch when I visited the college counseling department, a place I always tried to avoid. I felt much as early peasants did when they entered a cathedral. Faced with an all-powerful and inscrutable God, I hoped to propitiate the deity and leave before hellfire and brimstone rained down on me.

Parents were willing to swallow the school's price tag of twenty-seven thousand dollars because of the yearly results of the college counseling department, which placed, on average, half of the senior class in an Ivy League college. While most high schools struggled to place one student a year in a place like Harvard or Yale, Academy X often sent ten or more students to one of those schools.

In a simpler age, the department had been called the college admissions department, but the school had changed the name after a disgruntled parent had sued the school on the grounds that the name implied an ability to get students admitted to college. This parent's child, who had been caught cheating on two different occasions and had flunked at least one course a year since ninth grade, had been rejected from twenty-seven different schools. The suit was dropped after the student was admitted to a university following a generous donation from the parent (matched by the parent's corporation). The school decided to avoid any future confusion by taking *admissions* out of the name. And then a few years ago, the college counseling department was rechristened the Throckbottom College Counseling Department after a multimillion-dollar donation from grateful parents when their child, whose only distinction was an unending appetite for drugs and alcohol, gained admission to an Ivy League school. Both feats were engineered by the same man, Phil Snopes, the legendary head of the department, who was rumored to be the highest paid employee at the school.

Snopes always looked a little too slick—and not Armani-suit-and-polished-looks slick, but oily slick. He was a tall, heavy, sweaty man with lank black hair, and he used his size to full effect. He would grab your elbow, invade your space from above, and lean in closer and closer until you finally agreed to do whatever he asked.

In other times and in other professions, he would have been called a fixer. The administration called him simply the money man, a nickname that dated to a presentation that he gave to the school's parents in which he correlated school endowments with admission rates to top colleges and convinced them to open their pocketbooks as never before. The students called him Mr. Ivy or, after a particularly impressive coup, God. And the faculty called him various unprintable names based on his ability to make or break various classes and, thus, various teachers. One teacher had made the mistake of criticizing Snopes at a faculty meeting. The next year, the enrollment in her senior elective dropped from twenty to three. The following year, the enrollment dropped to zero. The year after that, the teacher decided to seek employment elsewhere. All it took from Snopes was the suggestion that a certain class wouldn't look good on a transcript, and the class was doomed.

Despite the all-devouring nature of the college admissions process and the all-seeing eye of the Throckbottom College Counseling Department, I did my best to remain invisible to Snopes and his minions.

"John, good to see you," said Snopes from behind an enormous desk when I entered his office.

"Good to see you, too," I said uncertainly.

"You probably know why I asked you to come in."

"No," I replied.

Snopes smiled at me benevolently, as if he was about to bestow an invitation to a rich banquet.

"John, you don't really know much about what we do here."

"That's true."

"F. Scott Fitzgerald once said that the rich are different than you or me," Snopes said.

"To which Hemingway replied, 'Yes, they have more money.'"

He grimaced.

"Do you know what the best indicator is that a student will go to an Ivy League school? Parental income. You see, wealth buys a number of advantages . . ."

I already knew this, of course, so I didn't pay much attention as he droned on for a while. The advantages that wealth brought were legion—more AP classes, more after-school activities, Japanese rather than plain old Spanish or French, SAT classes, tutors, and on and on. And from Snopes's point of view, teachers were on the list of possible purchases as well.

"You see, John," he continued, "we're in an arms race. Our students used to be virtually guaranteed a spot in the Ivy League, even if their grades weren't particularly good. That has changed in recent years. Not only are far more students applying to these colleges, but the colleges have decided that they want a more . . ."

He paused briefly as he chewed on his next words.

". . . *diverse* student body. To maintain our competitive edge, we have to maximize our advantages."

I had a horrifying vision of Academy X as an academic Soviet Union attempting to bludgeon college admissions committees into submission—or perhaps I should say admission. I thought of those poor boys and girls from Nebraska and South Dakota who were the cold war equivalent of Trinidad and Tobago. And I thought of

33

Academy X parents who had the option to go nuclear by making a strategic donation in the six-, seven-, or eight-figure range, depending on just how glaring the shortcomings of the student were. Frankly, it made me wish I could write a recommendation letter for that poor kid in South Dakota. Wasn't it punishment enough to grow up in South Dakota? I consoled myself with the thought that if I lived in South Dakota, I wouldn't even want to go to school in the Northeast. I'd want to go to a place like the University of Miami, where, according to my imagination, even professors wore bathing suits to class.

"Perhaps most importantly for our purposes, wealthy schools have smaller classes, which means that teachers know students better and can write more personal and heartfelt recommendation letters," he said, giving me a significant look.

I looked back at him blankly. He sighed.

"Caitlyn Brie," said Snopes.

"Great girl."

He looked at me expectantly.

"Great girl," I repeated lamely.

He smiled to himself at my ignorance.

"As you know, Caitlyn has been accepted to Wellesley," he said.

"I know," I said, "I think she will really like it there."

Snopes began drumming his fingers on his mahogany desk.

"Caitlyn doesn't want to go to Wellesley. She thinks she can do better. Her father thinks she can do better. I think she can do better," he said. "She wants to go to Princeton. And I want you to help make that happen."

"I wrote her a very strong letter of recommendation," I replied.

"I know. And everyone appreciates that. I've been on the phone to one of the admissions officers and made . . . certain inquiries. But I need your help."

"Sure," I said without conviction.

"We need another letter, a stronger letter. Something about how

34

you have seen incredible development over the course of the last year. That she is possibly the best English student you have encountered. You know the sort of thing I am looking for."

"I'm happy to talk about what an excellent student she is."

"One of the best. Maybe the very best," he said firmly.

"Well, I don't know about that. I mean, she is very good."

Snopes sighed loudly.

"John, you don't seem to understand," he said with some exasperation. "I need some strong ammunition."

I fidgeted in my chair.

"So you want me to lie?"

"Lie? No, I don't want you to lie. I would never ask that," he said soothingly. He came around from behind the desk and took hold of my elbow. He leaned in as if he was going to embrace me. "I want you to shape the truth a bit, stretch it just a tiny amount. A slight exaggeration perhaps. That's all."

He leaned in closer. I felt a fine spray on my face.

"Teachers do it all the time. Admissions officers expect it. They automatically discount what you are saying, so you have to exaggerate if you are going to get them to see the student honestly. I know some teachers who find a new student or maybe even two or three students each year who are the best students they have ever had. Teachers who know how the system works."

I eyed him suspiciously.

"Teachers who don't know how to play the game, who make life difficult," continued Snopes, leaning in closer still, "well, if you want to be one of those teachers . . ."

He left the thought unfinished. I pushed my chair back and gasped for air.

"I'll think about it."

"Good," he said, smiling. "Why don't you drop the letter off with me before you send it, so I can make sure that it sounds the right note?"

I didn't bother to argue that recommendations were supposed to go straight to the intended school. I couldn't take any more of the Snopes treatment. I turned to leave.

"Oh, by the way, John, are you a basketball fan?" Snopes asked.

"Yes," I replied hesitantly, hoping desperately that I wasn't going to be asked to add that Caitlyn was the best basketball player I had ever seen.

"Good."

I waited for him to say something else, but he turned to the work on his desk as if I had already left the room. I ran into Günter in the hallway.

"What were you doing in there?"

"I don't think you want to know," I said.

"Candide, I already know," he said. "And I just hope you haven't done anything to throw a monkey wrench in the works. You have no idea the lengths that he will go to."

"I think I have some idea."

"May fifth."

"What?"

"May fifth."

I gave him a baffled look.

"I realize that it appears to be a completely insignificant date, although I had hoped that after all of our time together you would at least remember that May fifth was Karl Marx's birthday. It also happens to be the birthday of one of the top admissions officers at a very prestigious university that I am too discreet to name. And every year, on May fifth, he gets a rather extravagant gift from Mr. Ivy. And that's just the tip of the iceberg. Snopes knows personal information that can be turned to advantage on admissions officers at every top school in the country."

"Oh, come on," I said. "You make it sound as if he is head of the KGB."

I had already heard plenty of stories about Snopes's various methods, of course. Infiltration was one of his favorite tactics. Every member of the counseling department used to be an admissions officer at one of the top colleges. And when Snopes couldn't hire someone directly from a school, he would work out a consulting arrangement with their admissions office, hiring one or two people from their staff to come to Academy X over the summer to discuss how to improve the department. The consultants would spend a week going to fancy dinners and Yankees games and then receive a fat check from the school for their trouble. But was Günter suggesting blackmail?

"Just don't get in his way," warned Günter.

ALL THE KING'S MEN

I felt a slight flutter in my digestive organs that afternoon, which was either the result of an ill-advised go at the lunchtime pudding or unease at the upcoming department meeting. I still shuddered when I thought of our last meeting, a two-hour affair when we debated whether the term paper should be five to seven pages or six to eight pages. Consensus was never reached, and we were slated to revisit the issue in June, at which point I planned to develop a mysterious kidney ailment that would necessitate my absence.

I left my office. Caitlyn was waiting for me outside the door.

"Hi, Mr. Spencer," she said. She gave me a warm smile.

"Hello."

I waited for her to speak, but she seemed happy simply to smile.

"Was there something you wanted to talk to me about?"

"I was just wondering if you had talked . . ." She drifted back into silence.

"Yes?"

"Never mind. It's nothing," she said.

"Are you sure?"

She nodded

"All right. I'm off to a meeting," I said, turning away.

She put her hand on my arm to stop me.

"I really love *Emma* so far."

"Good," I said, as I gave her hand a bewildered look and wondered how to remove it, while trying not to notice her low-rider jeans, which were riding very low indeed, so low in fact that they were bumping up against that which even the lowest of low riders was supposed to cover.

"See you tomorrow," she said as she walked away.

As I entered the chair's classroom, I surveyed my colleagues with a familiar sinking sensation. On one side sat Sylvester Johns, a nebbishy character reminiscent of Dickens's Uriah Heep, whose most pronounced trait was unending obsequiousness toward the chair. He was seated next to Edwina Strude, a thin, pinched woman, who believed that the decline in Western civilization could be traced to the failure to use the semicolon properly. Next to her was Dylan O'Brien, whose large, florid face was set off by a mop of white hair. By this point in the afternoon, he had undoubtedly fortified himself with his usual restorative tonics and was falling asleep in his chair.

I sat down with a sigh next to Dakota Andrews, a voluptuous woman with pre-Raphaelite hair, and immediately regretted my choice. Andrews considered it her duty to attend to the emotional needs of her colleagues, and she spent a great deal of time urging everyone to share their feelings. When people refused, Andrews eventually shared her feelings, often accompanied by tears, which then required a further sharing of feeling—a cycle that usually left the victims in a misanthropic state for a number of days.

"John, what's the matter?" Andrews whispered.

I forced my face into an expression of Buddha-like contentment.

"Absolutely nothing."

Andrews raised an eyebrow, but I was saved by the entrance of the department chair, Donald Samson. At seventy, he had become a little long in the tooth, and the students claimed that he sometimes lost his train of thought and stood silently at the blackboard for five minutes at a stretch. Tall with a slight stoop and a well-groomed head of gray hair, Samson thought of himself as the keystone that held the school together. He still resented the fact that he had been passed over for the position of Head of School.

"We'll talk after the meeting," whispered Andrews.

I sank a little lower in my seat.

"All right, everyone, let's get this meeting started," said Samson. "The first order of business is the Button Turbridge Student Essay Prize. Edwina, Dakota, and John will once again be selecting the winner."

I cursed under my breath for allowing myself to be roped onto the committee.

"I like to think that the excellence of the entries reveals the fine job that we are doing as a department. And I like to think, if I may say so, that the policies that I have instituted have contributed their small part to this success," Samson remarked. Most department meetings were largely taken up by Samson discussing the wonderful job he was doing, seconded at regular intervals by Johns. "My stewardship has always been marked by—"

O'Brien jerked awake with something between a loud snort and a hiccup. We all stared at him as he wiped some spittle from his chin. Samson frowned at the interruption. Johns bowed at Samson.

"You were commenting, Donald, on the department, which I have to say is running with its usual high efficiency. I hope you don't mind my saying so," simpered Johns, bowing again. "I feel an enormous debt of gratitude for being allowed to serve under your tutelage."

"Thank you, Sylvester. Not that I like to compliment myself, but I am tremendously pleased with how I have—"

Before he had a chance to work up a full head of steam, Strude interrupted him.

"I am still concerned that we need to increase the amount of time we spend on grammar," she said. "And I'm not just talking about split infinitives and run-on sentences. The proper use of the colon and the semicolon, not to mention the comma, the ability to handle the subjunctive . . ."

I sank even lower in my seat and prepared myself for another long department meeting. I spent most of it trying to think of how to escape Andrews. A change in tone brought me back to attention.

"There is one last item that I want to discuss," Samson said. "As you know, I have been thinking about retiring for the last couple of years."

Samson's hobbyhorse. He had talked of retiring for years, believing that we would appreciate him more if we thought he was leaving. I had come to assume that the only way he was departing was in a box and that his final breaths would be spent in one last fervent avowal of the magnificent job that he had done.

"I have decided that next year will be my final year," he continued. "I have spoken to the Head about this, and we have decided that the department should try to agree on a new chair by the end of the year, so that he or she can work alongside me to learn the ropes. So, please give some thought to whom you would like as your chair. I will canvass all of you informally over the next couple of days."

He stood up and left. Even O'Brien had been shocked out of his stupor. Everyone had developed a calculating squint and was trading shifty glances with one another. The extra money alone would have been incentive enough, but the post had so many added benefits: a reduced course load, the choice of what classes to teach, the best schedule, and the ability to make life miserable for your enemies.

Sensing a window of opportunity to rid myself of Andrews, I stood up and moved quickly toward the door. Just as my hand reached the knob, Andrews called out to me.

"John, wait for me!"

I wedged myself into a corner of the hallway. If I could hold the position, there was a small chance I would not want to kick a dog later. Andrews attempted to curl her arm around mine, but I pressed myself into the wall as if it would collapse without my support. The other teachers followed behind her and scurried to their offices. Somehow, while I was distracted by this movement, she managed to get her hand around my arm and began pulling me toward her class-room with the relentlessness of the grim reaper himself. A voice called out behind me.

"John."

I turned and saw Samson motioning for me to join him in his office.

"So sorry," I said. I wrenched her hand from my arm and hurried down the hallway.

"Don't wait for me," I called over my shoulder. I entered Samson's office and sat down.

"Now, John, I wanted to talk to you about the chair. As you know, I'm quite proud of the direction of the department. In fact, I like to think that my steady stewardship has been a key reason, well, perhaps *the* key reason, why things have gone so well. To be honest . . ."

I groaned inwardly. The interruption at the meeting had left him with pent-up praise for himself, which was now going to be directed at me. My eyes glazed over, and I wondered what was on television that night.

". . . And that is why I think you would make an ideal chair," said Samson suddenly after several minutes of self-congratulation.

If I had been savvier, I would have realized that I was a likely can-didate simply by process of elimination. Johns hadn't been at the school long enough. Andrews had forced her feelings on Samson so often that he had developed a facial tic whenever she approached. O'Brien had insulted Samson on a number of occasions when drunk, most spectacularly at a Christmas party a few years ago when he had placed an ancient Irish curse on Samson that involved a num-ber of very salty references to Samson's mother. And Strude was al-ways correcting Samson's grammar. It took a moment for Samson's comment to penetrate my semicatatonic state.

"Well," I said, churning through my mind to come up with a compliment for him. "To take over for you, it's an honor, although obviously no one will ever be able to fill your shoes once you are gone. It will be a tremendous blow to the school."

"Thank you," said Samson. "So, you agree with the plan I have laid out?"

I had trouble keeping a horrified look off of my face. He had laid out a plan?

"Plan . . . Yes, of course, the plan. So important. Perhaps you have it written down? I could frame it, have it always before me as my guide."

I laughed nervously.

"I don't have it written down!"

He looked at me as if I was a blockhead. I decided to show him that I was not a blockhead, that I was a man of initiative, that I had, as they say, "the vision thing."

"Well, I also have a lot of ideas for things I would like to change," I said. That was, of course, a complete lie. I was happy to see things continue in pretty much the same way. But I thought it sounded good. Samson looked intensely annoyed.

"John, the reason I chose you is because I don't want anything changed," he said icily. "I have not created this department so that some jackass can come along and screw everything up! Now, if you find that too hard to accept, I'm sure that I can find someone else who will not."

My primary job qualification had become plain. A complete lack of interest in all departmental matters turned out to be my main selling point because Samson assumed that my failure to express an opinion in meetings meant that I had no opinions at all.

"No, of course not. You're absolutely right, as always," I replied, trying to walk a fine line between respectful and cringing servility. "The department needs to carry on in your image. Always in your image."

I had visions of myself high atop the Kremlin wall wearing a fur hat and endlessly saluting a mural of Samson. I thought I cut quite a dashing figure in one of those fur hats. Was New York cold enough to justify a hat like that? Were they expensive? I wondered what Amy would think of the hat. Would it impress her? Or would she think it was a ridiculous affectation? I suddenly realized that Samson was giving me an annoyed look.

"Yes, always in your image. What is there to change? The department is run to perfection, thanks to you. Any changes that I make would only be to continue your work."

"No changes," he said petulantly. "No changes. No changes. No changes. Are you clear on this?"

"Yes, of course." At least I knew what the plan was.

"I hope you don't give me any reason to reconsider my decision," he said ominously. "You know how I don't like to do that."

I had never seen him change his mind during my years there. About twenty years ago he had apparently decided to have tenth grade students read *Great Expectations*, instead of *Oliver Twist*. Since then, nothing. It would be a dubious distinction to be the cause of a second change of mind in twenty years.

"No need to reconsider. I'm your man."

"Now, there is one small problem," he said.

Problem? I had just promised to be his man. I was perfectly content to install a lifesized statue of Samson in my office and to genuflect to it daily.

"The Head," he said, rolling the word around his mouth as if it was an unpleasant bit of food, "seems to think that she should have some say in this matter."

He shook his head, unable to believe that someone had actually questioned him about a departmental matter.

"We've compromised," he said, although the word sounded like a curse the way that he spat it out. "She has to approve of my choice. You'll have to meet with her. Ridiculous formality, really."

"No problem."

"Well, in any case, John, I'm glad we see the department the same way. And I'm sure a year by my side will give you a firm grasp of the Samson way, so that after I am gone, you will carry on exactly as if I was here."

I nodded and tried to look suitably worshipful.

He looked like he was ready to begin another panegyric on his efforts as chair, so I stood up and left. Although I had not launched myself with the strongest start, I couldn't help but think that it would be smooth sailing from here.

DECLINE AND FALL

When I left the main building, it was a perfect spring day, the kind that made romantic poets fall in love with the world. I tried to think of some suitably inspiring ode from Wordsworth or Keats, splendor in the grass and all that sort of thing, but couldn't come up with anything better than there once was a man from Nantucket. I liked to think of myself as the sort of chair who would have pearls of poetic wisdom tripping off his tongue more inspiring than an obscene limerick, so I had my work cut out for me. I heard shouts from the athletic field and wandered over to take a look.

The girls' lacrosse team, dressed in the school's colors of green and white, was playing a game, and parents stood clustered on the other side of the field watching their daughters. Caitlyn was out in front of the other girls. She shook off a whack to the shoulder from a beefy defender, grabbed the ball off the ground, and fired it past the goalie. The parents cheered, and her teammates clustered around her and patted her on the back. Later, when the referee wasn't looking, she tripped the defender with her stick and sent her sprawling to the ground. When the referee turned around to see what had happened, Caitlyn smiled at him sweetly and offered a hand to the girl. As she was running past me, she waved, although, after seeing what she had done to the other girl, the gesture seemed slightly menacing.

Günter sidled up to me.

"*Lord of the Flies* would have been a much more brutal novel if the island had been populated by girls rather than boys," he said morosely.

After Caitlyn had broken up with him, Günter had tried, unsuccessfully, to heal his ego with misogynistic theories on female cruelty, but he remained enthralled by Caitlyn, despite his best efforts. As he plaintively told me once, the heart was not a rational organ.

"What are you doing here?" I asked.

"I could ask you the same thing," he said. "Why aren't you standing on the other side with the parents?"

I shrugged.

"Really? I think I see Andrea Vern's mother over there. As well as some other potential trouble spots."

"You can hardly blame me."

"On the contrary, Candide, I think you are beginning to show some signs of development. By the way, did you see what Caitlyn did to that poor girl?"

"Günter, are you stalking her?"

He gave me an offended look.

"I am here in my journalistic capacity, covering the game for the newspaper," he replied haughtily. "The fact that Caitlyn is a member of the team is purely coincidental."

"Shouldn't someone more junior be doing that? You should be doing something lofty. An editorial on the excesses of homework or something."

"That would deny me the opportunity of enjoying this spring day."

"You hate being outdoors. You always tell me that the world of the future will be entirely enclosed and climate-controlled."

"A youthful affectation."

I noticed the school's sensitivity counselor, whose job seemed to consist solely of telling people that they had been insensitive, standing down the sideline from us and busily taking notes on a clipboard. Her major coup that year had been a mandatory middle school assembly on sensitivity and mental health after a number of sixth graders had given out Valentine's Day cards that said they were "crazy for you." She and Andrews were fast friends.

"What's she doing here?" I asked in a lowered voice.

"Apparently, one girl called another girl a fathead at the last game," whispered Günter, "although it is unclear if the girl intended to insult the other's girl intelligence or her weight."

"So, why don't they punish her?" I asked.

"They did," he answered, "but they want to make sure they avoid what happened to Trinity."

That past winter, Trinity students had heckled a Jewish basketball player from Dalton. Genteel heckling, of course. They called a turnover a "Passover." A shot was kosher or not kosher, and a basket by Dalton was cause to "light the menorah." This caused a round of angry letters and even an article in the *New York Times*, which was followed by the usual punishment for privileged children (community service), which was followed by mandatory school meetings on tolerance, which was followed by the feeling on the part of many Jewish students that they would not mind being a little less Jewish.

The half-time whistle blew, and the girls ran over to the sideline.

"Now, if you will excuse me, I have to get some quotes," he said, licking his lips as he looked at Caitlyn.

"Do you really think that is a good idea?"

"Quotes are essential. They give a certain authenticity——"

"I'm not talking about quotes."

"Don't worry yourself, Candide. I have a well-thought-out plan."

"That's what you said when——"

"I think you had better leave. I see Andrea's mother bearing down on our position."

I saw a small, tan, irritable-looking woman hobbling across the field as quickly as her four-inch heels would carry her.

"Thanks," I said, turning and beginning an undignified sprint to the subway, the one place I could be sure never to run into a parent.

"And congratulations on the chair," he called out after me.

I was too busy fleeing the Furies to wonder how Günter knew. Besides, Günter always knew things before anyone else did.

As I rode the subway home, I tried not to gloat. I had always cultivated a low profile. Uneasy lies the head that wears the crown—that was my motto. I wasn't even sure that the Head knew my name. Sure, I had served unmemorably on a couple of committees. And I had helped organize a Fiesta Day for the Spanish students, although a food-poisoning incident had cast a shadow over that foray into civic-mindedness. And then there were my literary failings. I hadn't read all of Shakespeare. I still didn't understand *Ulysses*. I didn't even like Henry James. But now that entirely undistinguished record was being rewarded for the fine achievement that it was. I couldn't help but feel that I was striking a blow for underachievers everywhere.

I got off at my stop and walked to my apartment, a two-bedroom, third-floor walk-up on the Upper West Side. My neighbors to the right and to the left paid about thirty-eight hundred dollars a month in rent, way out of my range. Luckily, a number of big-time real estate brokers sent their children to Academy X. A few years ago, one of them happened to have a child in my class, took a liking to me, and helped put me into a rent-stabilized apartment at a fraction of the going rate. Although I initially had some qualms about the arrangement, I was a good New Yorker and recognized that real estate trumped any ethical concerns. Besides, the broker's child was already doing well in my class, so there was no danger of a quid pro quo, although I was a little overenthusiastic in my college recommendation letter. I consoled myself with the fact that it was an inflationary medium, as Snopes had pointed out.

I dropped my things in the hallway and walked into the living room. My desk was doing a very good impression of the leaning tower of Pisa. My mind began to picture what a department chair's apartment should look like, and I realized that I was going to have to buy some new furniture. Framed photographs of obscure writers. A big, imposing desk. A chair that looked like a throne. Nothing excessive—tastefully grand. The desk was covered with ungraded papers and lesson plans that needed to be finished, but I decided all of that could wait and called my parents to tell them the good news.

"Hello," my mother said into the phone.

"Hi, Mom," I said.

"John, what a pleasant surprise."

"I have some good news."

"Really? You're dating someone."

"No, Mom, I'm going to get a promotion. I'm going to be department chair," I said.

"That's great, John. So, are you dating anyone?"

"Mom!"

"Am I not allowed to ask?"

"Can we just focus on the promotion?"

"You know, Mrs. Vanille's daughter just moved back to Chicago."

"I live in New York!"

"Well, you could come visit us. You could meet her when you are home."

I was too annoyed to argue.

"Will you put Dad on?"

"All right," she said, "but I want you to think about when you are going to visit. I'm going to talk to Mrs. Vanille this week. I will tell her that you are very interested."

She passed the phone to my father before I could protest.

"Hi, John."

"Dad, I'm going to be promoted to department chair."

"That's great. Does it pay a lot more?"

"Yes, a few thousand."

"A few thousand? That's all?"

"Well, there are other benefits."

"You know you could make a lot more doing other things."

"Women like men who make a lot of money," my mother called out.

"What about the Internet? You're a smart guy. You could make that work."

"Dad, the Internet bubble has burst. It's over."

"Your friend Ryan is starting a new Internet company. I'm sure he would hire you."

Ryan—one of the banes of my existence. The guy flunks out of college and takes some low-level job at a no-name company. They pay him peanuts and give him worthless stock options. Then the Internet becomes big. The little-known company turns out to be AOL, and his options are suddenly worth millions. He decides to enjoy his newfound wealth by buying high-quality pot and getting stoned every day. The company gets fed up and fires him. Out of pure spite and against the advice of everyone, he decides to sell all of his stock, saying something about how it will hurt the price because it will show that insiders are selling. When the stock moves higher and against the advice of even more people, he decides to short it—two weeks before the Internet bubble bursts—quadrupling his fortune. Everyone, including my parents, thought he was a genius, even though his main activity continued to be getting stoned. His new "Internet company" seemed to revolve largely around playing video games on his enormous plasma TV.

"Dad, I'm not going to work for Ryan."

"He's very successful," he said.

"He's dating a very nice woman," my mother called out.

"Just think about it," my father suggested.

"Look, I've got to go," I said.

"All right. Let me know if you want me to say something to Ryan."

It was not quite the affirmation that I had been hoping for, so I called Kate and Ron and asked them to meet me at our favorite bar.

It was somewhat seedy and emitted a strange odor on warm nights, but it had the cheapest beer in the area—always an important consideration when you are a teacher. You can be an alcoholic, but you have to do it on a strict budget. The bar had additional attractions for the two of them. The smell of the bar helped cover up the faint aroma of formaldehyde on Ron. And Kate liked the idea of slumming it because her boyfriend was an investment banker, and she always felt guilty about consorting with a capitalist oppressor. They were already most of the way through the first pitcher by the time I arrived.

"All right," said Kate, after I sat down, "what is the urgent piece of news you refused to tell us over the phone?"

"Well, after—"

"Who says we need to have an excuse to meet for a drink?" Ron gave me a broad wink. He tended to get a little loopy after his first beer.

"As I was saying—"

"Have a beer," said Ron. "Wet your whistle before you tell us."

He emptied the pitcher into my glass.

"Looks like we need some more," he said. "Barmaid! Barmaid!"

An annoyed waitress came over.

"Yes?"

"Another pitcher, please."

"Okay."

Ron watched her walk away.

"Attractive woman, huh?" His head nodded unsteadily in the direction of the waitress.

"Oh no you don't," said Kate. "We've been down this road before. We can't go to our favorite brunch place or our favorite coffee shop because of your embarrassment at seeing waitresses there. We can't lose our favorite bar as well."

"What are you talking about? Who said we can't go to those places?" Ron asked.

"You did," said Kate with exasperation.

"That's just silly," Ron said. "Of course we can go there. Now, if you will just let me . . ."

He tried to stand up, but Kate had a tight grip on his sleeve.

"I'll just have a little chat with her when she comes back."

Kate sighed.

"John, you were saying," she said, keeping a firm grip on Ron.

"Samson wants me to replace him as department chair," I said.

"You!" Ron and Kate said in unison, as if I had just told them that I was running for governor of California.

Ron was so stunned that he didn't say a word to the waitress when she brought another pitcher.

"That's wonderful," Kate said unconvincingly. "Congratulations."

"Yes, congratulations," Ron said weakly.

"What? That's it? That's all you're going to say?"

"It's just that . . . Well, you know. There are perhaps a few qualities you lack," she said.

"Very small," added Ron.

"It's not that you would be a terrible chair," Kate said, "but you aren't the most . . . disciplined teacher."

"A bit cavalier," offered Ron.

"And your history at the school . . . there have been some incidents," she said.

"A bit dodgy actually, not the sort of person you would expect to be chair."

"And you don't like your colleagues," she said.

"Hates them. Loathes them. Despises them."

Okay, so I could barely stay awake in meetings, and I avoided my colleagues like the plague. Was that any reason to expect this kind of treatment? The Spencerian bosom was wounded. Grievously wounded. Kate gave me a sympathetic look.

"We're probably just jealous," said Kate.

"Yes, that's right. This definitely is cause for celebration. I think I'll go find our waitress and order some additional libations," said Ron, getting up.

"No," Kate cried out. But she was too late. We watched him weave his way unsteadily toward the bar.

"John, I'm sorry. This is wonderful news," Kate said. "You know, the fact that you never seemed ambitious for this kind of thing is probably a sign that you are going to be a terrific chair."

She leaned over and rubbed my back, and I felt a little better.

"And you have a lot of wonderful qualities as well. Your students love you. You are kind and generous and are the least likely person ever to abuse your position. Not to mention the fact that you are the only person who still speaks to everyone in your department."

Ron reappeared without any beer but with a large wet spot on his pants.

"We need to go," he said sheepishly.

Kate gave him a quizzical look.

"I don't want to talk about it, but we really need to go," he pleaded.

I stood up and put my arm around Ron.

"That's all right. I never liked this place anyway," I said.

THE IMPORTANCE OF BEING EARNEST

I walked bleary-eyed from the subway to my office and, much like Prometheus, felt that an eagle was pecking at my liver all the way. It was only eight A.M., but the heat was already making the sweat run down my back. I had forgotten to pick up my laundry and found myself encased in a pair of blue wool pants, which seemed to thicken with each step. I staggered to the main entrance dreaming of air conditioning and saw Günter looking at me with an amused smile.

"Did we celebrate a little too much last night, Candide?"

"Is your task in life to torment me?"

"No, to educate you, *mon ami*. But don't worry. I'm not here for you. I just enjoy the morning procession."

I looked at the jumble of arriving students and wondered where the procession was hiding.

"I find Tocqueville so illuminating on this, much more than Veblen. Don't you?"

I hoped it was a rhetorical question.

"Only in a country devoted to equality do people pursue status and distinction with so much energy," he continued. "And watching the students arrive is to see the social and economic hierarchy displayed in all its finery."

I tried to look knowing, but I felt too queasy.

"I know you like to pretend that all of this escapes your notice, but denial is hardly a mature response," he said.

He glanced at me quizzically.

"I see that you have made the somewhat strange choice of wool for this humid spring morning. But no matter. Sit down for a moment."

He opened his backpack and pulled out a Gatorade.

"Drink this. It always helps with a hangover."

"Please don't say that, Günter. I like to retain certain illusions about you."

"Sorry. Let me rephrase that. My father claims that it always helps him with his hangovers."

I took a long gulp and felt the iron band around my brain loosen a bit.

"You see, the parental chariot tells you everything you need to know about them, at least in the reductive Marxist sense of class position."

"That reminds me," I said, trying to change the subject, "Don't you still owe me a paper on Marxism and Dickens?"

He gave me a reproachful look. We watched a BMW SUV roll by with its windows rattling from the bass of the stereo.

"A BMW or Mercedes is a pretty obvious statement, wouldn't you say? Of course, there are those students who are driven to school in town cars and limousines. I'm not sure which group should be placed higher. It depends on how you value leisure versus consumption. But I'm more interested in the subtle distinctions. You see those busses over there?"

He pointed at a long line of school busses belching out black exhaust and students.

"Certain busses go to the right neighborhoods, and other busses go to neighborhoods that aren't the right neighborhoods. And it may be too much time spent reading Marx, but I can't help feeling that the students on the right busses look happier. And if that is true, do they always look that way? Or is it that students naturally assume their place in the hierarchy only when they are at school?"

"I think you need a girlfriend," I said.

"I try to help you see what is going on all around you, and this is the thanks I get," complained Günter, getting up and moving to the door.

"Thanks for the Gatorade," I called out to his quickly departing figure. "And don't forget to turn in that paper."

As I was about to enter the building, I noticed Johns arrive. He surreptitiously looked himself over in a car window, smoothing down a lapel (given that he was wearing a rather ill-fitting polyester suit, I wasn't sure what effect he thought he was achieving), and crossed the street, quickening his pace to catch up with the Head. She was dressed in an understated but elegant dress and had the athletic look of someone who grew up on the playing fields of Andover. Her red hair was pulled back, as always, in a tight bun, and her pale face was set in its habitual frown. Johns followed her into a different door of the building, bowing and simpering the entire way.

I walked into school and checked my mailbox. There was a note from the Head asking me to meet her in her office after school. There was also a letter from Snopes, which I was hesitant to look at in my current condition. After another fortifying swig of Gatorade, I ripped it open, and two courtside tickets to the Knicks' play-off game fell into my hand. I was appalled—and thrilled. After holding them reverently for a few moments and fantasizing about how I would befriend Spike Lee, I decided to do the right thing. I imagined various self-righteous ways I could return the tickets, although I knew I would simply give them to his secretary. I tucked the tickets into my pocket and went in search of another Gatorade. By the time my class on Austen rolled around, I felt almost human. I grabbed my copy of *Emma* and walked into the classroom. Although David remained comatose, the rest of the class was bubbling with excitement.

"Mr. Spencer, if the senior class invited you to the prom, you would go, wouldn't you?" Rebecca asked.

I laughed uncomfortably as I remembered the last time I had attended the prom as a faculty member. Luckily, they were too young to remember.

"We will cross that bridge when we come to it," I said. "Now let's turn to *Emma*."

"Actually, the world of the prom and Austen illuminate each other, don't you think, Mr. Spencer?" Caitlyn asked, smiling at me sweetly.

"That's true. Maybe that can be a useful way into the book. Let's see how Austen's world compares to our own."

I walked to the board and grabbed a piece of chalk.

"So, what do all of you want from the prom?"

"To get drunk and hook up," crowed Jacob.

The girls looked at him with such disgust that he bowed his head.

"Would any of you go alone?" I asked.

"No way. I would feel like such a loser," said Ally, whose sexual spelunking had already secured her multiple offers.

"Does the boy always have to be the one to ask?"

"That is such an outdated notion," Laura said. She had already ridiculed the prom on a number of occasions, although her distaste had more to do with her lack of a date than with her feminist principles.

"A girl can't ask a boy," Ally said indignantly.

"And what about Austen?"

"Emma has to wait for Knightley to propose to her," said Laura.

"Ah, this brings us to a central problem for the women in Austen's novel, who are always at the mercy of men, always having to wait for men to make the move," I said. "So, it looks like maybe Austen's world isn't so different from our own."

"Yeah, you can end up without a date for prom," Rebecca said gloomily.

"Or an old maid in Austen's time," added Laura. "She never married."

"That's right," I said.

"I'd be happy to play the passive role," Marcus remarked quietly.

"I don't think that would help you much," Jacob laughed. Marcus reddened.

I frowned at Jacob, and he fell silent.

"So, girls, how does it feel to have to wait?" I asked.

"It's better than having to ask," said Ally. "That would be awful. You don't know what the person would say. You might get rejected."

"No," said Rebecca, "it's awful to have to wait."

She had been waiting for a certain boy to ask her, and with each passing day she became more anxious that he would not.

"Caitlyn, you're awfully quiet. What do you think?" I asked.

"I think that, if you know what you are doing, you can make a boy do anything you want him to," she said, looking at me in the way that a cat might eyeball a canary, "and by boys I mean all men."

The class fell silent, as the boys furtively imagined the things that they would be willing to let her make them do, and the girls wondered how they could learn the same trick.

"Uh, yes, well . . . What other things are part of prom?" I asked.

"Oh, yeah," Ally said, "limousines and stuff like that."

"And what about Austen?"

"There are carriages," said Rebecca.

"Does a carriage mean anything in Austen's world?"

"It's a sign that you are from a certain class," Laura said.

"And what about a limousine?" I asked.

"No, everyone who goes to the prom gets a limousine," said Rebecca. "It doesn't mean anything."

"Not everyone," said Laura.

"Well, it's not like it's a class thing," Rebecca replied.

"Do you know how much a limousine costs?" I asked.

"No," she said, "we just put it on our parents' credit cards."

"Are you sure it might not have some of the same significance as a carriage?" I asked.

"I guess," she said hesitantly.

"There are a lot of other expensive aspects to prom, aren't there?" I asked.

Ally squealed.

"Oh my God, I got the most perfect dress at Bendel's last week. It's strapless and has—"

"But it is so much more than clothes now," Caitlyn said. "There are so many other things we have to do."

"It's true. Manicures, pedicures," Rebecca said.

"Eyebrow waxing," added Ally.

"Or threading—"

"Hair straightening—"

"Facials—"

"Mud baths—"

"Hair extensions—"

"Tanning salons—"

"Spray-on tans—"

"Teeth whitening—"

"Teeth capping—"

"Cosmetic surgery—"

"Yeah, breast enlargements," Jacob said with a smile.

The girls in the class looked at him with revulsion.

"What? They started it," he complained.

"Massages—"

"Eyebrow tinting—"

"Bikini waxes—"

"Full Brazilian bikini waxes—"

"From the J. Sisters!"

Rebecca, Ally, and Caitlyn began laughing hysterically. I had no idea what a full Brazilian bikini wax was or who the J. Sisters were, but I was fairly certain that the classroom was not where I wanted to find out.

"Okay, so you could say that the world of the prom also has a great deal to do with class distinctions," I said. "Let's look—"

"But, Mr. Spencer, that only scratches the surface," said Rebecca. "We haven't even talked about which spas you have to go to. You can't just go anywhere. And what about diets?"

Rebecca looked as if she subsisted on one ounce of yogurt a day.

"Yeah," said Ally, "it's not easy figuring out which diet is right for you. Even little kids have their own diets. I have a five-year-old cousin who is a little porky, and she has her own nutritionist and is in a special yoga class."

She sounded jealous.

"Her mother probably breast-fed her too long," Rebecca said. "My mother said that can make children food-obsessed, so she always stopped feeding me before I was completely full."

Despite my best efforts, we spent very little time discussing *Emma* and a great deal of time learning about the various spa treatments available to New Yorkers with money and time. And many of the students at Academy X had both. Some students' "allowance" consisted of twenty thousand dollars or more deposited in their own checking account at the start of the school year.

After class, Laura followed me back to my office.

"Mr. Spencer, I need to ask a big favor," she said hesitantly.

Laura never asked for anything, not even an extension on her paper when her grandmother died, which meant that, short of committing a felony, I was pretty much prepared to do anything she asked. And I was willing to consider the felony. I also appreciated the fact that, despite being attractive, she never bared anything untoward, even though that undermined her popularity with the senior boys

"You see, I got into Wellesley."

"I know. I think that's wonderful," I said.

I had written her a recommendation letter, and she had told me weeks before about her acceptance. I still felt bad that she hadn't been accepted to her first choice, Dartmouth. Other students with weaker academic records had been admitted, but Laura didn't have any special pull. And the weaker students had had a lot of pull—and a lot of money. I used to feel more outrage about that kind of thing, but I had seen it happen so many times that I had come to accept it as a matter of course.

"I found out the other day about my financial aid package . . ."

She stopped, so I nodded my head encouragingly.

"Well . . . it wasn't quite what I had hoped for."

Laura fell squarely into the worst category for financial aid—the solidly middle class. Too wealthy to qualify for substantial financial aid but not enough to swallow the nearly forty-thousand-dollar yearly price tag without choking on it, especially with a younger brother coming up behind her.

"What can I do?"

"The school has a scholarship fund, but it requires a special letter of recommendation from a teacher."

"I'll be happy to write the letter, Laura."

"There's one other problem . . . You see, I just found out, and the letter is due . . . Well, it's due Monday."

"That won't be a problem."

She gave me a look of relief.

"Mr. Spencer, thank you so much! Really. You don't know . . ."

"Laura," I said, "I'm happy to do this. You don't need to thank me."

"It's just so hard sometimes, you know," she said. "I mean, all these other kids. They don't even think about these things."

She dropped her head to hide the tears in her eyes. Against my better judgment, I rested my hand on her shoulder.

"It's not fair. You and I both know that. But that doesn't mean that we can't do everything in our power to make sure that things work out for you."

62

She looked up at me and gave me a teary smile.

"Okay," she said in a small voice.

We talked for a few minutes about other scholarships she could apply for, and she left looking almost happy.

After she shut the door, I checked my voicemail and was thrilled to hear the honeyed tones of Amy Grancourt telling me that *The Narcissism of the Nipple* was overdue. The book was a dense treatise on the nipple as liberator by a German feminist, which had recently been translated into English. Günter recommended it to me, although I suspect that he liked it because it provided an outlet for his raging hormones after the breakup with Caitlyn. There were disturbing drawings of breasts in the margins in Günter's distinctive handwriting. I found the book incomprehensible and stopped reading it after a few pages.

I grabbed the book, found a somewhat furry-looking breath mint rolling around in one of my drawers, and walked to the library. I spotted Amy alone behind the circulation desk. A group of students was huddled over the computers at the other end of the room where I did not have to worry about them overhearing our conversation.

I sauntered over to her as casually as I could. These visits often threw me off for the rest of the day, as I obsessively examined our conversation for any signs of a budding relationship. I had wasted one entire lunch trying to convince Kate that Amy had stamped my book in a deliberately provocative way.

"Hello, Amy."

She looked up. She was wearing a sleeveless blouse and was lightly tanned. I noticed for the first time a hint of freckles on her forearm and was overcome by a surge of tenderness as I thought of her lying in the sun without adequate sunscreen. And of how I would lovingly cover her entire body with whatever SPF she wanted. Or of how I could walk discreetly beside her holding an umbrella over her head. I began to imagine the dizzying array of heroic, sun-protective things I could do for her.

"Is there something you wanted? Why are you staring at my arm?"

"I . . . I . . . You have to be careful of the sun," I blurted out. "You need someone to protect you. I mean *something*. You need something to protect you. From the sun."

She looked at me as if I had spent a little too much time in the sun myself, although that was a decided improvement over her normal hostility. I forged ahead boldly.

"So, did you do anything interesting this past weekend?"

"I went to a show on Chinese textiles at the Met," she replied coldly.

I could hardly imagine a more crushingly boring exhibit. I had spent most of the weekend watching the NBA play-offs.

"Oh, yes," I said warmly, "I thought that looked interesting. I find textiles fascinating."

"Really?" She raised a skeptical eyebrow. "Most men would find that boring."

I leaned on the table.

"Well, I guess I'm not like most men," I said in what I hoped was a manly and husky tone of voice, thereby countering the emasculating effects of having claimed to like textiles.

"Your arm is on the ink pad," she said.

I looked down and saw a purplish stain spreading across my elbow. "Damn."

I stood up quickly.

"No matter," I said casually. "I do that sort of thing all the time."

"You put your arm on ink pads all the time?"

"No, I mean I think nothing of such . . . such trifles," I said, as I realized that this had been one of my few remaining unstained shirts. "In fact, it's like a Rorschach test. What do you see in my elbow?"

I held my arm up in a way that I hoped would show my elbow to its best advantage.

"I see you've decided to return that book I called you about," she said curtly.

"Ah, yes, very astute," I replied, "you pass the test. Although I suppose that one can't pass or fail a Rorschach test."

A look of distaste crossed her face as she glanced at the book.

"Nipple," she said in a way that made the word seem positively shameful.

"Yes, ah . . . Theoretical work, very interesting actually," I said.

"Really? And what exactly is it about?" She gave me a severe look.

Damn Günter. Damn Günter and his teenage fixations. Why did I continue to listen to him?

"It's about, uh, the nipple, you see. Yes, the nipple and its relation to . . . Well, its symbolic meaning as . . ."

"Liberator?"

"Yes, liberator," I said.

"I see that you almost made it through the title."

"Well, it's very complicated. I don't want to bore you."

"That would be terrible. To have you bore me."

I don't know what came over me at that moment. Out of the corner of my eye I saw students walking to the desk, and this was the longest conversation we had ever had. I took the fateful leap.

"We should go look at the textiles together," I said.

"I've already been to the show."

"Some other show then," I continued desperately, unable to stop myself now that I had made the first, icy plunge.

"I'm very busy."

"What about the Knicks? Courtside seats?"

"Courtside seats?" She raised a skeptical eyebrow.

"Here. See for yourself."

I thrust the tickets at her. She looked at them for a long time. If she had had a loupe, I think she would have taken it out to give the tickets a closer examination.

I was stunned by my own boldness. Stupid, stupid man, I thought. I had gone too far. I had carefully cultivated her for months, and in one rash moment I had ruined it all. Better to worship from afar with

65

the dim hope of success than to have my hopes blasted in one fell swoop. I bowed my head and pretended to look at the book to avoid having to face the rejection head on.

"Okay," she said.

We made the necessary arrangements, and afterward I stumbled into the hallway as if waking from a dream. I ran into a rising tide of students heading off to classes and was sideswiped by a couple of backpacks. The rush subsided, and I saw Günter leisurely strolling down the hall.

"Aren't you supposed to be in class?" I asked.

"I never go to class on time. You can't expect me to be jostled by the hoi polloi. It's undignified," he said. "Go see Samson. He wants to talk to you about the meeting."

He continued his leisurely stroll down the hallway. When I walked into Samson's office, he seemed upset. He attempted a reassuring smile, although it filled me with foreboding.

"Ah, John, just the man I wanted to see," he said. "Sit down. Sit down."

"Did you tell Günter that you wanted to see me?"

"Why would I tell that pretentious, preening know-it-all anything?" Samson demanded. "The meeting with the putative Head today. I thought we should have a little chat about what you are going to say."

"Great," I said, thankful that for once Samson was actually going to be helpful.

"Don't worry. Mere formality. Department already runs like clockwork, not that I mean to pat myself on the back, although it sometimes feels like I have to."

He gave me a lugubrious look.

"Yes, yes," I said a little impatiently. "Runs like clockwork, thanks to you."

He frowned at me.

"Not that my accomplishments aren't known, but people take for granted what I have done—"

I had to interrupt him. There was no telling when he would stop. One time, he tried to convince me that he had discovered John Updike.

"So, about this meeting," I said.

"What meeting? I was talking about my tenure as chair. When I was first appointed in—"

"My meeting with the Head!"

"Oh, yes, I told you. It's nothing. She'll ask you a few questions about your educational philosophy. Simply tell her that your philosophy is to keep doing things exactly as I did them. That ought to satisfy her. What more can she expect? When I think of the changes that I have wrought, how I have shaped and molded this department . . ."

He seemed to be talking to himself, so I decided to slip out while I could. Samson had let the Head know how much he disliked her through the occasional snide remark at faculty meetings, and she more than returned the feeling. Telling her that I would do things exactly the same way did not sound like a promising strategy.

As I walked to lunch, I tried to figure out if I even had an educational philosophy. My only thought the first year had been to avoid getting fired, which had been modified over the years to a general rule to avoid doing anything stupid—a little imprecise, yes, but a useful general reminder. The most important subsections of this general rule, added after painful personal experience, were threefold: 1. Never get into a fight with the child of a trustee. 2. Never do anything social outside of school with students. 3. Never date anyone you work with (this in reaction to my brief fling with Kate). The appearance of Amy had caused me to modify the last rule, so that it now applied in my mind only to my colleagues in the English department.

I walked through the student dining room and gazed longingly at the food. Caitlyn was surrounded by a gaggle of girls. Marcus sat by himself off in the corner. I waved at him. In his excitement to return the wave, he spilled milk over himself and grinned at me sheepishly.

I nearly ran into Rebecca as I was about to enter the faculty dining room.

"Hello, Rebecca," I said.

"Hi, Mr. Spencer," she whispered.

"Is everything all right?"

Her eyes began to well up, and I was filled with terror that she would cry. Then, in all decency, I would have to give her a hug. In front of everyone in the faculty dining room. A young teacher— okay, youngish—who hopes to be appointed chair of his department should not be seen manhandling a teenage girl wearing only a tube top and terry cloth shorts. I tried to give her a reassuring pat on the shoulder before things came to that.

"The prom . . . I thought . . ."

Her crush had obviously asked someone else. I was actually somewhat relieved because he had a reputation for browbeating girls into doing things—sexual things. Besides, one of my favorite seniors, Tom Jones, had an enormous crush on her.

"Rebecca, I know a number of young men who would love to go to the prom with you," I said.

"No one wants to go with me," she said, sniffling.

"You are a beautiful girl," I said. I was a little worried that I had just said she was beautiful, but I had at least called her a girl. "And I know for a fact that a number of senior boys would kill to have you as their date."

"Really?"

"Absolutely," I said confidently, "and if you want, I could let them know that you are unattached."

"You would do that?"

"Sure."

I gave her another pat on the shoulder. The hopeless look left her face, and she walked to Caitlyn's table.

As I entered the faculty dining room, the pungent odor of curry slapped me across the face. Kate sidled up beside me.

"Leo is still exploring his cuisines-of-the-world cookbook," said Kate. "Let's just be thankful that we don't have a faculty meeting today."

We each grabbed a tray and shared a dubious glance as a viscous curry stew was ladled onto our plates. As we were about to sit down, one of the deans pulled Kate away to talk about a disciplinary problem, and I was confronted with the task of choosing a table. Given the current wrangling over the chair, I decided to avoid my colleagues, and I headed toward an empty table when I felt a hand on my elbow. I turned around and was startled to see Johns.

"Come join me." He bowed. "Unless you prefer the company of some other table."

I followed Johns to a table in the corner. I sat down and stared glumly at the food.

"So, I heard the news," said Johns, bowing again.

How could Johns know already? Günter was one thing, but Johns?

"Don't worry. It's going to be public soon enough," he said.

"How did you find out?" I asked.

"That's not important. What's important is how pleased I am." He bowed again.

I wasn't sure whether to be pleased that my appointment already looked like a slam dunk or concerned that Johns was pleased about it. The smell of the curry was cutting off my oxygen supply and making it difficult to think.

"Mainly, I just wanted to congratulate you," he said with as much warmth as his frigid personality could muster.

"That's very nice of you," I said.

Johns smiled at me, a sickly, sad spectacle.

"I think the two of us might be able to help each other out."

"Oh," I said as neutrally as I could manage. Helping Johns out tended to be good for Johns and bad for everyone else, as I had already found out more than once.

"I want to tell you that you can count on my support for the position. And I hope I will be able to count on you later."

"Hmm," I said noncommittally.

"Just be careful in your meeting with the Head."

How did he know about that?

"She hasn't been completely happy with the way things are going in the department. Just reassure her. Tell her how you want to maintain high standards, demand the best, that sort of thing."

"Mmm," I said, trying to look inscrutable. It was as if the devil was whispering in my ear.

"Good luck. I've got to go to class. Let me know how it goes." He stood up and walked away.

Ron and Kate joined me at the table.

"So, why do you look so happy?" Kate asked.

"Amy has agreed to go on a date with me," I said.

Kate gave me a stunned look.

"I'm going to die alone," moaned Ron.

"You won't die alone," said Kate.

"Yes I will. I'll be surrounded by all those other single men living at the YMCA."

"Perhaps some of them will be willing to offer the love that dares not speak its name," I said.

Ron sank into a deeper gloom, and Kate gave me an angry look.

"Look. Don't worry," I said. "I'm sure Amy has all sorts of girlfriends that I can introduce you to."

I regretted the offer almost immediately. I had already set Ron up a couple of times with disastrous results.

"Really?" He looked happy for the first time that trimester.

"Trust me, Ron," Kate said, "Amy is not the kind of girl to have girlfriends."

"What's that supposed to mean?" I asked.

"Women just know these things."

"You've never even spoken to her."

"I can tell by the way she walks."

"That's ridiculous."

"We'll see," she said.

"Thanks for extinguishing my only hope," Ron complained to Kate. "Now I'm back to dying alone."

"Ron! You are not dying alone," said Kate. "You know, Dan has some women that he works with who would love to meet a guy like you."

"I don't think that would be a good idea," Ron said nervously.

"Why not?"

"You know why. I can't date women who make that much money. It goes against the biological imperative of the species. Men are supposed to provide for women, not the other way around."

"Ron, you've got it all wrong," I said. "We've evolved beyond biology. What could be better than a wealthy woman who can take care of you financially?"

"We ignore biology at our peril," Ron said darkly. "And if dating these women is so great, why don't you do it?"

"I'm going out with Amy."

"What? You two have something exclusive?" Kate asked sarcastically.

"Of course not."

"So, let me set you up. Just to give Ron some reassurance."

"The thing is, your past setup—"

"What was wrong with her?" Kate demanded.

"She was, well, uh, how to put this," I said hesitantly. I tried to come up with an answer that wouldn't make me sound too shallow. "Big-boned."

"No she wasn't," protested Kate.

"And she had more facial hair than me."

"She was not that bad," Kate laughed.

"I would kill for big-boned right now," said Ron. "I could even live with a mustache, as long as it wasn't larger than my own."

Ron sported the type of mustache that hadn't been seen since *Starsky and Hutch* went off the air. He thought that facial hair was a sign of virility and that women were instinctually attracted to it. Since he hadn't had a girlfriend in several years, either he was wrong, or women were very successfully repressing their instinctual natures.

"Were you talking to Johns earlier?" Kate asked.

"Yes."

"What's that about?"

"He wants to ingratiate himself with the rising power," I said. "His sucking up is so ingrained that Samson's departure won't derail it."

"Classic alpha male behavior. Show of subservience from other males. Probably explains Amy as well. He's irresistible now. Kate will probably start hitting on you next," said Ron.

"I don't think John needs to worry about that," Kate said decidedly.

"Well, it doesn't matter," Ron said to me. "Since society doesn't allow for polygamy, you should only focus on one woman anyway. Other males might get upset if you monopolized the females."

Kate rolled her eyes. "How did you get the ice queen to melt?" she asked.

"The usual Spencer charm."

She raised an eyebrow.

"And where are you taking her?"

I studied my curry intently.

"John?"

"I'm sorry. Did you ask me a question?" I asked. "You know, this food isn't agreeing with me. I think I'll go find something else."

"John!"

"Yes," I said innocently.

"Where are you taking her?"

"The New York Knicks game," I mumbled.

"You got Knicks tickets!" Ron shouted. "Those must have cost a fortune. Did you go to a scalper?"

"Not exactly," I said.

"How did you get them?" He asked.

"Does it matter?" I laughed hollowly. "The important thing is that I'm going to the game with Amy."

"I'm just curious," Ron said.

"Yes," Kate said suspiciously, "so am I."

Biologists were always so annoyingly literal-minded. They had to know all of the stupid, unimportant, completely insignificant details. And Kate was just, well, she was just annoying.

"I got them from Snopes," I said.

"Snopes!"

"John, you can't," said Kate.

"I was going to give them back. And then somehow I asked Amy to go to the game. And now . . ."

"Somehow asked?" Kate snorted.

"Maybe he should use them," said Ron. "It's not as if there was some quid pro quo."

"Well, that's not entirely true," I said. Or almost said. I couldn't speak, you see. My mouth was filled with curry, lovely, delightful curry.

Ron looked at me with concern.

"John, you really shouldn't eat that."

THE BOOK OF THE COURTIER

I entered the Head's office feeling much as I did when I was choking down that bite of curry. The last time I had been in this office was after the fiasco of Fiesta Day when the sour cream scandal had almost landed me in the soup. The Head of School had changed since then, and the new Head had designed her office to reflect her own "educational philosophy." Gone were the dark wood, the hunting scenes, and the heavy furniture, replaced by a cool modernist look—blond wood, hard edges, and no clutter. Constance Van Huysen was talking on the phone and waved to me to sit down.

I decided to avoid the beige couch against the wall. Earlier that year, the Head had had a stormy meeting with a mother who was angry that her son had not been admitted to the advanced placement U.S. history class, a somewhat understandable decision given that the boy had almost flunked regular U.S. history the year before. When the Head had uncharacteristically refused to relent, the mother had decided to vent her feelings—literally—by urinating on the couch. This had landed her on a very special list of parents who were banned from the campus because of their behavior. The Head had the cushions dry-cleaned, but the stiff-backed chair in front of her desk still seemed more inviting. While I waited for her to get off the phone, I stared out the window at the school's shuttered greenhouse,

"I, uh, well, don't have a girlfriend per se. I have prospects. Women I am dating."

"Women?"

"Oh, not like that. I don't mean to imply that I am some sort of a Lothario. You know, just trying to find the right person. Age-appropriate and all of that," I said.

"So, no girlfriend."

"No, not at the moment."

"That's too bad," she said. She glanced back down at the file. "It also doesn't look like you are a particularly active member of the community."

"I wouldn't say that."

"Tell me, then, what you are involved in."

"There was Fiesta Day," I said.

"Was that the one with the food-poisoning incident?"

"Yes."

"And what was your responsibility?"

I winced.

"The food," I said, "but it wasn't my fault. Really. Some student left the sour cream in his car."

The Head looked back down at my file.

"Anything else you've done?"

"I also serve on the English department prize committee," I said.

"That's good," she said unenthusiastically.

She continued flipping through my file without saying anything. After a minute or two, she lifted her head. Her look was not reassuring.

"John, I've worked very hard to rebuild this school," she said. "The new classrooms, the auditorium, the library."

The Head took an inordinate pride in "her" buildings, which were already falling apart from the shoddy construction. The new auditorium had been built to give the high school a place where the whole student body could meet but was so poorly designed that it couldn't actually fit all of the students. Luckily, enough

77

students cut "mandatory" school meetings that crowding wasn't a problem. To sell the school as an arts school, she had pushed through a multimillion-dollar stage that lowered, although it had yet to perform that function in any school production. But it had managed to lower the school's credit rating. And the high-tech classrooms had a low-tech problem—there wasn't enough room for all of the students to sit. Apparently, twenty-seven thousand dollars a year did not quite cover seating. But the race is to the swift, so perhaps students learned a valuable lesson about punctuality. The school did boast the city's only indoor croquet court, although no one ever used it for that. It was, however, popular as a picnicking spot on rainy days.

"Obviously, good department chairs are crucial to that effort to rebuild," continued the Head. "So, let's talk about what your plans are if you become chair. Let's hear your educational philosophy."

There they were. The dreaded words. I had worked all afternoon on the perfect line and had even memorized it. Something that would reassure her without actually committing me to anything. Now, at the crucial moment, my mind went completely blank. Nothing. Nada. Zip. I could feel my pulse begin to race. Johns's words popped into my mind.

"That's a good question. I guess you could say that my main goal is to maintain standards. You know, demand the best from the children."

"Really? So, you think the school is failing to do that now?"

"No, of course not." I laughed weakly. "It's just something that, you know, you've got to watch out for."

"No, I'm not sure I do know. I think our students are already under enormous pressure, and I'm not sure that ratcheting up that pressure is what they need. In fact, I think it is the opposite of what they need."

"I can certainly understand your concern," I hurried on, "and I agree with you. I didn't mean we should ratchet up the pressure. Far from it. Exactly the opposite in fact. Not what I meant at all when I talked about maintaining standards."

"What exactly *do* you mean by maintaining standards?"

I had no idea what I meant. My mind was still reeling from my horrendous opening. I tried to regroup. I noticed a long silver envelope opener on her desk, and I imagined various ways that I could stab myself severely enough that I would have to end the interview.

"John?"

Behind her head, I saw a poster, and a single word caught my eye—*empowerment*. Before I even had time to finish the thought, I began to speak.

"I'm sorry for the pause. I should have realized that there might be a misunderstanding, because I forget that my idea of maintaining standards is somewhat unusual. Most people, I suppose, imagine that means more discipline or more work or something of that nature. I guess if I could sum up in one word what I meant, it would be empowerment."

"Interesting." The disapproving frown left her face for the first time.

"I think in the classroom, there is a certain . . . a certain synergy among the students that allows them to achieve, ah, to achieve . . ."

To achieve what? I had no idea. I could feel my body begin to grow warm and realized that in a few seconds sweat would begin rolling down my face. The intercom buzzed to life.

"Phillip Nostrum to see you," the Head's secretary said. He was the chairman of the board and the school's biggest donor.

"I'm sorry, John. We're going to have to cut this short. I don't want to keep him waiting. But I'm intrigued by what you are saying. I think we should have a meeting next week, so I can hear more about this."

"No problem. I'll set something up for next week." I tried to act suitably disappointed at not having had a chance to finish my explanation.

As I left her office, I bumped into Dean Wallenstein. He gave me a genial smile.

"So, John, I hear you are going to be joining the side of law and order," Wallenstein said.

"I hope so."

I suppressed a smile at the thought that Wallenstein considered himself an enforcer of law and order. The Head had replaced the old dean of the high school, a stern taskmaster affectionately nicknamed Dr. No by the faculty because of his response to most student requests, regardless of the relation of the student to the trustees or to prospective donors. So the Head had shoved him into early retirement and had replaced him with Dean Wallenstein—everyone called him Dean Wally—a genial man, who never said no to any student request. Occasionally, when he violently disapproved of some scheme, he would ask the students to think carefully before taking action, which they invariably saw as a license to do exactly as they wished, often with disastrous consequences, such as the time the students decided to show school spirit by dying the water in the pool to match the school's colors before a swim meet, a stunt that left the pool with a permanently ominous dark hue. His typical response to this type of disaster was to call it a valuable learning experience. I wished that my meeting had been with him.

"Well, I'm afraid I have some unfinished business," he said, giving me a forlorn look.

He walked into his office and closed the door. I looked through his office window and saw John North sitting disconsolately between his stony-faced parents. John should have been living the good life. Stanford had accepted him early, so theoretically the pressure was off. Only theoretically, though. John's parents had told him in no uncertain terms that he was expected to maintain his straight A average. When he had received a B in his physics class, his parents had done everything short of chain him to his desk and had threatened him with a variety of punishments too awful to repeat. He had panicked and was caught rifling through his teacher's desk looking for the next test. Now he found himself caught between the sound and the fury. Poor Dean Wally seemed uncertain where to place his sympathy, so he simply stared in a befuddled way at a picture on his wall of a sailboat in the middle of a stormy ocean, as if, through sheer good-will, he might help the boat reach the shore safely.

Long lines snaked out of the offices of the tenth- and eleventh-grade deans, the annual onslaught of parents whose children had been rejected from advanced placement classes. The parents knew that, if they complained long enough and loud enough, room would eventually be found somewhere. Many of them would return to these offices three or four more times during the summer until they wore the deans into submission. With the college counseling department advising families that at least two advanced placement classes a year were essential for any student who wanted to have a serious shot at the Ivies, you could hardly blame them.

As I walked back to my office, I ran into Amy, who was staggering under a load of books.

"May I give you hand?" I asked gallantly.

She gave me a sly look.

"That would be great," she said, handing me some of the books.

As we strolled toward the library, I searched for something witty to say.

"So, how did a nice girl like you end up in a place like this?" I had to stifle a groan. What a line. Appalling. I wouldn't be surprised if she bounced a book off my head after a line like that.

"Who said I was that nice?" She gave me an arch look, as she deftly grabbed the books from me and disappeared into the library.

I stifled the urge to run after her, drop to my knees, and declare my love. I had to play it cool. I would wait until next week to do that. That wasn't so long. One week. Just one. Of course, who knew what villainous cretin was even now lying in wait to do the same thing? Someone much less devoted, much less worthy. Some careless play-boy who was good-looking and wealthy in some superficial and un-satisfying way. What about carpe diem? Marvell certainly didn't dither for a week pursuing his coy mistress. Why not tomorrow? Or, better yet, today. Right now even! Yes, the impulsive gesture of the true romantic! It was time to gather my rosebuds while ye may. As I reached for the door, a hand grabbed my arm.

"What did you tell the chair?" Samson demanded.

I looked at him blankly.

"About your educational philosophy!"

"Not much. We got interrupted."

"I thought we agreed that you had my educational philosophy," he barked. "Not that I want to go on about my own achievements, but I thought you appreciated everything that I have done for the department, what I have created."

"I do."

"So, why are you talking to her about empowering students? Have you ever heard me say that? Does that sounds like my educational philosophy?"

How could he possibly know what I had said already? His voice was rising, and his face was beginning to take on an unhealthy, blotchy color.

"Well, the thing is, you see, I . . . That is to say, that one can only . . . Um . . ."

Samson glared at me and stormed off. The carpe diem had been knocked right out of me, and I wandered back to my office to find Kate standing by the door.

"I wanted to see how the meeting went," she said. She looked at my face. "Oh."

I opened the door without saying anything, and we sat down.

"It couldn't have been that bad," she said. "I'm sure you did fine. Gave her the old Spencer charm. What did you say to her?"

"Well, I started talking about maintaining standards."

"Maintaining standards," she laughed. "You're joking, right? You know how much the Head dislikes that sort of thing. Maintaining standards just mucks up the whole college admission process with lower grades and harsher evaluations. It upsets students. It upsets parents. It

82

upsets the college advisers. It upsets the development office. Why would you say something like that?"

"I panicked, and all I could remember was what Johns had told me at lunch," I said glumly.

"*Johns*," she said incredulously, "that conniving, no good, despicable—"

"—man who wants to be the next chair of the department," I said.

I spent that night trying not to think about my miserable performance by working on my recommendation letters. Laura's letter flowed from my pen like the proverbial milk and honey. But Caitlyn's letter left me completely flummoxed, as I repeatedly tried and failed to strike a balance between giving Snopes what he wanted and maintaining my self-respect. After a slew of false starts, I found myself composing imaginary recommendation letters.

Smith College, Massachusetts
Dear Sir or Madam,
Although Hugh Hefner's high spirits have led him into certain indiscretions, I believe that a female environment would perfectly suit his talents and add immeasurably to the student body . . .

Harvard Business School, Massachusetts
Dear Sir or Madam,
Despite his lack of experience in the world of free market capitalism, Joseph Stalin has shown the kind of bureaucratic panache that would make him a titan of the corporate world. Especially during this time of mass layoffs . . .

Berkeley Montessori School, California
Dear Sir or Madam,
While Adolf Hitler has gotten off on the wrong foot, I believe that the

right educational environment can turn him around. A diverse student body with whom he can learn to appreciate difference is just the ticket . . .

Tuskegee Institute, Georgia
Dear Sir or Madam,
Although Orval Faubus has said some harsh things about African Americans, he assures me that he counts many of them among his best friends. I am confident that his contribution to what he lightheartedly calls "those people" will redound . . .

CIA, Virginia
Dear Sir or Madam,
Osama bin Laden has shown a gifted ability at just the type of black box operations for which the agency is justly famous. Although he is unable to submit to an on-site interview, he would be more than happy to arrange a satellite call . . .

After a few more of these, Caitlyn's letter no longer seemed quite so daunting, and I ground out a letter that left me with only mild feelings of shame, roughly on a par with enjoying a long night of reality television.

PRIDE AND PREJUDICE

The next day, the class was painfully slogging through the opening pages of *Emma*. Most of them hadn't even opened the book yet.

"All right, class, let's try this one more time," I said. "Laura, will you please read the first paragraph?"

" 'Emma Woodhouse, handsome, clever, and rich, with a comfortable home and happy disposition, seemed to unite some of the best blessings of existence; and had lived nearly twenty-one years in the world with very little to distress or vex her.' "

"Thank you," I said—at least I could now be sure that everyone had read the first paragraph, or almost everyone since David was even more comatose than usual.

"Handsome?" Jacob sneered. "That's a word for a guy. Maybe Emma's a guy. I mean, does the book ever mention her breasts or her va—"

"That's enough," I shouted. The students giggled and exchanged looks with one another. Earlier in the semester, when I had explained the meaning of the word *specie*, Ally had chimed in with a burst of poetical whimsy that the word *specie* rhymed with *feces*, and the remainder of the class became—well, imagine if Dr. Seuss had written a book devoted entirely to bodily functions. I didn't want to think about what might happen when the V word was out.

"When you think about it," I continued, "she is not unlike many of you. Close to the same age. Blessed with talent, a comfortable home, loving parents, all the things one hopes to have. So, do you like Emma?"

"Not really," said Rebecca, "she is so full of herself."

"Yeah," said Ally, "like she is the only one who understands what everyone should be doing."

It was the most active class participation we had had (not involving the discussion of spa treatments) since I had provoked the class by telling them that romantic love was a modern invention to serve the needs of an industrialized economy (a line I had stolen from Günter). Caitlyn smiled with amusement, but before she could say something to derail the conversation, I pushed on.

"Does she have any reason to be so full of herself?" I asked.

"No, she is totally wrong about everything. She doesn't even know what she wants," said Laura.

"But she is rich," I said.

"So what? Like that gives anyone a greater knowledge," Laura said.

"Yeah, what makes rich people think they know everything? It's just like kids at this school . . ." said Marcus, trailing off as he glanced at Caitlyn.

"Does Austen give us any sense in that opening paragraph that something may not be quite right?" I asked.

"Her life looks pretty good to me," Ally said.

"What about the word 'seemed'?" I asked. "What does it mean to 'seem' to unite some of the best blessings, rather than simply to unite some of the best blessings?"

"It means that she doesn't, right?" Rebecca asked. "Gwyneth looks like she has everything all figured out, but she doesn't."

"Very good," I said, happy that she had made the point, even with the wrong name. "This novel is all about the education of Emma Woodhouse, about her realizing that she still has much to learn. Part

86

of what we are going to study is how she changes over the course of the novel."

"But isn't perception all that really counts?" Caitlyn gave me a sly smile. "I mean, it's all well and good for people to think that they know something about someone, but is it ever more than perception? It's so arbitrary."

"It isn't arbitrary," said Laura. "Hard work, things like that, they tell you about a person."

Caitlyn looked at her indulgently.

"It's nice to believe that," she said, "but that is hardly the real world. Look at all these corporate scandals. If their stocks were still riding high, no one would be on trial. Sure, you can say that now we know the truth, but that is only because our perception already changed. It doesn't really matter what you do. It only matters what you can make people think you have done."

"But that's completely amoral," Laura said.

"But it's true," said Rebecca. "Remember when everyone thought Julie was a slut because she did it with those two guys at the club, and, even when she said she didn't, it didn't matter because everyone already believed that she had?"

"Laura has a good point, though," I said. "Perception obviously shapes how we view things, but that does not mean that we should—"

"Mr. Spencer, you're not going to give us one of those life lessons, are you?" Caitlyn asked.

Her comment brought the conversation to a grinding halt. I almost regretted the glowing letter I had given to Snopes that morning discussing Caitlyn Brie as a student who "seemed" to be one of the best students I had taught. I would have given her a disappointed look, but I was trying to avoid looking at her altogether. The warm weather had brought out an even skimpier wardrobe than usual. At this rate, she would be down to a loincloth by graduation. I looked over at Laura with gratitude. Sure, she wore tight T-shirts and short skirts. What girl at Academy X didn't? But at least they covered all the essential areas.

"Besides," Caitlyn continued, "what if Emma simply wasn't clever enough?"

"That goes against the whole novel," protested Laura. "Her problem is not just that she plays matchmaker but that she is such a bad matchmaker and doesn't even know her own heart."

"But what if she had been a good matchmaker? What if she had been more clever?" Caitlyn asked. "What if she had nothing to learn?"

The class bell rang.

"Don't forget. Creative writing exercise on *Emma* due at the end of the week," I said.

The class groaned. I stopped Rebecca on the way out. I had convinced Thomas that he should ask her to the prom, and I wanted to see if my matchmaking had met with success.

"So, Rebecca, how are you doing?"

"Fine." She looked at me blankly.

"Do you have a date for the prom?" I asked.

She smiled.

"Yes, I do."

"So, you and Tom . . ."

"Tom?" she said laughing. "You've got to be kidding me. I don't know what he was thinking asking me to the prom. What a joke."

As she left, I saw Günter smiling at me.

"I could have told you that was a mistake," he said.

"You don't even know what we were talking about," I said.

"All right, but I would avoid Tom for a while."

It served me right. Had I learned nothing from *Emma* after all these years?

"So, am I to assume that you have a paper for me?" I asked.

"You can assume anything you want," said Günter. "You can't ask me to produce for a deadline. I'm an artist. I can't abide these bourgeois capitalist notions of putting people on the clock."

"And yet you meet your deadline for the newspaper every week," I said.

"A foolish consistency is the hobgoblin of little minds," he replied airily, as he sauntered away. "By the way, good luck next week with your talk."

As usual, I had no idea what he was talking about. I entered my office and discovered that my red voicemail light was on—always a worrisome sign. I picked up the phone and heard the voice of the Head.

"John, I've been thinking about our meeting. I was very impressed. I had no idea you had such progressive ideas. I think these are exactly the sort of ideas that our own faculty needs to hear more about. So, I've scheduled you to give a talk to the faculty next week. You can call my secretary for the details. Barring any unforeseen developments, I think we should be able to announce your appointment as chair by the end of the week. Good-bye."

As long as the talk went well, I would be chair! Excellent news! Spectacular news! But . . . but . . . but . . . I would have to give a talk to the faculty. Terrible news! Disastrous news! It was one thing to stand in front of a group of teenagers who wanted me to give them a good grade. It was quite another thing to stand in front of my colleagues. Most of them hated staying after school, and a few hated me.

As I walked to the cafeteria, my mood worsened. I tried to pass through the students' side without noticing the food on their plates. Caitlyn waved me over to her table, where a number of girls sat deferentially around her. It looked as if none of them had touched their meals. I wondered how rude it would be if I ate some of the food off of their plates, and my hand twitched at my side.

"Mr. Spencer," said Caitlyn, "you are looking at me as if you haven't eaten in three days."

She laughed, and the other girls laughed with her.

"I mean, looking at my *food*," she said with a giggle.

The girls around her exploded in shrieks and screams.

"Save my seat. I need to talk to Mr. Spencer," she said.

We walked to a quiet corner of the room.

"Sorry about today," she said.

"Caitlyn, don't say you are sorry. Just don't do it again. You know, you could learn something from *Emma*."

"Please," she said. "Don't think I didn't hear about your own little matchmaking debacle."

"Which only proves my point," I said.

"Does it?" She smiled. "Who do you think set Rebecca up with her date?"

Another moral lesson down the drain. Next time, I was going to assign *Pilgrim's Progress*. No chance of mistaking the moral lessons there.

"Don't feel too bad. Your heart was in the right place," she said, putting her hand on my arm. "But that's not why I wanted to talk to you. I just wanted to say thanks. Mr. Snopes told me about your letter. And I really appreciate it."

"I hope things work out for you," I said, pretending not to notice her hand.

"I wish there was something I could do to show you how much I appreciate it," she said.

"Just try to be a better influence in class."

I was not happy to learn that Snopes had found time to talk to Caitlyn when he had refused to talk to me about Laura. I had tried to discuss her situation when I dropped off the letter, but he had claimed that he was too busy. And when I had pressed him, he had replied that he did not get involved in that kind of thing, tapping me on the chest with my own recommendation letter to emphasize the point. To hide my irritation, I looked across the cafeteria and saw Günter staring forlornly at Caitlyn.

"And be nice to Günter," I said.

"I thought you learned your lesson about that sort of thing," she said with a laugh.

"I just want you to be nice to him. I didn't tell you to go out with him."

"Sometimes I am very nice to him," she said.

She turned away, and I walked into the faculty dining room and shivered when I saw the menu, El Dorado fish sticks. To misquote Samuel Johnson, fish, like guests, tends to stink on the third day, and this fish was well past the third day. In fact, if smell was any guide, the fish had come on a slow boat from China whose refrigeration system had failed in the sea of Japan.

I sat down with Ron and Kate and told them about the phone call from the Head.

"An all-school meeting about empowering the student?" Kate asked. "How in the world did you let yourself in for that?"

I cataloged my various missteps. It was an impressive list after only a few short days. I was like the anti–Dale Carnegie.

"It's okay, John," said Kate softly. "We'll get you through this."

When she used that tone, she could be very reassuring.

Ron glumly speared a fish stick and sniffed it warily.

"As a biologist, I really can't recommend eating fish that smells this way. Do you know the microbes that can develop in rancid fish—"

"Stop!" Kate pleaded. Ron liked to regale us with the lethal biological organisms lurking in our food, so that we could only eat now with a fragilely maintained amnesia.

"I'm just saying that the flesh of fish is very fertile ground—"

"Ron!" I interrupted.

"Sorry," he said.

"You don't share this sort of information when you are out on a date with a woman, do you?" I asked.

"She has a right to know! You can't trust the cleanliness of a lot of those restaurants," said Ron.

I was starting to think that we should try to set Ron up with a woman who didn't speak English.

"Let's return to John's problem," said Kate. "I don't think we have enough time today to work on Ron's dating technique. First, you need to go see Samson and reassure him that this 'empowering the student' thing is only to keep the Head happy."

"Right," I said.

"The talk should be fairly simple, too. We'll grab a little empowerment lingo from those education journals, and you'll be fine."

"What if someone asks me questions?"

"When is the last time anyone asked a question after a talk like this? Everyone is desperate to get out of there."

It all sounded reasonable.

"What about my fear of public speaking?"

"John," she said with exasperation, "I can't literally give the talk for you."

That afternoon, I was flipping through some education journals that I had checked out of the library when Strude popped her head into the office to remind me that the Button Turbridge Student Essay Prize Committee was meeting. I trudged unwillingly behind her. We entered one of the classrooms, and I groaned when I saw the stack of candidates in the middle of the table—at least fifty this year. I cursed the relentless ambition of the students.

I sat down between Strude and Andrews. The two would have made a great English teacher if they could have been combined into one person. Strude had taught at the school for twenty-two years, and her dry, puckered face made it seem as if her students had slowly been sucking the lifeblood out of her. I wouldn't have been surprised to see a picture of her in her youth when she was a blooming, rounded, blushing beauty. Her passion for the correct use of grammar extended far beyond strictures about things like the semicolon; for instance, she liked to argue that rap music had sprouted from the split infinitive. She had taken it as her personal mission to stamp out such degeneracy one paper at a time.

Andrews was Strude's opposite in every respect. She was in her early thirties and still dressed as if it were the sixties—lots of billowy peasant blouses and jangling bracelets. She had come to the school directly from Hampshire College. She liked to go to experimental poetry readings in the East Village and, like the Talmudic scholars of old, did not believe a razor should touch any part of the body. I still regretted the manner in which I had become aware of that fact. Andrews did not care at all about the correct use of grammar but only concerned herself with, as she liked to say, the creative flow. Last year, during a particularly heated argument, Strude had asked Andrews how she thought the comma should be used, and Andrews had replied that it was like fairy dust: You should sprinkle it on liberally and not worry too much where every little bit of it went.

The prize included a plaque and a two-hundred-dollar gift certificate to a local bookstore. But that hardly explained the appeal to the students. Much more important was the wall of fame. Every winner had his or her picture placed on a wall with previous winners, which would not have been a big deal, except that Academy X had produced a number of famous writers in past decades, all of whom had won the Button Turbridge Prize. In the right society, students could coast on that win for years—invited to all the right young author parties, cushy jobs at publishing houses, magazine articles. All in all, a nice way to launch yourself into the world.

Strude and Andrews took the prize almost as seriously as the students and saw themselves as the anointers of future greatness. They studied the essays as if they were decoding the Gnostic gospels. I, on the other hand, didn't even want to be on the committee. Not that I minded being thought of as a literary sort. Technically, I was still a Ph.D. candidate. The circumstances that had brought my scholarly ambitions to an abrupt end made it highly unlikely that I would return to finish my degree. But I liked to tell people that I was working on my dissertation, although this claim was starting to wear a little thin over the years. And I still daydreamed about publishing a well-received scholarly book. All of this allowed me to present myself as a writer, while not actually having to write, which was just about the best of all possible worlds. But, as I found out, no good exaggeration goes unpunished. I had written a couple of brief book reviews for an obscure academic journal run by a grad school friend of mine, and I had fallen into the unfortunate habit of dropping the occasionally discreet reference to my work "as a reviewer for a literary magazine." One time Samson overheard me, and before I knew what had happened, I found myself ensconced on the committee.

"Now," said Strude, "I believe we can have all of these read by next week, and we can begin to make some preliminary selections."

She paused and looked significantly at Andrews.

"Let's remember that this award is for analysis and that clear writing is the very foundation of effective analysis."

Andrews returned her stare.

"Actually, the award is for *original* analysis, and as I'm sure both of you will agree, creativity is essential for any truly original work."

I attempted to look thoughtful as Strude and Andrews renewed their annual debate. I thought to myself that, except for these meetings, the assignment wasn't so difficult. Next week, I would stop by to chat with both Strude and Andrews and would find out what their favorite essays had been. Usually, they would both like at least a few of the same ones, although those would rarely be among their top choices. I would then read those few with only two questions in mind: Is its use of grammar correct enough to satisfy Strude? And is it creative enough to satisfy Andrews? I would let the two of them exhaust themselves in debate and, at the last moment, enter my dark-horse candidate, which the two of them would accept with gratitude. Only my latest and tenuously maintained vow of discretion had kept me from bragging about all of this to Günter. Candide indeed!

"Well, we won't settle this today," Strude said with an annoyed tone after they had hammered away at each other for a while. "I will see you both here next week."

I returned to my office and had just finished packing up when Andrews popped her head in.

"Do you have a moment?" she said.

"I'm sort of in a rush," I said, moving toward the door.

Unfortunately, the room was so narrow that the only way I could have escaped would have involved violence to her person. She edged me back into my chair like a skillful lion tamer.

"I just need a couple of minutes," she said.

I slumped into my seat. Although this had the advantage of protecting me from any physical contact, it also left me vulnerable to the lean-in, and I soon found myself eyeball to eyeball with Andrews in all of her sympathetic glory.

"Is everything all right?" She oozed concern all over me. I tried to push my chair back, but she edged after me.

"Fine, great. Couldn't be better. Right as rain. Tip-top," I babbled inanely. There were few things more painful than sympathy offered at point-blank range from Andrews.

"Good, I know you are under a lot of pressure with the impending promotion," she said softly. Was it just my imagination, or did she bat her eyes at me? And how did she know about the promotion? Couldn't anyone keep a secret in this place?

"Ah, well, nothing to worry about there. Place runs itself. No need to supervise the likes of you," I said, trying to look encouraging while edging my seat back again. She pulled her own chair closer.

"That's exactly what I am concerned about," she whispered with tears in her eyes. "You are so nice. People take advantage of that niceness, John."

It was somewhat reassuring that the murderous thoughts raging in my head were not, apparently, visible on my face.

"You need someone to protect you," she said even more softly. I watched with dread as her hand reached out for my arm, bringing her even closer. She leaned forward, so close to me that I could see every pore on her face. I could smell her—her perfume, her makeup, her conditioner, and (was it possible?) the faint odor of cat. I tried to edge my chair back, but I had reached the wall.

"Someone to watch over you, nurture you," she cooed.

"Very kind, I'm sure. Great to know you are looking out for me," I said, trying to stand. She dragged me back down with her hand.

"You don't realize the forces against you," she warned. "That vile O'Brien. The things he says about you."

"I'm sure it's not that bad," I said.

"Oh, it is," she said, looking at me with moist eyes. "It is."

"I want to be there for you, John." She paused and leaned in even closer. "In whatever way you will let me." She gazed deeply into my eyes. Her other hand suddenly made an appearance on my thigh. She began her final lean forward, and I let out an undignified yelp.

The door banged open.

"Oh, I'm so sorry," said Kate innocently, "I had no idea you were having . . ."

She gave me a wry look.

". . . a meeting. Do you want me to wait outside?"

"No!" I almost yelled before Andrews could say anything. "Don't go. We're almost done here, I think."

Andrews reluctantly released me from her grip—I was reminded of one of those nature shows when the lioness is forced to give up her prey to the lion. She stood up and walked toward the door. Before she could escape, Kate briefly clutched her arm.

"Thank you so much," she said, looking deeply into Andrews's eyes. "Soooo kind of you."

Andrews gave her a pained smile and left the room. Kate flopped into a chair and threw her leg over the arm.

"Ron is right," I said miserably. "I've become irresistible."

Kate laughed.

"Don't worry. I think that you won't struggle with that problem much," she said.

"It's probably only a matter of time before you throw yourself at me."

"More likely throw something at you," she said. "If you keep up like this, you'll become more insufferable than Samson."

I had a terrifying vision of myself in ten or twenty years holding forth at a department meeting. Not dreading the meeting but embracing it as another opportunity to elaborate on the benevolence of my reign. Long anecdotes about how I had single-handedly resuscitated the reputation of Tennyson.

"Don't worry," she said smiling. "I'm here to smack you around when you get out of line."

"I'm glad you arrived when you did. I had run out of room."

"I was out there all along. I just couldn't resist having a little fun," she said. She smiled when she saw the look on my face. "Oh, come on. Be a sport. How could I pass up an opportunity like that?"

I rubbed my shoulder, which had practically gone into a spasm to avoid the clinch with Andrews. Kate moved behind my chair, put her strong, confident artist's hands on my shoulders, and massaged my back.

"You've got to relax," she said. "At this rate, the stress will kill you before you can take the job."

I began to unwind under the insistent pressure of her fingers. After our fling, we had come up with all sorts of reasons why we shouldn't date each other, but at that moment I couldn't remember a single one of them.

"Let's go find Ron and have a drink," she said, letting go of my shoulders and moving to the door. The warm cocoon that had enveloped me evaporated.

"By the way, John, I want you to know that I'll be there . . . in any way you need me," she said huskily and laughed.

When I left the office a couple of minutes later, I heard a muffled shout. At the end of the hall, two boys were towering over Marcus. I hurried over before they shoved him into a locker or dipped him in the toilet.

"Excuse me!" I said angrily.

Marcus's glasses teetered on his face at a ridiculous angle. The two boys turned around. One of them was a beefy redhead who was the captain of the lacrosse team and the child of a trustee. The other was a hairy behemoth who seemed likely to be the winner in a future hotdog-eating contest.

"What do you think you are doing?" I demanded.

I worried that I would be stuffed into the locker with Marcus when I saw their nonchalance.

"Just having fun with our good buddy," said the redhead. He grabbed Marcus roughly around the neck. "Right, Marcus?"

"Take your hands off of him." I said. His arm lingered on Marcus's shoulders. "Or perhaps you like touching him?"

He removed his arm with a sneer.

"Perhaps the three of us should visit the dean?"

They both looked at me contemptuously. They knew that even if that happened, nothing would come of it.

"Get out of here," I said.

"Sure. Whatever," the redhead said.

The two swaggered down the hallway.

"Thanks, Mr. Spencer," Marcus said weakly.

"Are you okay, Marcus?"

"I'm fine."

"Do you want me to report them?"

"No, that will only make it worse."

"Marcus, it's none of my business," I said, "but if you changed a few things, you would be less of a target."

A brief look of hope flared in his eyes. Then I thought of Caitlyn. And Emma. And I was startled to realize that I had acquired a deep fondness for Marcus just the way he was, that I loved his cluelessness

98

because it kept him from developing all those hypercompetitive traits that places like Academy X fostered.

"You know what, Marcus? Forget I said anything. You shouldn't change a thing. You should just be yourself," I said.

"If you say so," he said without much conviction, pushing his wobbly glasses back into place.

"Trust me, Marcus, in the long run you will be glad."

He looked at me anxiously.

"I promise."

"Okay," he said.

"All right, I'll see you tomorrow." I gave him a pat on the back.

Caitlyn rounded the corner as Marcus disappeared down the stairs.

"Molding young Marcus," she said with an amused smile.

"Caitlyn, how long were you standing there?"

"Long enough."

"Long enough to help Marcus?"

"Don't worry. I intend to help him."

"And just when were you planning on intervening?"

"Oh, I wasn't going to intervene in this," she said with a breezy wave. "But I think I have found a prom date for Marcus."

"Are you sure that's a good idea?"

"She is very cute, although she doesn't speak much English." She bit her fingernail thoughtfully. "Then again, I think that might be counted as a bit of a plus. Don't want to put too much conversational pressure on Gandolf."

"You mean Goldorf."

"Whatever."

"I'm sure you have good intentions, but I think you would be doing him a greater service if you would protect him from the bullies."

She frowned.

"That's not really my thing."

"What's not your thing? Helping other people?"

"No, of course not! I donate part of my allowance to a soup

kitchen. I just don't like being a disciplinarian. You know, all stern and frosty."

I tried to give her my own stern and frosty look—or as stern a look as I could manage as she fingered her bra strap.

"I expect more from you," I said.

"Are you trying to mold me now?"

She smiled mischievously, and I sighed as I thought about what a complete failure my attempt to transform Caitlyn was turning out to be.

"Never mind," I said. "I'll see you tomorrow."

I turned away before she could begin fingering some other under-garment and went to find Ron and Kate. Later that evening, Ron made a very convincing biological argument that doing tequila shooters would help me overcome my fear of public speaking. The fact that the three of us had already split a few pitchers of beer had given his words a plausible air, and by the time I stumbled home, all my problems seemed far away. Before I had a chance to bury myself in the cool comfort of my sheets, my phone rang.

"Heerryyo," I mumbled.

"John, John, is that you?"

"Muuuthhher!" I said as brightly as I could manage, although I think it came out sounding like a vague murmur.

"Have you been drinking?"

"Whaddyatalkingabout?"

"You have been drinking!"

"No?" I'm not sure how this came out as a question.

"John, this is what I worry about. You, lonely, single, drinking yourself slowly to death when there are all these wonderful women who would just love to be with a man like you."

"I'm not lonely. I was drinking with friends," I protested. Although I had admitted that I was drinking, I had at least proven that I was not a sad, lonely, pathetic loser. At least I thought I had. Unfortunately, what my mother actually heard was something like, "So lonely, devastating end."

"Don't give up, John! You are not coming to the end. You are in the prime of life! Promise me you won't do anything rash. You don't have any pills or anything, do you? John! John!"

Although I had not wanted to kill myself before she called, it was becoming an increasingly attractive possibility. It would mean an end to this conversation. I could avoid the massive hangover that was coming. I wouldn't have to give my talk to the faculty. And then there were all of the intangibles. People would have to say nice things about me. The school might even set up some sort of memorial. And I would be deep, one of those brooding intellectuals. A Dostoevsky sort of figure. I pictured various people at my funeral. Kate would throw herself on the coffin and weep, repentant for all of the cutting things she had said over the years. And Ron would look on sadly—admittedly, Ron always looked sad. But this time he would be really sad. They would all—

I heard my mother yelling to my father to call the New York police, and he was yelling back that he couldn't call the police because she was on the phone. Then she was yelling at him to go next door. And then, well, you know how these things go.

"Mother!" I shouted. She continued to yell at my father. "Mother!"

"Don't get angry, dear," she said. "I did the best I could. Oh, you're not doing this because of me, are you? You know there is no greater love than that of a mother for her son. Whatever I did or didn't do, forgive me. Maybe I breast-fed you too long—or was it too short? I can't remember. They keep changing the rules. I'm a terrible mother. I can't even remember how long I'm supposed to breast-feed a baby. No wonder you turned out this way. I should kill myself. That's what I should do. Would that make you feel better?"

"Mother, just calm down. No one is killing anyone. Okay?"

The good news was that her hysterics had sobered me up enough to bring me back into the land of human speech.

"You're not going to kill yourself?" She whispered.

"No, mother, I'm not going to kill myself. I promise."

"Oh, thank God!"

She fell silent for a moment.

"John, would you mind if I called you back? Your father has gone next door to call the police, and I think I'd better stop him."

"Sure," I said wearily, "whatever."

When she called me later, I was so overcome by guilt that I promised to visit for three weeks that summer and to allow her to set me up with, as she called them, "very eligible young ladies." I also told my father that I would talk to Ryan about joining his Internet start-up. It was shaping up to be a banner summer.

CIVILIZATION AND ITS DISCONTENTS

The next day, I spent the morning trying not to move and reminding myself that it was Friday. When the bell rang for my Austen class, I stood up gingerly and shuffled to the classroom. Marcus looked woeful. His glasses were held together by duct tape, and a slight bruise colored one cheek.

"Marcus, you're looking more colorful than usual," said Caitlyn.

That was all the encouragement Jacob needed.

"Looks like somebody needed a beating!" Jacob crowed. The class laughed. I turned around and fixed my gaze on Jacob. Everyone fell silent.

"What? I was just joking. Right, Marcus?" Jacob said.

"Sure," Marcus said quietly.

I walked over to Jacob's seat and leaned menacingly close.

"Do you think that's funny, Jacob? That's a source of amusement for you?"

Jacob dropped his head.

"No," he mumbled.

"I suppose other people in pain is pretty hilarious. Isn't it? Cruelty to others is a real laugh, *isn't it*?"

"No."

"Well, I'm glad that you feel the same way. *Now, get out of my class, and don't come back until you can treat others with the decency and respect that they deserve!"*

The other students sat in stunned silence while Jacob slunk out of the classroom, at least temporarily cowed, although I could look forward to a phone call later from his mother. I just hoped that she wouldn't insist on reading me long passages from *Raising Your Spirited Child* again to convince me that his bullying was really a cover for his sensitive, artistic soul. I still shuddered at the memory of my last parent-teacher conference with her. Repeated face-lifts had pulled her skin so taught that a smile threatened to explode the whole apparatus. And she kept shimmying her shoulders during the meeting—she had received breast implants the year before and seemed to believe that they would be taken away if she didn't give evidence of their existence at all times. Worst of all, she insisted on repeating everything she said at least six times, a habit she had probably picked up from talking to Jacob, who had the attention span of a fruit fly.

"Caitlyn," I said sharply, "you should be ashamed of yourself."

She looked astonished, as if she hadn't been reprimanded since she had been potty trained. I was so angry about Marcus that I couldn't concentrate at all during class. I let them out early and tried to bury myself in the fuzziness of my hangover.

"Mr. Spencer?"

I turned around to find that Marcus had stayed behind.

"Yes, Marcus."

"I just wanted to say thanks," he said quietly. "I know it's not easy . . . well, you know, to have someone like me in class."

"That's not true, Marcus. I don't want you ever to think that about yourself," I said, although I had frequently thought the same thing. He gave me a grateful look that made me feel terrible.

I limped back to my office and found Caitlyn waiting for me.

"I just thought it would be a harmless joke. That's all," she said.

"It's never harmless when you pick on someone like Marcus. Especially when you gang up with someone like Jacob."

"That's not fair! I wasn't ganging up with Jacob! I like Marcus—sort of. I'm trying to get him a date to the prom!"

"Fair?" I said angrily. "Is it fair for the most popular girl at the school to pick on one of the least popular boys?"

"No," she sniffled.

"Do you remember the scene in *Emma* when Emma makes fun of Miss Bates?" I asked more gently.

"Yes, but that has nothing to do with this. It's a book, Mr. Spencer, not a guide to life."

"People look up to you. They follow your lead. You can't just ignore that," I said.

"I know," she said quietly.

"Good. Try to remember that the next time you are about to make a joke at Marcus's expense," I said.

She bit her lip and looked up at me.

"Mr. Spencer," she said hesitantly, "I was just wondering. You're not going to, you know, change your mind. About the letter, I mean."

"No, Caitlyn, your letter has already been sent. And I haven't changed my mind about you. I'm only trying to get you to change your mind a little about yourself."

I walked to the cafeteria wondering if Caitlyn's apology had been about Marcus or the letter and feeling that I deserved nothing but the proverbial sackcloth and ashes, so I prepared to do my penance by eating lunch. Kate banged her tray down on the table as I finished my silent prayer to whichever saint was supposed to be the protector of those who wore glasses and played Dungeons & Dragons in high school.

"I can't do it anymore," said Kate.

"Don't worry. It's almost summer," said Ron.

"Yeah, well, tell that to the three-foot dildo that has sprung up in my classroom," she said.

Ron and I looked at each other in confusion.

"Is there a midget in the high school?" Ron asked.

"Is that what we are supposed to call them?" I asked. "Aren't there height requirements? For the various categories, I mean. And I thought they wanted to be called little people."

"I think you're right," said Ron. "A midget is—"

"I'm not talking about a student. I'm talking about a dildo! A clay phallus! King Priam! Whatever you want to call it."

"Yikes! I'm not stopping by your classroom anytime soon. My masculinity is shaky enough without being confronted by that," Ron said.

I was about to laugh, but a quick glance at Kate's face changed my mind.

"I'm serious," she said.

"Well, three feet is nothing to joke about, is it?" I said.

"What is it about men and their penis," Kate said with exasperation. "Anytime the penis enters the conversation, men start acting like giggly twelve-year-olds."

Ron and I struggled not to giggle.

"I'm sorry, Kate, really," I said. "Tell us what happened."

"For the last assignment, I told my students that they could sculpt whatever they wanted. And one of my senior boys decided that he wanted to sculpt the penis. Claimed it was art!"

"Interesting philosophical question," I said.

"Yes," agreed Ron.

"If art can be elephant dung smeared on a picture of Christ, who is to say what art is?"

"Why elephant dung?" Ron asked. "Is there significance in the choice of dung? I mean, why not dog or cat or horse dung? They're a lot easier to get than elephant dung."

"Bulk discount?"

Kate sighed with exasperation.

"What makes it even worse is that he used to be one of my favorite students. I wrote him a recommendation letter. And then he got into a good college, and now it's like he has become a different person."

"Don't beat yourself up," I said. "There's not much you can do, so let him have his fun and ignore him. He'll get bored with it and move on to something else."

"Maybe the vagina," Ron said.

"I tried that, but it's getting worse," she said. "A few days ago, he brought in porn magazines. He claimed that he needed pictures to make it as realistic as possible. As if teenage boys don't play with it so much that it's burned into their memories. Today, he went around the class asking everyone to save their pubic hair. Says he wants to add it to the completed sculpture."

"Pubic hair?" Ron said squeamishly. "That's disgusting."

"You have to admire his commitment to the realist aesthetic," I said.

"And he is really good. I mean, that thing is lifelike. It practically throbs," she said.

"At least that shows what a good job you've done as a teacher," I said.

"Do you know how hard it is to stare at a three-foot dong every day when your own boyfriend won't touch you and when you haven't had sex in months?" she whispered fiercely. "What's wrong with me? I'm hideous, aren't I? I should just become celibate. Devote all of my energy to my art."

Ron and I exchanged a worried look. The last time we had raised the possibility that Kate's boyfriend might be gay, she hadn't spoken to us for weeks. And she had told him everything, which meant that whenever we saw the two of them, Dan spent most of the time glaring at us while Kate wasn't looking.

"There's nothing wrong with you. You're attractive, intelligent. Any man would feel lucky to be with you," I said.

"I'm sure Dan is just busy with work," said Ron.

"He *has* been working on a big deal," Kate said in a small voice.

"You see! That's all it is," I said.

"Do you really think so?"

Ron and I both nodded and stared intently at our Hungarian goulash, undoubtedly named for those heroic Hungarian nags ridden by Cossacks across the vast steppes before arriving on our plates.

Later in the day, I was sitting in my office when O'Brien staggered through the door. He had clearly had his "lunch," and his face was even more flushed than usual.

"Well, Johnny, as the immortal bard wrote," he said, meaning Yeats, not Shakespeare, whom O'Brien thought was an imperialist hack, "the ceremony of innocence is drowned."

"Too true, too true," I said.

"The best lack all conviction, while the worst are full of passionate intensity," he continued.

"Hmmmm." I tried to look wise.

When I first met O'Brien, I was deeply impressed by his mastery of poetry. He always had a line or two at the ready. After a few months, though, I realized that he actually only had about ten lines at the ready and simply recycled them again and again.

"Hard at work," he remarked. "Good to see. Important to have a good work ethic. Like Dylan Thomas, singing in your chains like the sea. It will help us protect your innocence."

He gave me a knowing look and leaned in to give me a confidential wink. In his condition, it came across as more of a leer. Although it wasn't quite drowned, my innocence definitely felt soiled.

"As chair, you'll be working harder than ever."

O'Brien knew about the chair? Already? I thought that drunkenness alone would keep him out of the loop for another few days.

"Ah, yes," I said awkwardly, "nothing official. We'll have to wait and see what happens."

"That's a good attitude. Yes, Johnny boy."

I winced. Whenever he called me Johnny boy, he was sure to follow it with a request. Last time he called me that, he woke me up at two in the morning to ask me to call his wife and explain that he was sleeping at my apartment.

"A very good attitude. Shows a lot of wisdom, that. Yes indeed, Johnny boy."

Twice—that wasn't good.

"Reminds me of my school days in Dublin . . ."

This inevitably led to an interminable anecdote that involved drinking and potted meat.

"What can I do for you?" I interrupted.

"Ah, the question is," he said, "what can I do for *you*?"

His breath from that distance was making me woozy.

"You need my help," he said. "The fact is"—his eyes darted around the office conspiratorially—"there are dark plots swirling around you. *Dark plots!*"

"I'm sure nothing so sinister as that," I said, feeling a trifle unnerved by the maniacal look on his flushed face, which grew redder by the minute.

"You need someone to protect you," he said. "They are all against you. Johns. Strude. Andrews. They would slit your neck as soon as look at you. Mind you, I argue with them. I tell them what a fine chair you will be. Just the man for the job and all of that. But they won't listen to reason. So, let us follow Yeats and declare that there is more enterprise in walking naked."

Unfortunately, walking naked did not seem like an answer to any of my problems.

"Ay, I can see you know what I mean," he said. "Well, don't fear, my boy, don't fear. We had tougher hooligans than this lot in my day."

He leaned closer. I felt the full force of his eighty-proof breath.

"I'll take care of you," he whispered, "and when the time comes, I know you'll take care of me."

He gave me a broad wink and lurched out of the office.

ROMEO AND JULIET

Courtside seats! With Amy! It was shaping up to be a spectacular night. I called Kate to get her advice about what to wear. She was her usual supportive self.

"Oh, please, you're a grown man. Dress yourself," she said.

"I thought women liked giving advice about this sort of thing."

She snorted.

"I don't see what you need advice about. It's not as if you have some extensive wardrobe," she said, "but if you are too pathetic to pick your own clothes, I would suggest jeans and a nice T-shirt."

"Isn't that too casual? I want to impress her."

"It's a basketball game!"

After a few more comments from Kate along those lines, I hung up and got ready.

I met Amy outside the Garden. She was wearing a black, shimmering, almost see-through top that made me short of breath. We took our seats on the floor, and she smiled at me for the first time. Not the first time that night. The first time ever. It almost made me forget what those tickets had cost me. As long as some 240-pound power forward didn't land on us, the evening looked very promising. By the time I put her in the cab a few hours later, though, everything had gone horribly wrong. The first half was perfect. She knew about my promotion and kept making jokes about how I should hire her, how she would love working for me. At a few points, she even placed her hand on my thigh. After a couple of beers, I got into the spirit and made a few jokes about how I could never hire her because I had different plans for her entirely, and the next thing I knew she was flirting with some investment banker sitting next to us. Soon, she was resting her hand on his thigh.

I had a couple more beers to calm down, and I managed to convince myself that she was just doing it to make me jealous. Perfectly natural biological impulse, as Ron would say. I decided to play it cool and pretended to study the game intently. When she finally turned her attention back to me, I was looking—innocently, I might add—at the Knicks dancers. She muttered something under her breath about leering, which was completely unfair. I was actually thinking a number of high-minded thoughts about the terrible exploitation of women at sporting events. I had even made a firm promise to myself to go to a WNBA game that summer to show my support for female athletes.

I tried to make a peace offering by buying her a Knicks teddy bear, but I spilled my beer on it. By the time the game had ended, communication had broken down completely, and we walked silently out of the building. I felt a little ill. Some readers will probably jump to the wrong conclusion that I had too much to drink, but the blame lay entirely with an ill-considered smoked sausage I had eaten during the third quarter. After I hailed a cab, I leaned over to give her a kiss on the cheek, but she got into the cab before I could make contact and left me stranded on the street mid-pucker.

I called Kate after the date to figure out where I went wrong, but she just kept telling me that I was drunk and that I should go to bed. I'm not sure what happened next, but I woke up fully clothed in my bathtub. Only my pounding headache kept me from writing a strongly worded letter to Madison Square Garden complaining about that sausage.

By Sunday morning, I had recovered enough to begin facing the stack of unread papers on my desk. As penance, I read Jacob's paper first. It didn't have much to do with *Emma* and relied heavily on people saying, "Yo, mother f———!" I picked Caitlyn's paper off the pile with a smile. I could always count on her to be interesting and amusing.

Paper assignment: Imagine yourself as a character in Emma, and invent a new scene for the novel. You can set it in Austen's time or make it contemporary.

Emma's Awakening

by

Caitlyn Brie

I felt the cool night air as I stood in the window with the wind pressing my silk nightgown against my body. In the pale moonlight, my skin almost glowed. Knightley would enter soon, and we would enjoy our first night as man and wife.

The door opened, and he stepped into the room wearing a dressing gown. He walked over to me and placed his arms around me. Before he could speak, I put my fingers over his lips and kissed him. His hands slid down my body. A shiver of ecstasy ran through me, and I pressed myself against him, pulling open his robe. I felt . . .

I stopped. I was appalled. Okay, I admit it. I was also a little turned on, although that is not proof of anything. I *know* I said I thought of being Knightley to her Emma, but not like that! I didn't know if I should read the rest of the paper or burn it.

SENSE AND SENSIBILITY

On Monday, I wanted to call in sick rather than see Caitlyn after having read the first few paragraphs of her paper. Well, in truth, maybe I read the first page. All right, if you must know, I read it all. But only because I had to figure out what to do.

I brooded about it in my office and tried to think of something serious and high-minded to keep myself from dwelling on the sexual details of her essay—land mines in the former Yugoslavia or starvation in Africa or flooding in Bangladesh. But my high-minded thoughts soon became entangled in my low-minded ones, so that Bangladesh appeared as a sexual Shangri-la where buxom girls wearing wet T-shirts went swooshing through the flooded streets as if they were on some giant waterslide.

There was a quiet knock on the door, and Günter let himself in, giving me a solicitous pat on the shoulder.

"How are you doing, Candide?"

"I've been better."

"I know. Look, don't worry about it. If I were you, I would just ignore it. It's a provocation. She wants you to react."

"What are you talking about?"

"Caitlyn's paper," he said.

"How do you know about that?"

"You are always asking that question, and it is never the pertinent one. The question is, what are you going to do?"

"I'm sure you will figure that out before I do," I said.

"Do you think I could see the paper? I just want to—"

"Günter!"

"Well, it's not as if she and I—"

"I don't want to know what you two did! Aren't parents supposed to be taking care of these kinds of things?" I asked, feeling exasperated.

"You can't really blame our parents. They are fighting an uphill battle. It's easier just to go along."

"Can't they at least impose some control on wardrobes?"

Günter laughed.

"You should enjoy it. Other men your age do," he said. "There are girls here who date men in their twenties and thirties."

He was right, of course. That year, one senior girl was dating a man in his fifties. He was famous, an artist, and French—each quality apparently taking about a decade off of his age.

"Günter, can we please talk about something else? And can we pretend to have a normal teacher-student relationship?"

"If you insist," he said as he stood up to leave. "Are you sure I can't—"

"Günter!"

I entered the class and looked at Caitlyn.

"Caitlyn, we need to talk after class," I said.

"Oooh, the teacher's pet is in trouble," said Rebecca.

"Am I in trouble?" Caitlyn smiled innocently.

"Not exactly," I said, feeling flustered.

"Is this about my paper?"

What was she doing? I didn't want to talk about this in class.

"Let's talk about it after class," I said.

"Your paper? What could you write in a paper that would get you in trouble?" Ally asked.

"I wrote about Emma's first night as a married woman," she said. The class looked at her uncomprehendingly. "You know, sex."

"Oh my God!" Ally screamed. "You wrote about sex. That is so great! That is so great!"

Laura shook her head in disbelief.

"Maybe we should read it in class," said Jacob.

"No," I said.

"Can I read it?" he asked Caitlyn.

"Of course not," she said, "you're not mature enough to read something like that. I thought Mr. Spencer was, but apparently I was wrong."

She gave me a disappointed look.

"All right, everyone, let's drop this, and talk about the book," I said. "Caitlyn and I will talk about the paper after class."

"I just don't see why sex should be off-limits," Caitlyn insisted. "All of these Austen books are about men and women forming relationships, but we never see anything physical going on. Presumably, people in the nineteenth century had sex. They obviously didn't live in a time when they could discuss sex. But we don't live in that sort of time, so I was simply filling a hole in the literature of the period."

"Filling a hole," Jacob giggled.

All the girls looked at him with disgust.

"She's right, Mr. Spencer," said Ally. "Austen is in denial."

"It's not denial. It's decorum," I said.

"But you can even read about it in the *New York Times*," Caitlyn said. "Remember that article about how middle school girls give boys blow jobs as a way to have sex but keep their virginity?"

I had tried to blot that article from my memory because, if middle school girls were giving blow jobs, I was frightened to think what high school girls were doing. I certainly didn't get any blow jobs when I was in middle school. Then again, I wasn't really getting any blow jobs as an adult either.

It didn't help that it was spring, which the students responded to like young animals in heat. Sex was in the air. If you didn't want to catch students at it and haul them in front of a dean, you generally tried to avoid using any out-of-the-way stairwells late in the afternoon. It was also best not to notice the Kama Sutra–esque entwining of limbs under the lunch tables.

"Even our parents talk to us about sex," said Rebecca, looking far more horrified by the parental involvement than she was about the sex. "My mother kept trying to talk to me about the advantages of various forms of birth control. Like I want to hear about that from *her!*"

"Can we please talk about something else?" I asked.

"Mr. Spencer, you need to learn to be more comfortable with your sexuality," Caitlyn said. "We're all deeply sexual beings, you know."

She looked at me so intently that I was forced to find refuge in the Freud poster above her head.

"Whatever happened to the innocence of childhood?" I asked desperately, although I knew that the idea would sound about as relevant as a quilting party.

They all gave me a blank look.

"You know, that time before you started to worry about college and . . . and . . . sex. And there weren't any expectations, and you could play. Just be a kid," I said.

"No expectations?" Rebecca said.

"Just play?" Ally said.

"Yes! You know, kite flying, jumping rope, whatever," I said.

"My mother has had me tested every year since I was three," said Rebecca. "You can't just send a kid out to play and expect that child to get into a school like Academy X."

"Tested for what?" I asked incredulously.

"You know, when you learn to walk, when you learn to talk, to color, when you are potty trained, all that sort of stuff," Rebecca said.

"Doesn't that just happen?" I asked, wondering when infancy had become a developmental hurdle.

"Sure, it happens," said Ally, "but you just can't wait around. It makes a big difference if you start falling behind your peer group. You don't want to have to tell the admissions committee that your child didn't start talking until two. You want to be able to tell them that your child started talking by the twelfth month."

Toddlers now had to worry about keeping up with the Joneses?

"You can't control those things," I said.

"Of course you can!" Rebecca said, looking at me as if I needed some remedial training myself. "When I was five, I didn't do well on some of my coordination tests, so she put me in a special class."

"Yeah, I had to take child yoga," Ally said. "My mother promised me that I would thank her later."

"My aunt put her twins on a special diet of foods that were supposed to be good for brain growth. Well, and also because they were a little chubby," said Rebecca.

Brain growth? It sounded like a bad 1950s-era science experiment.

"Babies are supposed to be fat," I said.

"Yeah, maybe when they are one," said Ally. "Not after that. I know a lot of mothers who ration their kids' food."

I wondered what Wordsworth would say. Trailing clouds of glory indeed.

After the class, Caitlyn followed me back to my office. We sat in silence for a few moments. I was having trouble figuring out how to reprimand her without revisiting some of the more salacious parts of the essay.

"Caitlyn, you must realize how inappropriate your essay was."

"I don't agree. I followed the assignment. Wasn't it well written?"

"Of course, it was well written. That's not what I'm—"

"And didn't you tell us we could write about anything we wanted?"

"Just because I haven't explicitly forbidden writing about sex doesn't give you permission to do it. That's like saying that you have to be reminded not to rob a bank."

"I find it interesting that you would compare sex to robbing a bank," she said.

"Don't try to change the subject by psychoanalyzing me."

"Well, I'm not the one who put a poster of Freud on the wall."

"This isn't about Freud. This is about your pornographic essay."

"It wasn't pornographic! It was artistic!"

At that moment, I was filled with sympathy for Kate as she faced her clay phallus day after day. And if it had been in front of me at that moment, I would have smashed it to pieces.

"I'm not going to debate this with you."

"You know, throughout history, men have been afraid of women's sexuality!"

"I know," I sighed. "I'm the one who taught you that."

"What's that thing Freud talked about?" She paused, and then her face lit up. "The vagina dentata! That's what this is!"

"Can you please not use that word?"

"What word? *Dentata?*"

She laughed.

"Caitlyn, this isn't funny."

"Don't think that Günter hasn't told tell me about your attempt to live in denial."

Damn Günter and his big mouth!

"I'm not arguing any more about this. I want you to rewrite the essay without any sex. Is that clear?"

"Yes," she said. "But that doesn't mean I agree with what you're saying."

After she left, I decided to forget about the essay and instead take to heart what she had said about how we are all sexual beings by spending a little time patching up my own romantic life, especially since I was quickly coming around to the Head's point of view that a high school was no place for a single man. I walked to the library. Amy was behind the desk stamping books with uncommon grace, and I couldn't resist watching her for a few moments. The image of her as a Knicks dancing girl popped into my mind, and I felt myself flush.

"John? Are you all right? You look distracted," Amy said.

"Oh, yes," I laughed, "I'm fine. Just wanted to return this book."
I handed it to her.

"Are you sure you're all right? You're sweating," she said.

"Ha, this is nothing. You should see me when I really sweat," I said.

Did I actually say that? Did I just put the image of myself dripping with sweat in her mind? Disgusting.

"It's supposed to be healthy to sweat," she said.

Yes, healthy. Short step to robust. Perhaps even virile. I puffed out my chest and tried to project a manly vigor.

"That's right. It's important to secrete, um, that is . . ." I said, drifting into silence. Secretion did not seem like a more promising tack to take.

"Toxins?"

"That's right. Toxins," I said thankfully. "Anyway, enough about sweaty old me."

Sweaty old me? Did I want to die alone? Surrounded by unused kitchen gadgets that my mother had sent me? I could feel myself on the verge of releasing a whole new batch of toxins, so I thought I should get to the point immediately.

"I, uh, that is to say, the other night, you know, when, well, anyway, I just thought, uh . . . You know . . ."

"I know. I feel bad about it as well," said Amy.

Incredible! We were totally on the same wavelength. I was absolved—she must have known that I hadn't been leering rudely. Staring thoughtfully was about the most you could say. And clearly it was the sausage, not the beer. And, and, and . . . maybe the date hadn't been a disaster after all. Looking back, it almost began to seem like a great first date story that a couple will tell laughingly to their other couple friends. I plunged ahead boldly.

"So, I, uh, well, I was thinking that, um, it might be, well, you know, that we might, uh, that is—"

"That we should go out again," she said.

"Yes!"

"Maybe you could get tickets to another Knicks game."

Was she kidding? Maybe if I sold one of my kidneys. I hadn't really expected us to patch things up so easily, so I hadn't stocked the old mental cupboard with date ideas. Although it would have been nice to suggest something along the lines of a perfect café with a garden in the back, the truth was that my entertainment consisted mainly of Ron and Kate and television, so brilliant ideas were not cascading off my tongue. The only thing that came to me was takeout and a movie from Blockbuster. I cursed myself for being a cultural Neanderthal. My frantic gaze fell on a flyer for a Velázquez exhibit at the Met.

"I've really wanted to see that Velázquez exhibit at the Met," I said.

"So have I." She smiled.

"Great."

We made arrangements, and I walked back to my office trying to convince myself that my strangled inarticulateness was actually winsome charm. Günter was waiting for me with an amused smile.

"So, quite a class today," he said.

"Please don't make me relive the experience," I said. "And thanks for selling me out."

"You can't let yourself get so upset about it. It's no use pretending that your students are in some happy, preadolescent state. Frankly, just getting students to have safe sex would be an improvement. If you knew the number of kids on antibiotics for some sort of—"

"Günter! I can't maintain my already fragile belief that teenage dating consists of hand-holding if you keep thrusting all of this in my face."

"Well, you better not read next week's paper. We're running a double-page spread that connects the sexual dots among the senior class. Once you include the usual array of drunken one-night stands, dances, overnight trips, and summer flings, it's a testament to the unflagging sexual ardor of—"

"Günter, please!"

Sure, I could have stopped pretending. I could have simply faced the facts. But it was much easier to teach a roomful of teenagers who, in my imagination, went home to evenings of roller-skating and watching cartoon network than to a roomful of kids downing vast quantities of illegal substances and using various orifices for purposes that the Church likes to refer to euphemistically as the non-canonical path.

Before I could go home that day, I had to make it through a final meeting with Strude and Andrews to select the winning essay. I sat quietly through an hour or so of the usual arguments, biding my time, waiting for the moment when exhaustion would finally outweigh obstinacy. And the moment was at hand. The corners of Strude's mouth were white with dried saliva, and she looked even more dessicated than usual. Andrews's peasant blouse had dark stains under the armpits. They were deadlocked between two final students—Caitlyn and Laura.

There was so much to recommend Caitlyn—the warm glow of her regard, not to mention her influential father and the possible benefits his regard would have for me. On the other hand, Caitlyn would have things her way her entire life. She didn't need the boost that the prize would give. The sun would always shine brightly on Caitlyn Brie. Laura was another story. She would always be overshadowed by the Caitlyn Bries of the world. The prize could help rectify that to some extent. It would allow her to cross to the sunny side of the street, at least for a while.

I also felt guilty about Marcus. The purplish bruise. The duct tape. Something stirred within me, some long-lost part of me that had been hibernating or kept on starvation rations. A part with a much more active sense of right and wrong and of how to draw the line between the two.

"I think we should pick Laura," I said, interrupting an interminable harangue on the use of the dash by Strude. Both women

122

looked at me in surprise. Not only had I not spoken for the last half an hour, but I had already given every indication that I thought Caitlyn should win. Both were silent, as they quickly adjusted their strategies. I saw my opportunity and pressed on.

"I think both candidates are magnificent. I wish we could split the prize," I said, "but I find Laura the superior writer in two key respects. First, I was a little dismayed at Caitlyn's occasionally too liberal use of the comma. Edwina has convinced me of the importance, indeed the necessity, of proper grammar if we are to move forward not just as individuals but as a society, that grammatical correctness is akin to moral purity."

I thought I might have gone too far and passed into the land of irony. I turned to Strude with what I hoped was a look of fawning respect, and she smiled. Andrews was about to explode. I leaned over to her and placed my hand on her arm.

"Equally important," I said, as I gave her a look meant to convey not just respect but a deep physical attraction restrained only by my own unworthiness, "I find Laura a superior writer in terms of her creativity. Although Caitlyn has picked the more exciting topic, Laura has a correspondingly much more difficult task. To wring poetry from a Freudian reading of *Great Expectations*, well, I think we can all agree what a challenging task that had to be.

"Not to be too personal," I said, staring at Andrews and blinking rapidly as if holding back tears, "but I found myself learning not just about the book but about . . . yes, about myself."

Once again, I worried that I might have overdone it, but I saw that Andrews had tears in her eyes as well. I knew that it was only a matter of time. I sat back and allowed the two of them to come up with their own justifications. They talked for another half an hour, expanding and elaborating on what I had said, which gave me time to bask in the glow of my own self-regard. I am a good person, I thought, a very good person.

DANGEROUS LIAISONS

At school the next day, I felt enormously pleased with myself. Chalk one up for the little guy, compliments of John Spencer, humanitarian. I entered the room and surveyed the students with a benign smile on my face.

"Today, I want to talk about Emma's realization that she loves Knightley," I said. "So, any thoughts?"

"He is so much older," said Ally, "isn't that kind of gross?"

Rebecca was studiously silent—her father had remarried a woman who was at least a couple of decades younger, and he insisted on bringing her to school events.

"Is it any different from what goes on today?" Laura asked. "Look at all of the older men with younger women."

"And older women with younger men," Jacob chimed in, "talk about disgusting."

"At least they are both from the same class," said Caitlyn.

"We haven't talked much about class in the novel yet, but that has a big effect, doesn't it?" I asked.

"People in that world are not supposed to aspire to something outside of their station," Laura complained. "You're just supposed to accept it."

"Yeah, but it's not that way anymore," Rebecca said. "We talked about this in U.S. history. The Revolution changed all of that. We're a meritocracy."

"Really? What about this school?" I asked.

"Class is everywhere at this school," said Laura.

"And if you're in the wrong group, there's no escape," said Marcus forlornly.

"That's what losers say," replied Caitlyn.

Marcus looked like he wanted to crawl under the table.

"Caitlyn," I said angrily. "I want you to apologize to Marcus."

"I have nothing to apologize for."

"Then you can leave," I said.

"Fine," she said, packing up her books and walking out.

"Can I leave?" Jacob asked.

"No!"

The rest of the class was subdued and uncomfortable. Afterward, I walked back to my office in a funk. Günter was waiting for me. He gave me a pat on the arm.

"You should have just taken the holiday today," he said.

"What are you talking about? There's no holiday," I said.

"Perhaps not an official holiday, but it is the week after a number of students were notified if they would be accepted off of the waiting lists," he said.

I gave him a confused look.

"You are familiar with the college admission holiday season? A day off *before* the SATs to rest. The following Monday to recover from the strain. When college letters arrive. A few days off in the fall to visit schools and then another few days to revisit schools in the spring. The day off before college interviews to relax. Is any of this ringing a bell?"

"But getting off the waiting list?"

"Hey, I don't make the rules."

"If this is some 'holiday,' what are you doing here?"

"Oh I'm not going to classes," Günter replied, "I'm just here to work on the newspaper."

He gave me another sympathetic smile and left. A few moments later, there was a knock on my door, and Caitlyn entered.

"I'm very upset with you," she said.

"Frankly, Caitlyn, I don't care. Your behavior in class today was totally inappropriate. I've never been more disappointed in you," I said.

"Oh, it's just one stupid class."

"This isn't about one class! This is about showing respect for your fellow students."

She shrugged.

"Whatever."

"Why are you acting like this?"

"Why should I tell you? You don't care about me."

"Of course I do. You're one of my favorite students. You know that."

"Not your very favorite."

Actually, she probably still was, despite her recent behavior. The previous year, she had single-handedly saved my junior English class by using her charm to turn the boys into literary world-beaters. We sailed through the poetry section after she told them that poetry was the quickest way to a woman's heart. And when she convinced them that reading Homer would teach them to be real men, they asked if they could read the *Odyssey* after we had finished the *Iliad*. I even still had a faint hope that the lessons in *Emma* would not be lost on her.

"I'm not, am I?" she said.

"What are you talking about?"

"You didn't pick me."

"For what?"

"For the essay contest!"

She couldn't know about that. We had only picked the winner last night, and it wouldn't be announced for another week. Strude was a stickler for rules. And Andrews was—well, actually, Andrews was just the type of person to tell Caitlyn that she'd wanted her to win.

"First of all, you are not supposed to know about that, and second of all, a committee picks the winner, not me," I said.

"You had the deciding vote."

How much did Andrews tell her? I decided to appeal to Caitlyn's better nature.

"Caitlyn, you wrote a great essay. Really. One of the very best. I loved it. But Laura also wrote a great essay. Either one of you would have been an excellent choice. You have had so much success. Don't you think it would be great for Laura to have some recognition?"

I could see a struggle waging within Caitlyn. After years of being trained to vanquish all of her opposition, some small part of her was fighting against that instinct. I was about to congratulate myself on being the cause of such remarkable personal growth when Caitlyn shook her head violently.

"But she cheated!"

"That's ridiculous."

"Oh, please," she said, as if I was hopelessly naïve, "people like her . . ."

She left the thought unfinished, but she didn't have to say any more.

"You have to investigate," she insisted.

"Caitlyn, please don't do this."

"Do what? I'm just telling the truth."

She stood up.

"I expect you to look into this," she said. Then she smiled. "See you tomorrow."

I shouldn't have been surprised. Academy X was, after all, the kind of school that had created the type of woman who slammed her SUV into a crowd outside a bar in the Hamptons, called the injured victims white trash, and then drove away from the scene of the crime. Share your crayons. Play nicely with others. Those types of sentiments were all well and good most places, but this was New York City.

Of course, I had no intention of doing anything about her accusation. Unfortunately, Laura stormed into my office moments later.

"What's going on?"

"Nothing."

"According to Caitlyn—"

"Don't get caught up in her little games."

"That's easy for you to say. You're not the one she has accused of cheating!"

"Look, the important thing to remember is—"

"It's because of that stupid essay contest. Isn't it?"

"Laura, I know you are upset. But I think we need to focus on—"

"So does anyone get to make accusations against someone else? Or is it just *some* people?"

"That's not fair."

"Fair! Caitlyn gets whatever she wants. Is that fair? Everyone treats her like a queen. Is that fair?"

"No." I sighed. "It's not fair."

She paused.

"You know, I'm not the one who plagiarized," she said. "You should be talking to Caitlyn."

"Can we just drop this entire matter?"

"Why don't you check both of our papers?"

"I have no intention of checking either paper."

"So I never get a chance to clear my name? I have to put up with her whisper campaign against me."

"Let's just forget all of this nonsense," I said. "Laura, I want you to be the bigger person. I want you to rise above it. I know it isn't fair, but I also know that you aren't like her, that this sort of thing is beneath you."

Laura looked at me and went through her own internal struggle.

"No," she said.

"No?"

"No."

"What does that mean?"

"I want you to check the papers—both papers. Promise me!"

"I'm not going to promise you. I wasn't going to do anything about Caitlyn's accusation, and I'm not going to do anything about yours."

"Please, Mr. Spencer," she said, giving me a desperate look. "You know what she is capable of. I don't want to walk up to receive the award and look out at all those people whispering to each other about how Caitlyn should have won the award."

"I'll think about it," I said.

"No, promise me!"

"All right," I said unhappily.

I couldn't believe I was actually making that promise to her, but if I really wanted to congratulate myself for standing up for the under-dog, I couldn't balk at the first sign of trouble.

At lunch, my mood was not improved by the plate of Lunchtime Delight. The name alone implied a certain vagueness about the in-gredients. The Delight consisted of brownish, shingle-shaped blocks covered in a greasy gravy.

"What if one of them has actually plagiarized?" I said.

Ron and Kate were still staring intently at the shingles.

"Is it a meatloaf?" Kate asked.

"Well, it's possibly a loaf, but I'm not sure about the meat," said Ron. He sniffed a piece suspiciously.

Kate lifted the side of her plate and watched the gravy ooze across it.

"Look, it's no big deal," I said, "watch."

I cut a large piece off with some difficulty and jammed it into my mouth. I can't really describe the sensation after that. It was a little like if you placed something in your mouth and then found that it had been pulled from one of the toilets in Penn Station the day after

New Year's Eve. I ran to the bathroom and spit it out, although my mouth was coated in something for the rest of the day that reminded me of the smell in my junior high locker room. When I came back to the table, Kate and Ron looked at me with concern.

"Are you all right?" Ron asked.

"No, I'm not all right. My two best students have accused each other of plagiarism," I said.

"Look, it's no big deal," said Kate. "I'm sure there is nothing wrong with either paper. Besides, you need to go to the library and get to work on your speech."

"And see you know who," Ron said.

"I think it's safe to say that John has burned that bridge," said Kate.

"What happened?" Ron asked.

"John had a little too much to drink, and—"

"Actually, we're going on another date this week," I said smugly.

"What? After what happened?"

"I guess Ron is right. Alpha male and all of that."

"Biologically speaking, that does uphold my theory. You see, when the female of the species—"

"Oh, shut up!" Kate said angrily.

After school, I sat hunched over a pile of education journals feeling sorry for myself. Amy wasn't even there to flirt with. For an hour or so I slogged halfheartedly through the journals that Kate had helped me find. Libraries made me sleepy, and I had the strong urge to lay my head down on the pages of *Education Today* and take a long nap. It was remarkable that I had made it through so many years of grad school. I thought bitterly of how movies had managed to glamorize research—fifteen minutes in some library before a eureka moment when the hero would dash back into the world of action, as opposed to months spent in the musty stacks reading endless numbers of boring books.

I glanced at my watch. I had been reading for a little over an hour, and I only had a couple of pages of random notes to show for it. The doodles outnumbered the notes by a ratio of three to one. I had done quite a nice picture of the Head being stretched on a rack.

Johns glided up to me in his usual reptilian manner.

"John?"

I gave him an annoyed look.

"I wanted to apologize. I gave you terrible advice the other day," he said. He made a slight bow.

"Yes, you did," I said. The guy had some nerve to think he could simply apologize about something like that.

"I beg forgiveness," he said, making another bow. "I'm looking forward to your talk. I've been doing a little reading on the subject myself."

To sabotage me, I thought grimly.

"How nice," I said.

"Well, I'll let you get back to work."

He made an even lower bow and backed slowly away as if I were some potentate. I watched him drop a book into the return bin at the front desk as he left. I hurried over and pulled it out—*Empowering the Student Within: A Child-Centered Classroom for a Child-Centered World* by Robert Hedges. Relief washed over me. Research done! And this time I was going to be prepared for Johns.

I went back to my desk, pulled out the papers of Caitlyn and Laura, and tracked down the books they had used. I checked the first few citations from Laura's paper and breathed a sigh of relief. They were fine—better than fine. With her usual diligence, she had footnoted anything even vaguely drawn from the book. I checked Caitlyn's paper. The same story. I felt as if a terrible burden had been lifted. Dealing with a plagiarism case would have been a nightmare, especially for seniors about to go off to college.

One of Caitlyn's books had been on my Ph.D. oral exams, and I leafed through some of the other essays when a sentence jumped out at me. I looked through Caitlyn's paper and found the same sentence. Word for word. I put the book down and took a deep breath.

Caitlyn was only weeks away from graduating. She was one of the most popular girls in the school and, in all likelihood, was heading off to Princeton in the fall, thanks in large part to my letter. Her father was obscenely rich and well connected. A plagiarism case could mean disaster for her. And it certainly wasn't going to do me any good either. I eyed the book unhappily. I had opened Pandora's Box, and I wasn't sure I was ever going to be able to get it closed again.

Evidence collected for the disciplinary hearing concerning John Spencer's conduct toward Caitlyn Brie. School counselor's confidential notes from the interview with David Lurch:

I can't say I was paying much attention . . . Look, I don't spend a lot of time thinking about the class . . . No, I'm not high! . . . I picked up that smell from some guy on the subway . . . No, I won't turn out my pockets. Who are you, some Nazi?

LOLITA

"Colin Firth is sexier," Rebecca insisted.

"How can you say that? Ewan McGregor is much hotter," replied Ally.

Normally, I would have called a halt to this discussion long ago, but I was busy trying to figure out what I was going to do about Caitlyn. It didn't help that I was already feeling a rising sense of anxiety because I had to give my talk that afternoon. My conscience, generally so accommodating, would not allow me to ignore the matter. I thought I had come up with a reasonable compromise between charging her with plagiarism and simply pretending I hadn't found anything. I would show her the book, talk to her about the importance of academic honesty, scare her for a while, and then tell her that I thought it was a mistake in judgment that could be handled between the two of us by having her write a new paper. She would learn a valuable lesson and I would avoid the wrath of her father, Snopes, and the Head for throwing a monkey wrench into Caitlyn's hopes for Princeton. It might even bring about the Emma-like transformation of Caitlyn that I had been hoping for, so that she would look back on her high school years and remember me as the teacher who had made a difference in her life. Surely, the goal of a teacher was not to punish but to educate. At least, that's what I kept telling myself

"I always thought Hugh Grant was very hot in *Sense and Sensibility*," said Laura.

"*Hugh Grant*," said Ally with derision.

"Yes," Laura said defensively.

"I sort of liked Emma Thompson in *Sense and Sensibility*," offered Marcus.

He smiled shyly at Laura, who was horrified that she and Marcus might actually share something in common.

"First of all, Marcus, we are talking about *male* actors. Second of all, Emma Thompson is *old*," said Rebecca. "And third—"

"Dude, what are you doing watching a movie about a Jane Austen book?" Jacob said, shaking his head in disbelief. "*Voluntarily.*"

"It wasn't voluntary," Marcus said. "My mother wanted me to go."

"*Your mother*," said Jacob, "you do what *your mother* wants you to do."

"Maybe you had better ask your mother to go to the prom with you," Caitlyn said. "I think she is the only one who will say yes."

"Caitlyn!" I said.

"I was just kidding."

I gave her a stern look.

"Oh, all right! I'm *sorry*, Marcus," she said with exaggerated politeness.

"Marcus's comment raises an interesting issue about the book . . ." I said, trying to get off the topic of Marcus and his mother.

Luckily the bell rang because I had no idea what that interesting issue was. Marcus approached me as everyone filed out.

"Thanks, Mr. Spencer," he said.

"Marcus, don't thank me. I should never have let it get to that point. I'm sorry that it did," I said.

"I should never have gone to that movie with my mother."

I smiled.

"Don't stop going to Austen movies. Women in college are going to love that about you."

"They are?"

"Definitely," I said. "And your feelings about Emma Thompson show you to be a hero in the true Austen mode, a man of taste and distinction."

"Thanks," he said.

"I'll see you on Monday."

Caitlyn was waiting for me at my office.

"Hi, Mr. Spencer, do you have a few minutes?"

She flashed me a dazzling smile.

"I have to give a talk today," I said, hoping to put off the awful moment.

"Please. It won't take long."

"Caitlyn, with Marcus today, you can't do that," I said, as I sat down.

"I know. But I'm incredibly frustrated with him! I tried to set him up with this great girl, and he refused to ask her out!"

"Finding it more difficult to be a matchmaker than you thought?" I asked with an amused smile.

"No, I just—Mr. Spencer, forget about that for now. I'll apologize to him later. What I really came here to tell you was that Mr. Snopes called me last night, and it looks like Princeton is going to accept me off the waiting list. I want to thank you. He said that your letter really helped."

"That's great," I said without much enthusiasm. The book she had used was sitting on my desk. I tried to drop my copy of *Emma* on top of it before she noticed, but all I managed to do was draw her attention to it. She gave me a horrified look. There was no escaping it now. I plunged ahead guided only by the thought that it would be best if I could avoid any crying because her outfit was so skimpy that there was no place for me to give her a comforting pat without touching some part of her I didn't think I should be touching.

"Caitlyn, when I confronted Laura, she insisted that I check your paper for plagiarism."

"But that's not fair! She can't just do something like that!"

"That's not the issue."

It seemed too cruel to point out that she had done the same thing and was the cause of her own undoing.

"What are you going to do?"

"I don't know," I said.

She smiled at me.

"Can't we just deal with this between the two of us? You know, with Princeton and everything," she said breezily, "can't we just call it a valuable learning experience?"

That was pretty much my plan, but she said it so glibly, so easily. Where was the suffering? The shame?

"So, in other words, you think I should just pretend this never happened. I shouldn't tell the dean. I shouldn't tell Princeton."

"But, Mr. Spencer, couldn't we figure something out?"

She tilted her head and gave me a conspiratorial look.

I scrutinized her for signs of remorse. Even a little insincere remorse, patently false and done solely for my benefit, would have been nice. Where was my Emma? Where was the moral growth? And yet I hardly wanted to be the one to ruin all her plans. I was about to let her off, to accept the fact that she would never live up to the role I had imagined for her and that even the undying gratitude I had looked forward to was likely to be perfunctory at best. I leaned forward to give her the news. She leaned forward and slid her hand up my thigh.

"You know I think so much of you . . ."

I stared at her hand. My mouth opened and closed, but no sound came out. This wasn't the scene I had imagined! Knightley-like chastisement followed by Emma-like repentance. That was all! Caitlyn wasn't supposed to put her hand on my thigh! Caitlyn smiled, taking my silence as a sign of my acquiescence and confidently sliding her hand higher. Somehow I had taken a detour from Austen to erotica.

"Stop!" I shouted, pushing her hand off my leg.

As my fragilely maintained view of student innocence came crashing down, I couldn't help imagining Günter saying that he told me so.

"I think you'd better go," I said.

"But, Mr. Spencer, I find older men so much more . . . interesting." She looked at me like I was a particularly tasty ice cream cone that she intended to lick.

"Go!"

She stood up reluctantly and left. I had to give my talk later that day, or I would have told Samson that I was ill and gone home. I couldn't even talk about it to Ron and Kate because then they would know about the whole plagiarism mess and might force me to turn her in, which was exactly what I was trying to avoid. I skipped lunch and fretted about Caitlyn, although I took a number of breaks to fret about my talk, about what Kate would think, and about how my whole life seemed on the verge of going down the toilet.

By the time I was sitting in the cafeteria waiting to speak, the look on my face did not inspire confidence, and even Ron and Kate were hard-pressed to do more than mumble good luck. I had the air of one of those WWII pilots in the movies, the ones who have one last mission before going home to their sweetheart, the ones you just know are going to get shot down. I felt the first bead of sweat roll down my back. I cursed myself for ever entertaining the ambition of being chair. It was like I was back in the exam room as a Ph.D. candidate. But only four people had witnessed that humiliation. Today there was a whole roomful.

I looked around at my colleagues. What were so many of them doing here? It was a beautiful May day. They should have been playing hooky. My anxiety ratcheted up another notch, and a few more drops of sweat rolled slowly down my back. I lowered my head to read my note cards, but everything in front of my eyes started to blur. I was dimly aware that the Head was moving toward the podium.

Maybe I could stab myself with a pen! That would buy me at least a few minutes. It had worked in fifth grade when I had wanted to get out of a math test. I reached in my pocket but couldn't find anything sharper than a quarter. I could swallow the quarter. I could choke on it. I could run from the room choking. But what if it actually became stuck? What if I choked to death? Was death preferable to giving the speech? There was something comforting in the thought of a permanent escape from my situation. But to die from choking on a quarter? It was a close call, but in the end it seemed better to give the speech.

"Thank you for coming," the Head said. She was so relaxed up there, so smooth and polished. "We are lucky to have our own John Spencer here today to speak to us about empowering children in our classroom. I'm looking forward to learning more about this, as I'm sure you are, so without further ado, John Spencer."

I experienced the sensation of my body moving. It was as if another force had taken over my body, as I watched numbly from some distant region. I walked to the podium, carefully laid out my note cards, and took a sip of water. I was dimly aware of my heart beating furiously. My shirt clung damply to my back.

"I would like to talk to you . . ." My voice came out as a squeaky croak, and I heard muffled laughter from a couple of my colleagues. I took another sip and tried again.

"I would like to talk to you about empowering children in the classroom." I was relieved to find that my voice had returned to normal. But with each passing sentence, I spoke more quickly until the words came out in a nonsensical blur, as if a drunken man on speed was reciting experimental poetry. More laughter. I remembered that old advice to relax by thinking of the audience naked. Unfortunately, I thought of this as I saw Bob Gruntley, whose laughing figure was now unclothed to reveal a 275-pound man with marginal hygiene in all of his glory. I took another sip of water. I became vaguely aware of rustling from my audience and saw the Head glance at her watch and then at Samson. I noticed Johns sitting in the front row and smiling in his simpering way. I felt a rising fury at him, as if he was single-handedly the cause of all of my misery.

I began again, imagining each phrase as a rock that I was throwing at him. I spit out the phrases with a furious precision. The tone of my talk would have seemed quite at home at a neo-Nazi rally, although I hoped the audience would see that as a sign of my passionate intensity. When I finished, I glanced around the room at puzzled faces. The Head, somewhat bewildered, stood up, shook my hand, and invited the audience to ask questions. Johns's hand immediately shot up. I smiled as I thought of the withering reply I was about to give him.

"Yes?" I asked.

"You rely heavily on Robert Hedges's book, *Empowering the Student Within*," he said.

"Yes."

Diabolical scheme foiled! Truth and justice triumphant! Hero richly rewarded!

"He has written an article recently in which he disavows his earlier work and refutes the central contention of your talk," he said.

Central contention? I had been shooting for bland overview. When did contention come into the picture? And what article was he talking about? I winced as I thought of the pile of unread journals—with the Hedges book, it hardly seemed necessary to read them.

I took a sip of water. The Head was eyeing me closely.

"I, uh . . . I'm not sure I would agree with that," I said weakly.

"Really?" Johns said. "I happen to have the article here. Hold on a second."

Johns pulled the journal out of his bag and leafed through it in a leisurely fashion.

"Let's see. Here it is. 'The recent studies on child-empowered teaching, including my own, are fundamentally flawed. In the end, there is no evidence that the strategies work and some evidence that they are counter-productive.' Would you like me to go on?"

"No, that's quite all right," I said. Silence filled the room.

I noticed Kate stand up to my left.

"John, if I may?" Kate asked.

"Of course," I said.

"I know that John is trying to spare our colleague any embarrassment, but I think it is important that we evaluate this technique on the most up-to-date information. John and I were discussing the recent article by Hedges. We both concluded that the preponderance of evidence was against his new stand and in favor of child-empowerment techniques, which John has already excellently illustrated. John, I know you know more about this than I do, but do you mind if I read something from the journal article that you gave me the other day?"

"Of course not!" I said, feeling quite jovial all of a sudden.

She pulled a journal out of her bag and flipped through it as leisurely as Johns had.

"Yes, here it is. This article is by another author in response to Hedges. He writes, 'New studies of child-empowered teaching techniques have revealed their effectiveness. Hedges's recent reversal notwithstanding, it is clear that classrooms should incorporate aspects of the new methods.'"

She looked up from the journal.

"Would you like me to go on?"

"No, thank you," said Johns, bowing slightly and sitting down.

"Quite right," I said cheerfully. "Perhaps when you are done with it, you can share the article with our colleague."

I smiled at Johns, who was tapping his foot impatiently.

"Any other questions?"

Thankfully, there were none. The Head stood up.

"Well, let's thank John for a wonderful talk. I think we all found that very informative," she said.

People applauded politely, and the Head came over to shake my hand.

"After a rocky start, you did a fine job, John," she said.

"Thank you."

"The official announcement won't be for a few days, and I would appreciate it if you wouldn't say anything."

"Of course," I said, wondering if there was anyone who didn't already know.

"I have one piece of advice for you. While I applaud your decency toward Johns, you have to learn to be a little more self-protective," she said.

"Right. Thanks."

As she walked away, I searched the room for Kate. I saw her laughing with Ron about something. I made my way toward her, but I felt a hand on my elbow. I turned to find Samson beaming at me.

"Well done, John, well done," he said. "I think we can safely say that my plan is working out. I particularly admire the way you subtly mocked what you were saying. Brilliant. Very effective. Completely over the head of Van Huysen, of course. Really showed me your loyalty. I'm touched. I had a few doubts, but I see that what I have so carefully created will be placed in capable hands. When I think of the many years, well, decades, that I have spent building this department from the ground up—do you know that before I arrived, students were reading *Oliver Twist* instead of *Great Expectations*—well, needless to say . . ."

I let Samson's words wash over me for a few minutes until he was distracted by someone talking loudly behind him and then slipped away. I didn't get far before I felt O'Brien's boozy breath over my shoulder.

"Johnny boy, brilliant performance," whispered O'Brien. "I'm behind you one hundred percent. Don't worry. I'm protecting you from those vipers."

A hand slipped through my other arm.

"I was moved by your talk," Andrews whispered breathily. "Don't trust O'Brien. He's nothing but trouble."

"Watch her," O'Brien whispered in my other ear.

They had hated each other ever since he had propositioned her at a faculty party by asking her to lie down with him in the foul rag and bone shop of the heart, and she had responded by filing a sexual harassment complaint with the school. As I attempted to pull free of them both, I came face-to-face with Johns.

"Very good talk, John," he said, bowing.

I scowled at him.

"I hope you weren't upset by my question. I was just trying to make sure that we have the most up-to-date information," he said meekly.

"Really," I said skeptically.

"Yes," said Johns. "I can't tell you how thrilled I am about your promotion. It will be not just an honor but a pleasure to serve under someone like you."

It was difficult to concentrate on what he was saying. O'Brien and Andrews were continuing to hiss away in my ears. At last I managed to get away and find Ron and Kate.

"We're so proud of you," said Kate. She kissed me on the cheek.

"Congratulations, Chairman," said Ron, as he slapped me on the back.

"You don't think I was shaky in the beginning?" I asked.

"No, you were fantastic," Ron said. "Total alpha male. You had the audience in the palm of your hand."

"Kate, I can't thank you enough. You really saved me," I said, "but why didn't you share that article with me earlier?"

"Oh, I'm sorry. Let me give it to you now," she said, handing me a spring fashion catalog.

When I got home, I decided to call my parents and tell them the good news. At the very least, it would reassure my mother that I was not on the verge of suicide.

"Hello?"

"Hi, Mom, it's John," I said.

"John, how are you?" Her voice was a soft whisper.

"I'm fine. You don't need to whisper."

143

"Don't get upset, John. You need to maintain your emotional equilibrium. Did you get those Deepak Chopra tapes I sent you? I think they will really help center you emotionally and lead you to your true soul mate."

My emotional equilibrium, which had seemed quite stable just moments ago, began to feel a little wobbly.

"I wanted to tell you how my talk went."

"Well, dear, whatever happened, don't worry about it. As Deepak teaches, it is not the result but the process that we must focus on."

"It went well, Mom. The Head—"

"Try not to be so goal-focused, John. The important thing is that you are on a path, a journey. You can't expect to meet the right person immediately."

"Mom, I'm trying to tell you about my talk today."

"You must put aside the extraneous, John."

She took a deep breath and let out a low hum.

"Would you mind putting Dad on?"

"Hello, John," my father boomed into the phone.

"Dad, I just called to tell you that I gave my talk at school today, and it went well. So, it looks like I will be chair."

"I thought you said you were chair."

"No, not exactly. It's not official yet."

"So, when do you take over?"

"Not until after next year."

"After next year? That's ridiculous. You can't run a business like that. John, you should give Ryan a call. I can tell you right now that he won't take a year deciding whether or not to hire you."

"You don't understand, Dad. Schools run on a different schedule."

"If you can call it that." He snorted. "John, when I went to work more than forty years ago . . ."

I sat through a few minutes of Dad's rise through the ranks and begged off when he started to lose steam.

Evidence collected for the disciplinary hearing concerning John Spencer's conduct toward Caitlyn Brie. School counselor's confidential notes from the interview with Marcus Lipschitz:

Of course he's not a pedophile . . . Yes, I know what the word means . . . You think I don't know about sex? Well, for your information, there was a girl last year at computer camp . . . Yes, there *are* girls who go to computer camp . . . Just forget it . . . Because you have already made up your mind . . . No, he didn't harass anyone sexually . . . Because I know! Look, high school is not an easy place. It can be ruthless. People say things and don't want to sit by you in class. And don't invite you to their parties. And, well, it's hard, you know. And some teachers see that and try to protect you . . . No, not in that way! . . . No, he never touched me . . . Look, are you going to listen to what I'm saying?

AN IDEAL HUSBAND

I spent Saturday thinking about my upcoming date with Amy—long conversations during which Amy gave rapturous accounts of my talk—and trying to forget what had happened with Caitlyn.

On Sunday, I crossed Central Park firmly in the grip of the pathetic fallacy. Everything around me was in a joyous state. I almost expected a bluebird to settle on my shoulder and twitter away. I even picked a few flowers for Amy.

I approached the museum and saw her sitting on the steps waiting for me. Her hair was drawn back in a loose ponytail, and her feet were tucked under her. She was wearing a white button-down and capri pants, and I paused for a moment and gazed longingly at her bare ankle, which at that moment seemed to be the epitome of beauty, at least as far as a bony protuberance can be the epitome of beauty.

She looked up at me and smiled.

"Hi, John. Shall we go in?"

I remembered the flowers in my hand.

"These are for you."

"That's so sweet," she said.

She gave them a wary look and held them at arm's length.

"I'm not sure they will let me bring these in. And they're a little dirty. Do you mind?" She dropped them into a nearby wastebasket. I couldn't imagine ever minding anything she did.

We stood in line for tickets, and I subtly worked the conversation around to my talk.

"So, what did you think of my speech?" I asked.

"Your speech?"

"You know, the talk I gave on Friday."

She gazed at me blankly.

"On child empowerment."

"Oh, right," she said at last, "I'm afraid I didn't see it. I had to leave early on Friday. How did it go?"

I swallowed my disappointment and told her about the talk, taking the opportunity to embellish the scene in a modest way by casting myself as a conquering hero who had vanquished his quivering nemesis.

"So, Johns came to your rescue? That was nice of him."

"No, Johns tried to sabotage me," I said. "Remember the part about him pulling the journal out of his briefcase?"

"Right, right," she said, as she looked over my shoulder at something.

We reached the front of the line, I pulled out my wallet.

"Two please." I glanced at Amy and was appalled to see her rummaging in her purse. She was going to pay for her own ticket! I was being downgraded from a date to a . . . a . . . what? Not even a friend. An acquaintance! A co-worker! Alpha male indeed! Ron was full of crap. I could forget about any sort of future with her, let alone a future filled with kinky delights.

She pulled out some lip moisturizer and smiled at me. Lip moisturizer! Balm to troubled lips! And sweet succor to a troubled soul! I smiled back at her as I paid for our tickets. I smiled back at those smooth, soft, red, well-moisturized lips and imagined them doing unspeakable things all over my body, sometimes with Amy in a nurse's uniform. And sometimes wearing black leather. And for a brief instant in a police uniform because I had apparently been a very, very naughty boy.

All those thoughts left me slightly dizzy as we entered the cavernous coolness of the museum. It was already proving to be a far more enjoyable visit than my usual narcoleptic stumble through the galleries when my mother came to town. And it was still early. There was always the chance that she would have to remoisturize.

I felt like Hector and was tempted to grab a shield from one of the suits of armor. We entered the exhibition, and the crowds soon separated us, which was fine with me. I had a lot to think about after that whole moisturizer episode. When I finally looked around for her, she was gone. I hurried to the exit and spotted her in the gift shop.

"Sorry to take so long," I said.

"Oh, don't worry about it. I've been debating whether to get this or not," she said, holding a poster of one of the Velázquez paintings.

"It's beautiful," I said, looking at her, not the poster. "Let me get it for you."

"Are you sure?"

"Of course, it will be a memento to remember the day."

"That's so nice." She pulled one of the framed posters from the bin.

Framed! We were talking about a framed poster?

"Do you mind getting me these postcards as well? It seems stupid to pay twice for just a few dollars."

"Sure, sure," I said as I tried to catch a glimpse of the price tag on the back of the frame.

She wandered away, while the cashier scanned the items.

"That comes to two hundred six dollars and fifty-seven cents. Will that be cash or charge?"

"Charge," I croaked.

I didn't even have that much in my checking account. My budding romantic impulses were snuffed out under the weight of my impending financial disaster. I began to calculate how much it would cost me to live on peanut butter and jelly sandwiches for the next month, although those calculations were soon shoved aside by my general despair about the relationship. Who was I kidding? Did I really believe that things were going to work out with Amy? Was it even vaguely possible that the framed poster was simply a friendly gesture as opposed to some pathetic, desperate attempt to buy her goodwill?

Then I looked at her as she bent over a book about the exhibition. Her hair was falling softly across her face, and her expression was so untroubled that I thought she could easily carry away the doubts and fears of one more person. Who could begrudge her anything? I was being promoted, and soon I would be making more money. Not a lot more, but enough. And every time she looked at the poster, she would think of me. And maybe soon we would be in her apartment looking at it together. And maybe not looking at it together.

I walked over to her, and she smiled at me in a way that made all calculation seem foolish.

"That was great," she said. "Do you want to come back to my apartment and hang up the picture?"

"Sure," I said casually, as I began thinking again about those well-moisturized lips.

She asked me about becoming chair as we walked to her apartment. She even made a couple of jokes about how she would be the perfect teacher to hire when Samson retired. We arrived at her building and walked up three flights of stairs to her apartment. Light poured through high windows, and everything in the room seemed to shimmer.

"Why don't you head into the bedroom? I've got to find a hammer and a nail."

The bedroom! My mind grew dizzy with the implications. Perhaps she had wanted the poster as a pretext to get me back to her apartment. Perhaps she had been having her own thoughts about my somewhat dry but still very kissable lips. I walked into the next room, which was also bathed in light. At the glowing center was a bed piled high with lacy pillows. It was so immaculate that I thought she must have another bed stashed somewhere.

"I think we should put it over by that window," said Amy as she entered the room. She walked over to the spot and placed the nail against the wall. "Here, I think. Why don't you take this from me?"

I put down the poster and walked over. As I changed positions with her, our hands briefly touched, and my breath quickened. I would have to tell Ron about the hammering. I was sure this was a sign, some sort of revelation about our growing relationship.

"Oh, I have a message," she said, pushing the button on her answering machine. I gave the nail a few tentative taps.

"Hi, Amy," said a male voice that sounded familiar. "I know you keep saying how busy you are, but I thought maybe we could get dinner. Give me a call."

I saw my prize slipping from my grasp.

"Why don't we have dinner?" I blurted out. I turned my head to see her response and felt a stabbing pain in the finger holding the nail.

"Ooooohhhhhh," I moaned. I dropped the hammer and squeezed my finger.

"John, did you hurt yourself?" Amy asked. "Let me see."

I held out my finger, which didn't look nearly as bad as it felt. She took hold of my hand with both of her own and examined it closely. Competing with the pain was my excitement at her touch.

"This doesn't look too bad," she said. "Let me get you some ice."

She left the room. I wanted to sit down, but the only place to sit was the bed, which still seemed too pristine for human contact. Amy came back with ice in a plastic bag.

"Here, put this on it."

She picked up the hammer and examined the wall.

"Well, you didn't leave too big a mark on the wall, and I think the poster will cover it up," she said. "I guess I shouldn't have asked an intellectual like you to perform manual labor."

I wanted to take the hammer to myself after that comment. No manual labor! Why had I wasted all those years reading novels, instead of carrying a tool belt and learning the manly arts? And the word *intellectual* dripped with sexual contempt. I would never be allowed to hammer for her again. I would never be allowed to perform any physical activities for her, especially any intimate ones. My dinner invitation continued to hang unacknowledged in the air, although now it was a dinner invitation from a guy who couldn't even hammer a nail into the wall. While she finished putting up the picture, I debated asking her again.

"There," she said, stepping back from her handiwork, "that looks good, don't you think?"

She was standing very close to me, and I caught a faint smell of her perfume.

"So, about dinner . . ."

"Oh, I would love to, but it's been a long day. I'm tired, and I think you should go home and tend to your wound."

Damn my finger! I would gladly have cut it off at that moment.

She walked to the front door, and I followed unhappily behind her.

"But we should definitely do this again. I had fun."

She put her hand on my arm and pressed her well-moisturized lips briefly to my cheek.

I spent the walk back to my apartment thinking about the word *fun*. It could mean so many things. Little children had fun. Adults also had fun. What kind of fun would we be having? Chaste trips to museums? Or covering your friend with chocolate and whip cream and then becoming the cherry on top kind of fun? I decided to ask her out again tomorrow to find out as soon as possible just what sort of fun we would be having.

When I got back to my apartment, there was a message from Kate.

"Hi, just wanted to hear how the big date was. Give me a call."

I reluctantly picked up the phone. I knew she was going to take a harsh view of things I wanted to gloss over. And I was still worried that I would tell her about Caitlyn in a moment of weakness.

"So, lover boy, how did it go?"

I decided to stick with vague generalities.

"We had an excellent date."

"Did you do anything after the museum?"

What was this? The Inquisition?

"I went to her apartment afterward."

"Her apartment? Did the two of you—Oh, what a slut! I can't believe—"

"Amy's not that kind of girl," I said indignantly—not that I would have minded if she had been that kind of girl. "I was only there to hang a picture."

I left out the part about banging my finger. Humiliation in front of one woman a day was quite enough for me.

"Right." She snorted. "What were you doing hanging a picture?"

I paused for just the briefest moment as I tried to explain what had happened. Somehow, removed from Amy's presence, my gift seemed a bit extravagant.

"I was hanging the picture there because we got it at the exhibit."

"We? Do you have a joint checking account?"

"No, I bought her the poster," I said.

"That's nice. Why are you being so weird?"

"No reason," I said too quickly.

"John, you're not telling me everything."

I realized at that moment that I needed to find a female confidante who would show a little more trust, one who was happy to leave things unspoken.

"Well, you see, it wasn't just a poster. It was a—How to put this?— I guess you could say I bought her a framed poster."

"A framed poster? From the Met? Who does she think you are?"

"I'm sure she didn't realize—"

"Do you think you are actually going to buy your way into a relationship?"

"As Ron would say, it is one more encouraging sign of how she is letting me be the provider."

"Stop quoting Ron to me! Why do you think he has so much trouble getting a date?"

"It's not as if I was trying to buy her affection," I said defensively. "We only went to a museum, and I didn't buy her flowers. I simply gave her some that I picked from the park."

"You picked flowers for her?"

"Yes."

"That's actually very sweet," she said. "I'm impressed. I think that strikes exactly the right note, even if you did go overboard with the poster. Did she like them?"

"I think so," I said with an unfortunate catch in my throat.

"She didn't like the flowers?"

"Of course she liked them. She just, well, you see, it wasn't convenient to have flowers and walk around the Met."

"What did she do with them?"

I paused, trying to think of how to put her actions in the right context.

"She put them in a safe place," I said.

"Did she throw them away?"

"I guess if you want to put it in those terms."

"And you bought her the framed poster after she threw them away?"

"Yes."

She became very quiet.

"It's not as bad as you think. Really. We had a great time."

Silence.

"She even showed a certain tenderness, helped me with an injured finger."

153

Louder silence.

"So, I guess you could say the whole thing was a great success. Really. Boffo. Rave reviews."

"Didn't you give me some crappy used bread maker for my birthday?"

I had a sinking feeling. It was basically new. It had been kicking around my closet for a few months at most. My mother had given it to me as part of a plan to provide me with all the necessary kitchen gadgets to take the place of a wife.

"Well, you see, the thing about it is . . ."

"Whatever."

I heard a click as she hung up on me. I felt a little guilty at first, but she had a boyfriend who bought her lots of nice things. Besides, the bread maker was a perfectly good gift. What right did she have to get upset about a gift like that? And where did she get off being so critical of Amy? What did Kate even know about the date? She wasn't on it. She was being completely unreasonable. Thank God things hadn't worked out between us. Like I needed to put up with that on a daily basis.

Evidence collected for the disciplinary hearing concerning John Spencer's conduct toward Caitlyn Brie. School counselor's confidential notes from the interview with Ally Alredy:

I like him . . . No, not *like* like. That is so gross . . . Of course I like Caitlyn. She is, like, the most popular girl in the school . . . I don't know what happened . . . No, I don't think Caitlyn would lie . . . No, I don't think Mr. Spencer would lie either.

BREAKFAST AT TIFFANY'S

On Monday, Caitlyn wasn't back, and her absence gnawed at me. I also made the mistake of showing a scene from the movie *Emma* in class. I was hoping to have a discussion about how you translate a novel into a film. Instead, the boys spent most of the time talking about how much cleavage the dresses of the time revealed. On the bright side, even David perked up enough to join the discussion.

After class, I stopped by the library to see Amy. She was sitting at the circulation desk, and I sauntered over for an intimate tête-à-tête. She didn't give me the dewy-eyed look I was hoping for, but I suspected that the professional code for librarians was very strict on the matter of dewy eyes. One more mark in her favor, I thought to myself. The perfect companion for a future chair.

"You look lovely today," I said.

"Ugh, I look terrible," she said. "I went out with a friend last night, and we drank too much wine. I feel like a mess."

Sweet vindication—I couldn't wait to tell Kate that Amy had girlfriends.

"So, where did you and your girlfriend go?"

"Actually, it was a boyfriend," she said.

I felt as if I had just been whacked in the head with a copy of *Clarissa*.

"A friend who is a boy, not a boyfriend," she said after she saw the look on my face.

"Of course, of course." I had a sickly smile on my face and was still staggering from the blow. Buck up, I told myself. Kate is your friend, and she is a girl. Nothing untoward there. Perfectly normal.

"How is your thumb?"

Yes! Solicitude! Must mention this to Ron. Clear sign that she was developing feelings for me, according to some study on primates or something.

"Well, I've had to cut back on my hitchhiking," I said.

She looked at me with confusion.

"Just joking," I said. Okay, stay away from the finger jokes. "Anyway, who needs a thumb? How important is it anyway?"

I felt vaguely disloyal to Ron, who was always going on about the importance of opposable thumbs in human evolution.

"Besides," I added, "in New York, the use of the middle finger is much more important."

She gave me another confused look. Again with the finger jokes!

"You know, when you, uh . . ." I didn't want to flip her the bird in the middle of the library, so I decided to change the subject. "I had a wonderful time yesterday."

There—was that so hard? A simple declarative sentence.

"Me, too," she said, giving me a look that, if not quite dewy, was promisingly moist. "Listen, there's something I want to talk to you about. Are you free for dinner tonight?"

Tonight! She could barely stand to pass an evening without me.

"That would be great," I said.

"Why don't you come by around seven? There's a great little Italian place near me."

The head librarian came over to talk to Amy and gave me a stern look. I had once accidentally left the library's copy of *Portnoy's Complaint* on the subway and then told her that the book had been stolen by a gang of Roth fanatics. Unfortunately, an Academy X student had already found it on the train and brought it in. It seemed like a good time to return to my office.

As I got ready for my date that night, in a freak return to adolescence, a zit appeared on my forehead. I took an aggressive course of action, which only made it quadruple in size, and then spent half an hour trying to undo my handiwork, including a run to the drugstore to pick up one of those cover-up sticks. After applying it, I looked as if I had some strange skin disease centered around a Mount Vesuvius–like bump. If only we were going to a costume ball, and I was wearing a Batman mask, which would show off my mouth to good advantage. I had often been told that I had a very nice mouth. One woman had even compared it to a ripe plum—or perhaps she had compared me to a ripe plum. I can't quite remember, but she definitely had said something very flattering about my mouth. I washed my face and tried not to look at myself in the mirror when I left the apartment.

On the cab ride across the park, I stared out at the fireflies flickering on the lawn. The fading light silhouetted a couple walking hand in hand, and I smiled as I thought about Amy and myself doing the same thing.

"Asshole," yelled the cabdriver, "pick a lane!"

We reached her building, and I got out and rang her buzzer.

"I'll be right down," she said.

When she emerged, she looked dazzling in a pair of jeans and a tight-fitting, sleeveless black shirt.

"Hi," she said.

"Hi," I replied suavely.

"The restaurant isn't far," she said. "I'll lead the way."

I had topped off my verbal bag of tricks with a little poetry memorized specially for the occasion, and I smiled inwardly as I thought of the charm juggernaut I was about to unleash.

"I look at you and think of what Pablo Neruda wrote," I said.

"That I want to do to you what the cherry blossom does to the spring."

She looked at me quizzically.

"Wait, that's not quite right," I said. "I want to do to you . . ."

Damn! This whole memorizing poetry thing was harder than it looked. Amy was staring at my frowning face.

"You're not thinking dark thoughts about me, are you?" She laughed.

"No, I'm trying to say . . . Well, let's just say that it involved cherry blossoms and spring, and it was really quite beautiful. And . . ."

And what? How hard was it to remember one line of poetry. My love is like a red, red rose? No. My mistress's eyes are nothing like the sun? Not even close. The voice of your eyes is deeper than all roses? Still not it. I can't get no satisfaction? True but not helpful. Let us go then you and I?

I noticed Amy looking at me strangely. How long had I been standing there gaping like an idiot? Clearly, long enough that my silence had continued down the street to awkward and then rounded the corner to embarrassing. I was going to spend the rest of my life scanning the personals. Some sad old man watching *Love Boat* reruns and flirting with post office clerks.

"Well, here we are," said Amy, giving me a concerned look.

"Great," I croaked.

The maître d' seated us at a table in a quiet corner.

"So, what do you recommend?" I said.

"I think the lobster here is great," she said.

Lobster! In New York City! Was she insane? Should I just take my wallet and flush it down the toilet?

"Really?" I said. "You know, it's not the season for lobster."

"Silly, it's always the season for lobster."

Always the season for lobster? Who was this woman, Holly

Golightly? She did realize I was a teacher, didn't she? She knew I wasn't just wandering the halls while I was away from my real job, right? I had taught courses in graduate school for less money than you pay for one lobster in New York.

The waiter appeared.

"Do you know what you would like?"

"Yes, I'll have the lobster," she said.

"And for you, sir?"

Well, I did love lobster, and I wanted to be agreeable. And seafood was supposed to be an aphrodisiac. Besides, I would soon be chair. Surely, chairs had lobster once in a while.

"I'll have the lobster, too," I said.

"Something to drink?"

"Bring us a bottle of the house chianti," I said.

"Very good."

"You know, I'm glad we're having dinner tonight," she said. "Even though we've gone out together, we haven't really had a chance to talk."

"That's true."

"So, how did you end up at Academy X?"

I decided it probably wasn't the time to tell her how my graduate training had come to an abrupt end.

"Oh, the usual story. What about you?" I asked.

"Well, it's funny that you ask . . ."

While she told a long story that seemed to have a lot to do with some English teacher she had back in high school, I drank most of the bottle of wine and nodded encouragement. She even held my hand for a few moments, although my fingers were so coated with butter from the lobster that it was difficult for her to get a good grip. I followed her back to her apartment with a giddy sense of anticipation.

The first kiss was almost the best part of a relationship before repetition dulled the pleasure. There was no such thing as a bad first kiss. Well, in my case, that wasn't quite true. I had been a little overenthusiastic with my first kiss in eighth grade. I had heard stories about French kissing and how a girl could always tell how experienced you were by how much tongue you used. So, I had launched my tongue into her mouth like a cruise missile and triggered some sort of gag reflex. After that, she had decided that she really liked another boy, who lisped slightly and had a large birthmark on his face, better than me. Still, I loved the first kiss.

We reached Amy's door, and as she was looking for her keys, I leaned into her. Actually, I sort of staggered. I probably had had a little too much wine. In my defense, the bottle was too expensive to leave unfinished. I nearly knocked us both into a bush.

"Sorry," I said. I picked up her purse and handed it to her. Still hopeful, I latched on to her arm and decided to give it another go. I leaned in again. I could smell her perfume, her soap, her skin. At the last moment, she turned her head. Despite my two lunges, I found myself with only a chaste kiss on the cheek. But she was still standing very close to me. Intoxicatingly close. I was on the verge of my third lunge.

"Care for a nightcap?" I said, trying to whisper in her ear but wildly overshooting the mark and speaking to the back of her head instead.

"I'm sorry," she said, "what did you say?"

I pulled myself upright by grabbing on to the bush.

"Nightcap?"

"Oh, no, thank you. By the way," she said casually, "I hear that it's about to become official that you will be the next chair."

I halted mid-lunge. Not the question I was expecting, but still very promising as far as that first kiss went.

"That's right."

"Congratulations." She smiled at me. "You know, I've always wanted to move up to a full-time teaching position."

" 'Course you do," I said. "Wonderful school. Absolutely natural desire."

"Maybe you could help me."

"Help you? I'll do more than help you. Talented woman like yourself would be a credit to the department. A credit! Can't imagine a better candidate. I would hire you this minute, if I could. Consider it done!"

I made a mental note to ask Samson how much say I was going to have in hiring decisions.

"Well," she said leaning into me in a way that threatened to undo my precarious balance, "when it becomes official, I'll have to have you over for a real celebration."

She stood on her tiptoes and brushed her lips across my ear.

"That was wonderful," she whispered.

She glided into her apartment and left me hanging onto the door for support.

Evidence collected for the disciplinary hearing concerning John Spencer's conduct toward Caitlyn Brie. School counselor's confidential notes from the interview with Rebecca Parker:

He was really nice . . . Like sympathetic when I had a problem . . . Did he touch me? I guess he might have given me a pat on the shoulder or something . . . Sexual? . . . Are you serious? . . . I think I would know the difference . . . Just because he touched me? . . .

THE DESCENT OF MAN

Caitlyn missed school again on Tuesday, and my anxiety was threatening to become a full-blown panic attack, especially when I got a call from Snopes's secretary to stop by his office. I found a security guard lounging by the main door of the college counseling department. Apparently, a mother had decided to express her unhappiness with her son's college choices by throttling one of the college advisers that week, which was not all that unusual. The year before, another mother had driven her daughter to her college adviser's house so that they could throw a brick through the window. The Board of Trustees always leaned on the advisers not to press criminal charges to avoid any embarrassing newspaper stories, and the advisers learned to keep a large piece of furniture between themselves and the parents at all times. When I entered Snopes's office, he smiled warmly at me.

"John, I have some good news," he said. "Caitlyn has been accepted to Princeton."

"That's great," I said, although I had a feeling that was not why he had asked me to come to his office.

"So, how is everything going for Caitlyn in your class?"

"Oh, fine, fine."

He paused for a moment.

"You know, Caitlyn stopped by the other day."

He gave me an appraising glance.

"She was . . . concerned about something that happened with you."

I tried to look inscrutable.

"It's just that, well, you know how these things are," he continued. "Kids are so excitable. They jump to certain conclusions about what happened. They tend to exaggerate their teacher's reactions. I'm sure that is all that is happening here. Right, John?"

Luckily, I didn't have to answer him. Snopes's intercom buzzed, and his secretary told him that he had a call from a parent.

"I told you I didn't want to be interrupted," he barked.

He gave me an apologetic look.

"I always want to make sure that I give you teachers my undivided attention. You are the heart of the school after all," he said.

He paused and seemed to consider his words.

"You know, John, I have been doing this a long time, and during all those years, I have only had three offers of admission revoked," he said. "I don't like it when offers of admission are revoked. It represents a lot of hard work down the drain. It's not good for the students. It's not good for the colleges. It's not good for the parents. And it's not good for us. Princeton is a very important client, John, and I don't want to give them any reason to reconsider our . . . special relationship. Not just for Caitlyn's sake, but for the sake of future students applying there. You wouldn't want to hurt the chances of future students, would you?"

He stood up and walked over to my chair.

"Now, John," he said, taking my arm and guiding me to the door, "I know you are a smart guy. On the rise, from what the Head tells me. I would hate to see you do anything stupid to screw that up."

He stopped at the doorway.

"So, how did you like those Knicks tickets?"

"They were fine," I said, feeling particularly loathsome.

"Good, good," he said, "well, I'll keep you in mind if we get some more. By the way, how is Jacob doing?"

I grimaced.

"If I can give you a little advice," he continued, "make sure that he does well enough."

He shoved me gently but firmly through the doorway, but I grabbed the doorknob before he could close the door.

"I really am quite busy," said Snopes.

"I know, I know," I said, realizing that this was probably going to be my only chance to say something to him about Laura and wondering how to help her without committing myself to some devilish bargain. Ann Landers didn't really delve into this sort of Machiavellian maneuver. And the closest I had come to reading *The Prince* was reading *Le Petit Prince*, which was absolutely useless for anything but the care of roses. "I want to talk to you about Laura Sturding."

"Laura? Why Laura?"

"Well, the thing is—"

"Hasn't she been accepted to Wellesley?"

"Yes, but—"

"But Wellesley's a wonderful school." He laughed self-consciously. "I mean, just because I don't think Caitlyn should go there doesn't mean that I don't think it's a great school for Laura."

"No, you see—"

"In fact, I think it is a perfect place for people like her."

"People like her?"

"Yes, you know what I mean."

I decided to let it pass. I had to keep my eyes on the prize.

"Laura doesn't want to go somewhere else. She wants to go to Wellesley. What she needs is additional scholarship money to be able to afford Wellesley."

"Well," he sniffed, "that's not really something that I have anything to do with."

"I don't understand," I said.

"I get people into college. I don't get involved in how to pay for it," he said, looking at me as if I had just asked him to clean the bathroom.

"I thought . . . at least I hoped—"

"Yes, well, you can see that you were wrong."

He tried to pull the doorknob from my hand, which was when I decided to make use of the only leverage I had, devilish bargain or no.

"That's too bad."

I smiled as he tried to jerk the door free.

"If you don't mind," he said, motioning to the door.

"You see, I think it is so great when people like you go the extra mile," I said.

"John, I really am quite busy."

"But maybe you're right. A firm line in these matters is perhaps the right approach. Maybe that's what I need to do with Caitlyn."

I gave him a cold stare, and his Adam's apple seemed to shoot up into his mouth.

"Yes, I can see now how I should handle this little matter," I said, taking my hand from the door.

"John, don't do anything you're going to regret."

"Why not?" I said.

We stared at each other for a long moment.

"I'll see what I can do for Laura." He sighed.

I gave him a warm smile.

"You're too kind. It's people like you who make Academy X the school that it is," I said.

Despite my minor victory, I walked to lunch feeling more uneasy than ever about Caitlyn. If Snopes was involved, things had already become far worse than I had imagined. I sat down at the table with Ron and Kate.

"So," Ron said, "when is your next date with Amy?"

"She's just using John," said Kate. "It's totally obvious."

"I wish a woman wanted to use me," muttered Ron, picking at his congealed macaroni and cheese.

I was in Ron's camp. If I didn't want to spend the summer at my parents' house squiring Mrs. Vanille's daughter around town—a daughter who was infamous in high school for a rather pronounced flatulence problem—I needed to make things work with Amy. And even if she was just using me, I figured that I could string the decision about hiring her out long enough that she might actually develop a genuine affection for me. At least that's what I told myself. Of course, I had no intention of sharing any of these thoughts with Kate, who already believed Amy was evil incarnate and became apoplectic every time I mentioned her name.

"But that doesn't mean she isn't interested in me," I said. "You can want to use someone *and* be attracted to them."

"Are you telling us this or trying to convince yourself?" Kate asked.

"All I know is that we went on our first date before she even knew about the chair's position. Maybe that just adds to my appeal," I said.

"Oh, please! What person would turn down Knicks tickets? Ron, will you say something to snap John out of his demented reasoning?"

"I have a better idea. Let's talk about what I should do for my next date with my girlfriend," I said.

"She's not your girlfriend," Kate said.

"Of course, she is."

"No, she isn't!"

"That's ridiculous! We just went on two dates in two days. I think that is pretty much definitive proof."

"Have you kissed her?" Kate asked.

"Yes," I said somewhat huffily.

"On the lips?"

"Well . . . No, not exactly, but definitely very close to the lips."

"Have you spent the night at her place?"

"Of course not, but that doesn't mean—"

"Do you talk regularly on the phone?"

"No, but we see each other—"

"Not your girlfriend," she said.

I looked to Ron for support.

"Sorry. Definitely not your girlfriend," said Ron.

"Can we please get back to the issue?" I asked.

"What issue?" Kate said.

"What's my next move? Things are heating up," I said.

"There is no next move, you idiot," said Kate. "She is using you. U-S-I-N-G you. You need to forget about her. Even if things do work out for a little while, as soon as you can't do anything more for her, someone else will come along who can, and she will dump you. And you will only feel worse because you will have had an actual relationship with her. And then you will have to see her all the time, and you will come crying to us at lunch every day. So, just do us all a favor, and don't go down that road."

"We all use each other," Ron remarked. "Simple biology."

"What are you talking about?" Kate asked.

"Evolutionary psychobiology," he said, brightening up considerably now that we were talking about biology. "You see, we are simply doing things to maximize the chance of successfully passing along our genes. Amy is using John. John is using Amy."

"What?" I cried. "That's ridiculous. I'm not using Amy."

"You are. You can't help it. None of us can. Hardwired into our systems," he said. "It's all about passing along genetic material."

"I don't even want to have kids," Kate protested. Ron and I glanced at each other. By dating a gay man, she had certainly chosen a genetic cul-de-sac.

"We'll leave you aside for a moment," Ron said tactfully. "You see, deep down, on a level John doesn't even realize, he wants to pass along his genetic material. So, he chooses the most attractive mate that he can because attractiveness is a sign of health. And health means that his babies will be born healthy and will grow up and have babies of their own."

"You know, Ron, I am planning on having safe sex—that is, if I ever have sex," I said.

"That's irrelevant. This is on a deeper level than conscious behavior.

And Amy is looking to ensure the survival of her offspring, so she naturally wants a man who can provide for her. And a department chair can provide much better than just a teacher. So, you are both using each other in perfectly understandable ways."

"Can we just forget for a moment evolutionary biology or debates about whether or not she is my girlfriend, which she is, by the way. What I need now is some *practical* advice about Amy."

"We've been over this," said Kate.

"Maybe I didn't tell the story about the date right. I'm not sure you understand—"

"Stop! I can't listen to this one more time," said Kate. "I'm sorry. I just can't. I can't hear one more time about your scintillating conversation or the time your hands touched reaching for a roll or whatever."

"At least he has felt the touch of a woman." Ron sighed. "I haven't had contact with a female since I dissected that cat."

"We're trying to eat here," Kate said.

"This is what scientists have to put up with. This is why I never have a date," Ron said.

"First of all, you are a high school biology teacher, not a *scientist*," said Kate, "and second of all, the reason you never have a date is because you won't shave your mustache and you are depressing to be around."

Ron's face assumed a curdled expression vaguely reminiscent of the mac and cheese we were eating. I looked at Kate in shock.

"Thanks a lot, Kate," said Ron.

"I'm sorry, Ron," she said, "I don't know what came over me. I'm just in a terrible mood today."

"No, you're right. It's hopeless. I don't know why I even bother. Of course, I'm depressed. I'm not dating anyone. The problem is I'll only find a woman when I'm not depressed. And I can't stop being depressed until I find a woman."

He sighed.

"I might as well just give up now. I don't know why you two even bother with me."

Kate gave me a desperate look. I wasn't sure what to say that would make Ron feel better. His therapist had failed at the same task for years, and I was supposed to do it during our forty-five minute lunch break after Kate had manhandled his self-esteem?

"Ron, you see . . ." I paused. "Well, that was Kate who said you were depressing to be around. Not me. I don't think you're depressing to be around. Maybe mildly downbeat."

Kate made a threatening gesture at me with her fork.

"Look, Ron," said Kate, "John and I love you. And we all have our flaws. You may be a little depressed right now, but things will change."

"That's right, Ron," I said cheerfully. "You're just having a run of bad luck. You're a great guy. Things will turn around."

Would they? Did they ever? The three of us had been having the same problems since we had first arrived at Academy X, and we would probably still be having the same problems ten years from now.

I noticed Günter staring at me lugubriously from the student cafeteria.

"Sorry, guys. I've got to go," I said, feeling fortunate to leave the table before saying something disastrously wrong.

Günter met me as I walked through the cafeteria.

"What have you done?"

"Nothing," I said.

"Are you sure?"

"What's the matter, Günter?"

"Caitlyn hasn't been to school for days."

"I know."

"And she won't take my calls. Or even instant message me."

"I wouldn't worry about it. She'll be back soon," I said as confidently as I could.

"The one time I did get her on the phone, she said something about you," he said guardedly.

171

I stopped.

"What did she say?"

"Nothing much," he said. "Just something about how she was upset and didn't want to see you."

Relief flooded through me.

"It's nothing, Günter. I promise," I said. I needed to end the conversation before he asked any more questions. "Now, what we really need to talk about is your paper."

"Sorry, I have to go. I'll try to get it to you tomorrow," he said, disappearing down the hallway.

As I was walking by the library, I ran into Amy. She smiled coyly at me.

"So, how are you feeling after last night? You certainly were a little tipsy."

"Tipsy? No. Took some cough medicine. Maybe a bad reaction," I mumbled.

She placed her hand on my arm.

"Why don't we have dinner tomorow night to celebrate your appointment? We can eat in and have a little more privacy," she said. "And maybe you can look into that other little matter we talked about."

Yes! Home-cooked meal. Definite sign of a budding relationship. And she wanted more privacy. I would be steps from her bedroom. A little wine. A little soft music.

"How about your place?" she said.

What had happened to the biological model? Wasn't she supposed to be taking care of me? Okay, temporary setback. I would have to clean my apartment—I was filled with horror at the thought of her seeing the weird, greenish mold that had taken over part of my bathroom in the last couple of months. Order some good takeout. A little wine. A little soft music. Candlelight. Only steps from my bedroom— I would definitely need new sheets before the date. There was a weird rip toward the bottom of my bed that I couldn't explain—as if I was running in bed while sleeping. Was that possible?

"Sure," I replied nonchalantly, "we'll have dinner at my place."

"You're going to cook me dinner? That sounds wonderful."

"Oh, well, no big deal," I said with much less nonchalance.

I was supposed to cook? What had happened to takeout? I couldn't cook. The last time I had attempted to cook I nearly set the kitchen on fire and ended up with a watery gruel that tasted suspiciously like wall paste.

"Great. We'll work out the details later," she said.

Despite my lingering worries about Caitlyn and my new worries about cooking for Amy, I felt lighthearted as I walked to my office. Kate was completely wrong about Amy. It was only natural that I would lend a helping hand to her. Why did that have to mean that she was using me? Wasn't Kate putting the whole matter in an unfair light? I was simply helping Amy. I would have done the same for Kate or Ron, and I wasn't trying to sleep with either of them. It made perfect sense if you just looked at in the right way.

In fact, if you took that view, I was a tower of virtue. Awarding Laura the prize. Helping a colleague improve her position. I was a great humanitarian. Altruistic even. Really, what are we here for but to help our fellow man or, in this case, fellow woman? And this was much more pleasant than working in some soup kitchen. The people around us needed help as much as the homeless. The crucial thing was doing your part. I reflected for a moment on John Donne's line that no man is an island and felt rather wise. A fracas was developing down the hall, but I was too busy with these profound thoughts to worry about that. I nodded benignly as I walked down the corridor and wondered what other good I could do that day.

Evidence collected for the disciplinary hearing concerning John Spencer's conduct toward Caitlyn Brie. School counselor's confidential notes from the interview with Jacob Dullwich:

I know why I'm here . . . My mother told me . . . I totally agree with what's happening . . . He's an asshole. I mean, come on! It's senior spring, and he expects us to work . . . Yes, I think Caitlyn's attractive. Who wouldn't? . . . This is confidential, right? No, I don't particularly like her . . . Because she is a stuck-up bitch . . . She just is . . . No, she never talks to me. Or anyone. Like she is too good for us. What a load of bullshit that is. My parents are as rich as her parents . . . I told you—he's an asshole . . . It's, like, a tone or something. It's hard to describe . . . I definitely felt a hostile atmosphere . . . Does this mean we aren't going to have to take our final exam? . . .

THE JOY OF COOKING

The next day, Caitlyn again failed to appear, and there was a message from Snopes offering me box seats to a Yankees game, which I decided to ignore. One moral crisis at a time. I would have panicked about the signs of growing calamity, but my anxiety was already being monopolized by the thought of cooking dinner for Amy. I went to lunch and prayed that Kate would have a magical solution.

"Do you cook?" Kate asked after I made my request.

"No," I said. "Not unless you count dipping a Pop-Tart in a glass of milk."

"Toasted?" Ron asked, as he chewed on a piece of ham.

"Huh?"

"Well, if it's toasted, it could count as cooking," said Ron, still chewing.

"Why haven't you cooked for us?" She asked.

"You don't seem to understand. I don't cook. That's why I need your help. You're a woman. You must have a secret recipe that's delicious and can be made solely with a can opener."

"Why don't you order in?" Ron suggested, after he discreetly spit the ham into his napkin.

"I already told you. Because Amy seemed to expect that I was going to cook for her," I said.

"Since when have you worried about what people expect of you?" Kate asked.

"Can we stick to the problem at hand?"

"All right," she said with a sour look, "I have a recipe that's idiot-proof. It's a chicken mango dish."

"This is all wrong," said Ron.

"Actually, I think that sounds good," I said.

"No, not the chicken. This date," he said. "It's all wrong. Terribly wrong."

We both looked at Ron with confusion.

"She should be cooking for you!" Ron said.

"That would be nice," I admitted, "but I think the train has left the station on that one. So, if we could just get back to—"

"I'm talking about the biological imperative," Ron said. "I'm talking about the deep and unalterable laws of nature."

"Yes, well, unless those laws can explain how to make mango chicken, I would like to get back to the main point," I said.

"No, no, let's hear Ron out," said Kate with evident pleasure.

"Women are the nurturers. Men are the hunters. Men go off and get all the things that the family needs. The women take care of the home and provide the babies," Ron said.

"Ron," said Kate, "you really need to enter the modern ages."

"It's true," he insisted. "When you go to a fancy restaurant and you see a beautiful young woman with an ugly old man, you know she is with him for his money. He is, in modern terms, a very successful hunter."

"Ron, this is all extremely interesting, but I don't see what this has to do with me or with mango chicken, so if we could—"

"That's just it. You're cooking for her. She isn't nurturing you. She isn't following her traditional evolutionary role, which makes me think that she hasn't developed any of the traditional feelings for you," he said.

"That's ridiculous," I scoffed, "all of that because I'm cooking a meal for her?"

"I think Ron is on to something," Kate said, smiling.

"What about me being the alpha male and irresistible and all of that?"

"Maybe I was wrong about that, too," said Ron.

"Look," I said. "This would have me worried—*if we lived in the stone age!* We're dealing here with modern woman, a very different species, liberated from biological imperatives. Can't cook. Doesn't want to have children."

"They're a statistical aberration," Ron said.

"Look at Kate," I said. "An aberration, I grant you."

"Hey!"

"Kate, who does the cooking?" I asked.

"Dan, most of the time," she said.

"And do you love him?"

"Yes."

"And yet you don't cook for him?"

"No."

"There you go, Ron," I said triumphantly.

"That's not a fair example, and you know it," he said.

"Why not?" Kate asked.

"Yes, Ron, why not?" I asked gleefully, fully aware of the trap I had set.

"Anecdotal evidence," he said nervously, "totally unreliable from a scientific standpoint."

Kate eyed Ron suspiciously, but Ron was unable to speak. He was busy chewing on another piece of ham.

I had everything planned to perfection for that evening. I would get home at four, clean the apartment for an hour, buy the groceries, prepare the meal by six, and leave myself plenty of time to get ready by seven thirty. I also needed to run by the video store to pick up

Casablanca—I planned to play Humphrey Bogart to her Ingrid Bergman, minus the renunciation, of course.

4:30 P.M. Damn. Bump into Andrews and only manage to pry her fingers off my arm when I pretend to be suffering from intense gastrointestinal distress and run into the bathroom. Still plenty of time.

5:30 P.M. Cleaning a disaster. Green mold in bathroom of supermutant variety. Resistant to all known cleaning methods. Appears to have grown while I have been cleaning it. Shut shower curtain and hope she doesn't look behind it. A few areas of success, notably cleaning off dining room table and living room couch, but that has only brought more disaster areas into view. Wonder if dim candlelight will give disorder a romantic glow, including zit on forehead, which has magically reappeared.

6:30 P.M. Video store out of *Casablanca*. Video store clerk belittles me for my choice, calls me a walking cliché, sneeringly suggests that I am having a woman back to my apartment. Notice that he appears not to have bathed for several days. Suspect that he has never had a woman back to his apartment. Still, feel instinctual need to respond to challenge: Choose *Die Hard* to prove him wrong. Realize that I didn't really want to watch a movie anyway. Much better to sit and linger over a bottle of wine. Very European and sophisticated. Damn—need to buy wine.

7:00 P.M. Grocery store feels like Bangladesh. What are all of these people doing here? Don't they have lives? Shouldn't they be out at restaurants or something? Forget ingredient list, but manage to remember the important items.

178

7:30 P.M. Return to apartment but realize that I have forgotten to buy mangoes. And wine.

8:00 P.M. Go to bodega to avoid bedlam at grocery store. Mangoes not particularly ripe, but decide it doesn't matter. Once they're cooked, it will all taste fine.

8:15 P.M. Go to wine store. Tell clerk that I would like a couple of good, inexpensive wines. Wine clerk tells me that I get what I pay for. In a huff, tell him I will find wines on my own. Completely immobilized by choice. Return humbled a few minutes later to ask his opinion. Find myself buying two ridiculously expensive bottles of wine. Cheer myself up by thinking of how much money I am saving by cooking dinner.

8:30 P.M. Arrive home. No time to shower. Barely time to change. Dinner completely unprepared. Wonder if it would be bad form to begin drinking one of the bottles of wine before Amy arrives. Question moot when Amy knocks on the door.

8:35 P.M. Amy looks at food with alarm. Order take out.

8:40 P.M. Calm Amy down after she pulls back shower curtain.

8:45 P.M. Open bottle of wine.

8:50 P.M. Mother calls and leaves message on the answering machine telling me that she hopes I'm not spending another night alone.

8:55 P.M. Make up long anecdote about myself to show what an active social life I have. Somehow mistakenly give her impression

179

that I am into group sex. Difficult to find delicate way to correct this.

9:00 P.M. Takeout arrives.

9:05 P.M. Try to impress her by using chopsticks. Consequently able to do very little eating. Amy asks why I am just picking at my food.

9:10 P.M. Mistakenly eat hot pepper. Intense pain. Amy finds my suffering amusing and calls me a card.

9:15 P.M. Open second bottle of wine.

9:20 P.M. Find way to eat food by using an egg roll as a fork. Amy gives me a quizzical look. Tell her that this is how Cantonese eat.

9:30 P.M. Make various promises about what I will do for her when I am chair.

9:35 P.M. Accidentally drop egg roll onto floor ending the dining portion of the evening. Romantic inspiration strikes. Under pretext of picking up the egg roll, move next to her on the couch, and put my arm around her shoulder. Attempt casual joke about etymology of Moo Shu, but effect somewhat undermined by suddenly squeaky voice. Undoubtedly the aftershock of the pepper.

9:40 P.M. Make out on the couch. Not sure how, but find myself holding egg roll again. Uncertain what's the polite thing to do with the egg roll. Finally manage to roll it under couch, and move into position for two-handed grappling.

9:50 P.M. Try to levitate her to the bedroom without her sensing that any movement is taking place. Plan foiled when I slip on the egg roll.

9:55 P.M. Amy disentangles herself from supposedly unbreakable wrestling grip—damn the WWF!—and stands up.

10:00 P.M. Amy whispers tantalizing promises of erotic delights to be bestowed when I become chair and leaves.

10:15 P.M. Fall asleep on couch.

12:30 A.M. Wake up with a headache and a furry mouth. Eat the rest of the takeout—greasy food supposed to be good for a hangover. And finish wine—hair of the dog and all that.

7:00 A.M. Wake up with a headache, a furry mouth, and an upset stomach.

Evidence collected for the disciplinary hearing concerning John Spencer's conduct toward Caitlyn Brie. School counselor's confidential notes from the interview with Laura Sturding:

It's frustrating . . . No, *he's* not frustrating . . . The worst you could say about him is that he is not much of a disciplinarian. It's the situation that is frustrating . . . Because it's totally ridiculous . . . No, I'm not jealous of Caitlyn . . . No, I don't have a vendetta against her! She has one against *me*! Just ask Mr. Spencer! . . . Because it all started with her accusing me of plagiarism . . . I just *know* . . . No, he didn't tell me . . . Of course it would be inappropriate for him to tell me . . . No, I do not think that means that we had an inappropriate relationship . . . I know what you are trying to imply . . . That's ridiculous . . . How am I supposed to prove that to you?

THE CASTLE

The next day in class, I continued to show *Emma*—my head felt too kung paoed for anything else. Caitlyn was still not back at school, and when I returned to my office, the ominous red voicemail light was blinking like a summons to hell. I picked up the phone and listened to the message.

"John, it's Robert Brie, Caitlyn's father," said a polished voice. "I would appreciate it if we could talk this afternoon. Would you mind stopping by my apartment? I live at 950 Fifth Avenue. The penthouse. Around five? Thanks. Good-bye."

I could have said no. He couldn't expect me to go see him at his apartment. On the other hand, he was one of Academy X's biggest donors and good friends with every important person at the school. The last thing that I needed as I was about to become chair was a call from Brie to the Head. And his message implied that I didn't really have a choice.

I skipped lunch that day—I was still worried that I might confess everything to Ron and Kate in a moment of weakness—and I spent the afternoon trying to figure out what I was going to say to Brie.

At five, I found myself standing in front of 950 Fifth Avenue and wondering how I had gotten myself into this position. What had happened to my plan to handle everything discreetly? The weight of the heavy stone building oppressed me, and for a moment I gazed at my rumpled reflection in the door. I could have told myself some reassuring things about the choices I had made, but all I could think was how much harder it was to be on the outside looking in, instead of the inside looking out.

I unrumpled myself as much as possible and walked through the door.

"I'm here to see Mr. Brie," I said—the Big Cheese as I couldn't help but think of him.

The doorman cast a skeptical glance over me and reluctantly picked up the phone. By the time I finally ascended in the private elevator to the penthouse, I felt poked and prodded out of any self-possession. The elevator opened directly into the apartment, and I was faced by a wall of windows overlooking Central Park. A servant met me at the elevator.

"Mr. Brie is on the terrace. Please allow me to take you to him," he said.

The apartment overwhelmed me with its voluptuous elegance—prints, paintings, sculptures, many of which looked familiar. I had the nagging suspicion that these were not reprints bought from a museum store. The servant led me to a terrace with a spectacular view of Central Park. Caitlyn's father was talking on a cell phone and motioned for me to sit down. If a Medici were reincarnated in modern-day New York, he would look something like Robert Brie, who radiated a casual confidence that made him appear equally capable of seducing a virgin or murdering a head of state. He clipped the cell phone shut and turned to me.

"I'm Robert Brie. Nice to meet you finally," he said. "My daughter is a big fan."

I remembered Caitlyn's hand snaking its way up my thigh. You have no idea, I thought.

He smiled at me and held out his hand. I stared at it. It looked so well manicured that I had to resist the urge to wipe my own hand on my pants.

"It's a pleasure to meet you," I said.

"Would you like something to drink?"

Time to take the firm line, I thought, not to be lulled by false conviviality. Show him I've got the backbone squarely in place.

"No, thank you. I think we should talk first."

"José makes an excellent mojito. Crushes the mint by hand," he continued.

"Really. I'm fine. We need to—"

"I insist, John—may I call you, John?"

"Of course. Should I call you Robert?"

"José, fix us a pitcher of mojitos."

"Yes, sir," said José, gliding silently off the terrace.

"Mr. Brie, I don't think—"

"Quite a view, isn't it? I like coming out here in the late afternoon. I find it calming. Gets me away from the daily difficulties of life."

He looked like a man who did not suffer too many of life's difficulties, but I nodded. José returned as silently as he had left and put a mojito in front of me. I later found out that mojito is Spanish for I-can't-remember-my-name-and-I'm-not-sure-where-I-got-this-tattoo.

"Take a sip," Brie suggested.

"Mr. Brie, I just want to talk about—"

"You know, John, in some cultures it is considered extremely rude to turn down someone's hospitality." He gave me a probing look.

I couldn't escape the ridiculous feeling that I was the princess about to drink the poisonous potion.

"Perhaps I'm old-fashioned," he continued. "I just thought that things would be a little more civilized. There is no reason to think that this can't be a pleasant meeting." He paused and gave me a questioning look. "Unless you've come here with the idea that you want to be unpleasant."

Well, when he put it like that, it seemed downright unchristian not to wet my whistle a little. I took a small sip and then a larger one and then a gulp. A pleasant thrill ran through my body. Brie did not take a sip of his own drink but watched me intently.

"Good, isn't it?"

"Yes." I took another large sip and put the drink down. José immediately refilled my glass.

"Do you know what the key to a good mojito is?"

"José?"

Brie laughed.

"No, ingredients. The freshest mint, the best limes, top-shelf rum. All essential. And to have good ingredients, you have to nurture them. Nothing can stand too much rough handling when it is young. I'm sure you, as a teacher, understand that better than most."

I nodded my head and took another sip of my mojito. I tried to remember what I had planned to say to him, the artfully constructed speech that I had crafted, which would allow me to extricate myself from this situation.

"Mr. Brie, about your daughter—"

"You've written a dissertation, haven't you?" Brie asked.

"Uhhhh . . . Yes?" I was preparing to launch into some very eloquent remarks I had prepared about academic integrity and was thrown off my stride by his question.

"Are you asking me?" He gave me the same smile that Caitlyn had dazzled me with so many times.

"Uhhhh . . . No?"

I seemed to be having some mojito-induced difficulty with the interrogatory.

"What's it about?"

I sat there mutely. I was having trouble remembering if I had even attended grad school. Brie waited patiently, as if he was happy to stay there all day waiting for my answer.

"Uhhhh . . . Victorian novelists?" I offered, "Austen. Dickens. Changing society. That sort of thing."

Four years in grad school, and that was the best that I could come up with? I took a large gulp of my mojito to console myself and immediately felt better. Sure, I was a little rusty, a tad off my game. That was to be expected. I hadn't even finished my dissertation. Once I had, it would become clearer, and I, correspondingly, would become more eloquent, a veritable Demosthenes. The fact that my usual thoughts on the dissertation had not, for many years, included the idea that I would actually finish it began to look like rank pessimism. José refilled my glass.

"Sounds fascinating," said Brie. "You know, my company does a little publishing, and this is just the sort of book that we are interested in."

His company was a vast conglomerate. One of its divisions published books, although generally only books that involved six- and seven-figure advances to famous authors.

"Victorian novelists?" I asked. "I'm not sure—"

"John, I could pay you an advance on the book." He gave me an appraising look. "Something along the lines of one hundred thousand dollars. How does that sound?"

"One hundred thousand!"

That was two years' salary! Intimations of the good life began to percolate in my brain. Of course, there was the small stumbling block of actually writing the damn thing. I only had about forty pages of the "book," and about half of those were a long and somewhat incoherent attempt to examine what would happen if *The Tale of Two Cities* were set in Vienna.

"I should warn you that I still have a lot to write."

"Of course you do," Brie said, smiling. "You academics are always such perfectionists."

"It could take me a long time."

"That's fine, although don't tell my other authors that I am doing this for you."

He laughed, and I almost thought I saw him wink at me—or was I only imagining it in the late afternoon sun?

"You know," he continued, "without a deadline or a contract, you could fail to deliver the manuscript, and there is nothing that I could do." He laughed again. "Yes, you really should keep our little deal to ourselves."

Deal? Did we already have a deal? Had I just sold my integrity for one hundred thousand dollars? To be honest, that was more than I had expected to get for it, since it was something of a bedraggled affair. He pulled an envelope out of a leather satchel by his chair and handed it to me.

"Here's a check."

Even in my mojito-induced haze, I was stunned that he already had a check for me.

"I don't know. It feels a little—"

"I understand. Take it home. Have a look at it. When you cash it, I will know your answer," said Brie. He paused and looked at me closely. "Don't disappoint me."

Brie stood up. I unsteadily followed.

"It was a pleasure, John," he said, shaking my hand. "José will show you to the door."

Moments later, I staggered onto Fifth Avenue like Cinderella after the clock strikes midnight. I took a cab home. With one hundred thousand dollars, I could take a lot more cabs. I glided through Central Park and thought about Amy. Our future together suddenly seemed much more promising.

That night, I sat in my apartment staring at the check. I know that the amount sounds paltry compared to what gets thrown around every day in New York. To me, though, the sum was astronomical. I didn't go into teaching expecting to become rich. I had the usual hopes of a house and a comfortable life. Nothing extravagant. Not to say that I didn't want money. Who doesn't want money? But it was a fantasy. I wanted it the same way that I wanted a girlfriend who looked like Cameron Diaz and cooked like Nigella Lawson. So, one hundred thousand dollars for doing what I was already intending to do was like winning the lottery. No more worrying about making my paycheck last until the end of the month. No more teaching summer school to earn a little extra. No more old clothes. In other words, no more me, or, at least, a chance to invent a new, better me.

I looked around my own apartment—my nice little two bedroom that had once seemed charming—and couldn't help thinking that it had crossed the fine line between cozy and shabby. The curtains, the furniture, the dirty, pitted walls, the leaky faucet, the missing tiles, the refrigerator that shook like the A train, the water stains from the bathroom upstairs. The whole place, which used to seem so comfortable, now struck me as drab and depressing.

Why shouldn't I take the money? Didn't I deserve it? I was a teacher. I helped other people. In the karmic balance, surely I was ahead of the game. Should I be disqualified from enjoying the same things that other people had? New York is a tough city to live in when you aren't rich. Everyone else seems to live life more fully than you do. Wasn't it my turn to live a little bit?

And yet a tiny doubt gnawed at the back of my mind. I was no moral exemplar. But this was different. Accepting the money would be accepting something about myself that I was not ready to accept. Or was I? My head was pounding, and the only thing I was sure of was that I would not have another mojito for a long, long time.

Confidential notes of a conversation with Caitlyn Brie taken by her lawyer in preparation for the interview with the school counselor:

I know I probably shouldn't have written the paper, but I couldn't resist. I could tell that he was attracted to me. I can always tell. I don't blame him. All the boys in the school are attracted to me . . . He's not a bad guy, but he's so obvious. Like when I wear a really short, tight top, he can't even look at me. He stares above my head as if he is looking at the poster of Freud. Freud! How funny is that? . . . And he is always trying to show us how cool he is . . . You know, he starts talking about some pop culture thing that he thinks we will relate to, and he is always saying things like he is so down with it. It's kind of sweet, but really it's pathetic . . . Am I attracted to him? I don't know. I enjoyed provoking him. I guess I thought he was cute. . . . To be honest, I feel like I am more of an adult than he is. I obviously have much more life experience . . . Has he even been with a woman? It's hard to imagine your teachers having sex . . . Can you flirt with someone by talking about Austen? Maybe. She would have to be really lonely, though . . . I know I haven't exactly walked the mean streets, but I still know a lot more than he does. For instance, the other day I was at a club . . . I know I'm underage. That's not the point. The point is that my friend was really drunk and passed out in the bathroom, and I had to go in and just handle it. We didn't want to call anyone because we would have been in so much trouble. We were all supposed to be having a sleepover at her parent's apartment. I think it's safe to say that Mr. Spencer has never been in that situation . . . I don't know what this has to do with the case. You're the one who asked . . . I guess you could say some of my behavior was inappropriate, but I'm only a teenager. Isn't this what we are supposed to be doing? Testing our boundaries? Exploring?

CRIME AND PUNISHMENT

As I walked up the hill to school, I could still feel an almost physical pull from the check on my kitchen table. I had decided not to cash it. At least, I probably wasn't going to cash it. Unless, for some reason, I really needed it. That was the right decision. I was sure of it. Or pretty sure. And I wasn't just going to let Caitlyn off the hook. I was going to make her sweat. Really teach her a lesson.

Günter was waiting by my door when I came back from lunch.

"Bravo, Candide," he said, smiling at me.

"What have I done now?"

"What have you done? Only returned the radiance to a life barren of hope, brought warm spring morn to desolate winter . . ."

"Günter, what are you talking about?"

"She has returned. My beloved has returned. And bestowed sweet succor on her valiant knight. And from what she has said, I have you to thank. And now the world bursts—"

I shut the door on him and got ready for class. There was a knock moments later.

"Günter, go away!"

The door opened to reveal Laura. She looked like the perfect all-American girl in her Wellesley sweatshirt, and I couldn't help thinking how much happier my life would have been if I had appreciated Laura's good nature more and Caitlyn's charm less.

"Mr. Spencer?"

"Oh, sorry, Laura. Is there something I can do for you?"

"I . . . I . . ."

She rushed over to me and gave me a hug.

"I just wanted to say thank you."

"For what?"

"I got the scholarship. I'm going to Wellesley."

"Laura, I'm so happy for you. I can't think of a more deserving student."

"Do you think . . ." She drifted into silence and bit her thumbnail.

"What's the matter?"

"Do you think I'll be happy there?"

"Of course! It's a wonderful school. I think it's perfect for you. Why are you worried about that?"

"I just . . . I don't know."

I had an inkling what the problem might be.

"You know, Laura, the rest of your life isn't going to be like high school. You're going to be surrounded by people who appreciate you for the kind, intelligent person you are."

She looked unconvinced.

"Yeah, I guess . . . Well, anyway, I'll see you in class."

She stood up to leave, and I smiled at her.

"By the way, Laura, you might find yourself a little lonelier at Wellesley," I said. "It looks like Caitlyn will be going to Princeton."

"Really? Are you sure?"

I nodded, and an enormous smile appeared on her face.

I walked to the classroom and saw that it was true. Caitlyn had returned. She looked radiant wearing a miniskirt and a T-shirt that were so flimsy they made her usual outfits look almost modest. Even David had stirred from his normal position to get a better look. I spent much of the class staring at the ceiling as if considering a particularly knotty passage in the novel.

"All right, let's talk about the lessons that Emma learns and about what Austen is trying to teach us about ourselves," I said.

"Not very revolutionary, is she?" Laura said. "The two leading people in the community get married to one another, and Emma is basically taught to bow down before the superior wisdom of her husband."

"Who is Knightley supposed to marry? Someone like Harriet?" Caitlyn asked, giving Laura a dismissive look.

Laura flushed.

"Laura raises an interesting point. Austen as revolutionary. Is that at all plausible?" I asked, trying to rescue the situation.

"She does find a lot to laugh at," said Ally.

"Very good, and where is that laughter often directed?" I asked.

"At the wealthy," Ally said.

"But is that really much of a revolution? I mean, it's not as if that world is changed by anything that happens in the book," said Laura.

"And what would a changed world look like?" Caitlyn asked. "A bunch of ignorant farmers running things?"

She stared at Laura.

"And the wealthy are paragons of intelligence, of virtue, of honesty?" Laura demanded. At the last word, Caitlyn flinched.

"What if we choose a different word?" I asked desperately. "What if we consider Austen not as revolutionary but as subversive of many of the usual orthodoxies about society and about love?"

"It's surprising that anyone can love Harriet," said Caitlyn.

"That seems a little harsh," I said.

"Well, at least she doesn't go around thinking that none of the rules apply to her and ruining everyone's life in the process," Laura said hotly.

"I don't think that is quite—" I said.

"If Harriet had never tried to rise above her proper station—" Caitlyn said angrily.

"Her proper station! I suppose that you think it is fine for certain people to rule and others to—"

"Quiet!" I shouted.

Laura and Caitlyn glowered at each other.

"Wow," Jacob said, "I had no idea this book was so good. I'm definitely going to have to try reading it."

When class ended, I returned to my office, and Caitlyn followed behind me. After I closed the door, I placed her paper on top of my desk.

I looked at her and couldn't stifle a wave of sympathy. Wasn't she a victim in a way? If Günter was right, and everyone around her was cheating as well, what was she supposed to do? Wasn't part of growing up making mistakes and getting a second chance? Not that all of that excused what she had done. Still, I felt sorry for her.

"I talked to your father last night," I said gently.

"I know," Caitlyn said, smiling.

My sympathy receded before her smile. Couldn't she at least show a little contrition?

"Caitlyn, you do not seem to realize the severity of what you have done. As a simple matter of ethics, it is completely unacceptable. And if that is unimportant to you," I said, pausing for dramatic effect, "then perhaps I need to remind you of the practical consequences. You could be suspended from school. Your admission to Princeton would almost certainly be revoked. Your whole future could be altered by this."

Caitlyn's smile curdled on her face. I was glad to see that I still had the knack for the old Sturm und Drang.

"So, now I am faced with a decision about how to handle this matter." A brief, forlorn vision of stacks of one-hundred-dollar bills flitted before my eyes.

I paused to let her think about that before telling her my decision. Don't let it be said that John Spencer can't wield the disciplinary cudgel when called upon to do so, even if it pained me to see Caitlyn suffer. But she would learn her lesson—at last. And I would be there to receive the warm look of thanks. She would look back on this moment and remember me as the teacher who had made a difference in her life, the one who had set her on a better path. I was feeling a warm flush of self-congratulation, so I wasn't quite prepared for Caitlyn's change of expression, which made her resemble her father at his steelier moments.

"My father said that you had made a deal," she said.

"Deal?" I felt a pang and thought of the check on my kitchen table. "Well, we talked. Exchanged views. That sort of thing."

"He said that the two of you had reached some sort of agreement," she said.

Was my new and improved, bribe-disdaining self to be chastised by her? Quid pro quoed? If Caitlyn thought she could give me the business, she was sadly mistaken.

"Agreement? No, you misunderstood."

She turned pale, and I realized that, whether or not she had learned her lesson, I didn't have it in me to punish her any longer. I passed a wistful moment thinking one last time of the check.

"Caitlyn," I continued, "I want to let you know what I've decided to do about your paper . . ."

My mouth continued to open and close, but words were no longer forthcoming. She had pulled off her T-shirt and was sitting across from me in a bra that seemed to be in the planning stages of construction. I tried to speak, but the only word that came to mind was *nipple*. She took another, slightly torn shirt from her Prada bag and pulled it on.

"I just want you to know that I didn't want to do this," she said.

"Caitlyn," I stammered, "your shirt . . ."

She was looking down at it and pulling at the tear until I found myself once again facing double-barreled trouble. My face flushed, and I was short of breath. She stood up and screamed. The door flew open to reveal Johns on the other side. Caitlyn, her shirt flapping uselessly, rushed up to him and began to cry. I sat there like the village idiot trying to sort through what had just happened.

By the end of the day, I found myself in the Head's office. I was flanked on either side by Johns and Samson. Johns positively glowed. Samson looked at me lugubriously.

"Well," the Head said, "this is obviously a very serious matter. Groping a student in a sexual manner. Frankly, I don't know what to say."

The gymnastics coach had been allowed to touch boys "accidentally" for years until he made the mistake of groping a trustee's child, but I realized that would probably not be an adequate defense.

"This is all a big misunderstanding," I said weakly.

"I hardly think that what I saw could be termed a big misunderstanding," Johns said loftily.

"Well, what exactly did you see?" I asked.

"I heard a scream. I opened the door. Caitlyn's shirt was torn. Your face was flushed, and you were breathing hard."

I had to admit that it was an accurate description of the scene. The Head stared at me with disgust.

"Is that true?"

Falling back on my graduate-school training, I chose the postmodern defense.

"Who can say what the truth is? We can know little truths, perhaps. I was indeed in my office with Caitlyn. But can we know big truths? Things like causality and intentionality?"

The Head looked unimpressed, so I fell back on the truth, ridiculous as it must have sounded.

"Look, Caitlyn tore her shirt herself. Not me."

"How do you explain your flustered appearance?" Johns asked.

"We were having a heated discussion."

197

They looked at me as if I belonged in the lowest circle of hell.

"She cheated," I said. "She was in my office because I was talking to her about her paper. She plagiarized."

The Head seemed, if anything, more disgusted.

"Tearing down the character of a student like Caitlyn Brie is not going to help," she said.

"Quite right," said Johns, bowing slightly to the Head.

I thought about grabbing the letter opener off of her desk and stabbing Johns.

"I can prove it," I said.

The Head gave me a skeptical look.

"All right," she said. "Prove it."

"Just give me a moment to go to my office," I said.

I stood up and, before anyone could object, ran out of the office. As I hurried through the hallways, I felt as if every eye in the school was on me, as if everyone was whispering about me. I reached my office. The door was ajar, and I stared stupidly at the desk. No paper. I frantically began searching. Nothing. I realized, even as I continued to look, that I was not going to find the paper. I sat down heavily in my chair. A one-way ticket out of town began to seem like an appealing prospect. Then, I had an epiphany. The contest! I ran downstairs to Strude's office. She was grading papers at her desk.

"I never thought much of you, John," she said. "I always thought your command of grammar was a little loose. That sort of slackness will out."

"Edwina, I don't have time to explain. But I need Caitlyn's paper from the contest. Do you still have it?"

"Yes, I still have it," she said, eyeing me as if I were a particularly unsavory, slithery creature that had somehow escaped from my cage. She pulled a box from under her desk and flipped through the papers.

"That's strange," she said.

She flipped through them again.

"Hmmmm. It doesn't seem to be here."

I walked slowly back to the Head's office. It finally dawned on me that Brie had prepared himself for any eventuality. Just as he had a check ready for me, he had a backup plan in case anything went wrong. I returned to the Head's office filled with a sense of impending doom.

"Well?"

"I can't find it," I said. I thought of the check from Brie but wasn't sure how to introduce it without making myself look even slimier.

"You can't find it?"

"No, it appears to be gone."

"Gone?"

"Gone."

Johns snorted.

"These feeble attempts to excuse your behavior are not going to help you in the end," she said.

I didn't know what to say, so I simply sat there.

"Given the evidence, the best thing for the school and for yourself is for you to resign. To drag this through a full-blown inquiry will lead to a lot of bad publicity for everyone."

"Resign?"

She turned to Samson.

"Donald, obviously we need to find a new chair, and we need to hire someone for next year as soon as possible."

"Resign?"

"John," the Head said. "I expect a letter from you on Monday."

I wanted to say more, but I was swept along as Johns and Samson left the office.

It began to rain as I walked from the subway to my apartment—a fitting end to the day, I thought grimly. I collapsed on a chair in my living room and watched the puddle of rainwater grow beneath my feet. The word *resign* continued to echo in my head. Sure, I had my boneheaded moments when I worried about being fired. But to be fired for this. I stewed in my growing puddle of rainwater and fantasized about revenge against Johns and Brie.

The school had forced a few other teachers to resign. Besides the gymnastics, there was the teacher who invited his class over to dinner. One of the students spiked the chili with acid as a joke, and the police eventually arrived on the scene to find everyone naked and finger painting on the wall.

My buzzer roused me from my stupor. I opened the door to find Kate and Ron standing there.

"I was going to let Kate come alone, but I was worried that you might grope her," said Ron.

"At this point, I would enjoy a good grope," said Kate.

"Come in—if you aren't afraid to be seen with me," I said.

"Not afraid to be seen with you, only afraid to use your bathroom, but I think from a biological standpoint I really should see that green mold," he said. "Be back in a moment."

Kate and I sat down and looked at each other in silence for a few moments.

"John, I hate to ask this, but I have to be sure," she said.

I looked at her.

"Did you do it?"

I laughed.

"Does it matter? They're going to get rid of me regardless."

"Yes, it matters very much to me and to other people as well."

Other people—Amy? Had she said something to Kate? I almost felt a moment of happiness, until I realized that even women in love did not generally marry disgraced teachers who were forced to take jobs as—as what? What did disgraced teachers do? Did we go west to escape our past and work on a cattle ranch spending long, lonely nights thinking about the past? I didn't really like horses, which was a problem. Maybe we worked on the margins of schools—as janitors doing things like cleaning chalkboards. A cautionary tale to the school community. There goes Mr. So and So. You know, at one time he was a teacher here. I didn't think I could take the humiliation. And ammonia always made me dizzy. Flipping burgers at McDonald's? Too old. Newspaper delivery boy? Too early. Cabdriver? Too stressful. Retail? Too annoying. As my mind eliminated one possibility after another, I began to feel that there was only one end to all of this. A life on the streets. Drunk, dirty, and dissolute. I wondered if I could be one of those charming drunks who is allowed to stay in rich people's homes, but that seemed unlikely.

Kate looked at me sadly.

"Is your silence your answer?"

"Of course not!" I said. "What kind of pervert do you think I am?" She gave me a hug.

"A wonderful, ordinary, everyday kind of pervert," she said.

"Look, I'm glad that I've satisfied your doubts, but that doesn't really change anything."

"Not yet."

"So, you have a plan?"

"Not yet."

"I'm supposed to resign on Monday. There is no yet for me. I don't get a yet."

"You can't resign," Kate said. "We need more time."

"What am I supposed to do? Just walk into school and pretend that nothing happened?"

"That's exactly what you do."

"But it's . . . I mean . . . I can't . . ."

"Of course you can. What are they going to do?"

"Grab me by the collar, and throw me out onto the street."

"They can't do that. To fire you, they've got to follow procedure."

"What procedure?"

"I don't know exactly. They'll have to collect evidence and have some sort of disciplinary hearing."

"Even if I go through with that, I might lose, and then where will I be? My reputation will be shot."

"And you think that resigning this way is going to be good for your reputation? Not to mention the fact that this story will make the rounds of all of the private schools within a day."

Kate shook her head.

"No, if we're going to make it through this, you've got to walk through those halls as if you don't have a care in the world."

"In case you haven't noticed, I'm not really the stoic type," I said.

Ron emerged from the bathroom.

"Actually, more of a celibate," he said, "which is interesting from a biological standpoint, because if you consider the imperative to reproduce—"

"Ron!" Kate said.

"Sorry."

"Look at this as your chance to stick it to them," she said. "It will drive everyone crazy if you refuse to resign."

It wasn't quite as satisfying as my fantasy of Johns and Brie being captured by an Amazonian tribe that still practiced cannibalism. Still, it was a role that had its appeal. A burr in the saddle was clearly better than a pedophile on parole.

"Listen, John," said Kate, "we're going to get you through this."

Over takeout pizza and beer, I recounted the whole affair—leaving out the check from Brie. I wasn't prepared to share my final shame with them. Even though I hadn't cashed it, I had brought it home with me, which was hardly a sign of moral rectitude. I got up to go to the bathroom.

"By the way, John, I think I might have clogged your toilet," Ron said.

What was next? A plague of locusts? Boils? I wondered if Job had any snappy answers for me.

THE SCARLET LETTER

After a weekend spent uselessly brooding about what I should have done differently, I slunk into school early on Monday so I could do the manly thing and take refuge in my office before anyone arrived. I barricaded myself behind a stack of blue books and felt quite pleased with my stealth—until my phone rang a few moments later. Apparently, I had not been stealthy enough. The Head's secretary told me that the Head was ready to see me. Dead man walking, I thought, as I retraced my steps.

"Thank you for showing up before the students, John. It will make this much easier," she said. "May I have the letter?"

"Yes, about the letter . . ." I drifted into silence.

"There is no need to drag this out. Give me the letter so we can get this over with before people start arriving."

"That's the thing. You see, I—well, it's difficult to explain. What I mean to say is that I, well, I . . ." I took a deep breath. "I don't have the letter."

The Head's face took on an expression I can only describe as flinty. Mount Rushmore–like even.

"I understand, John," she said. "It's a difficult letter to write. Unpleasant. I already have a letter typed up. All you have to do is sign it."

She slid a piece of paper across to me.

"Ah, well, that's the thing . . ."

"Why don't you read the letter?"

I picked it up. It all looked pretty standard, until the final sentence: "I also want to apologize to Caitlyn Brie for my grossly inappropriate behavior."

"Apologize to Caitlyn?" I asked.

"Yes," said the Head. "Given recent events, I think that is the least that can be expected of you. The family has agreed not to press charges, which is very generous on their part."

"Oh, yes, *very* generous," I said.

"Let's just put all of this behind us."

"You know what I think of this letter?"

I wadded it up and dropped it onto the floor.

"I'm not signing any letter. And I'm not resigning," I said, my voice beginning to rise, "This whole thing stinks, and I refuse to go along. In fact, I'm going to make things as difficult as possible. Even if you manage to fire me, I'm going to sue. And I'm going to publicize this case. Every detail of this place is going under the microscope. So, you go ahead and do whatever you want."

"John," she said soothingly, "you are making a big mistake. Not just for the school, but for your own career."

"Leaving a few weeks before the end of the year under the cloud of a sex scandal is bound to be a big bonanza for me, so thanks for looking out for my best interests. As for the bad publicity for the school, well, that's your problem. Now, I have a class to teach."

I walked out of the office after showing the door in no uncertain terms who was boss. According to the rumors, when the secretary entered a few moments later, the Head was still sitting there gulping at the air like a fish that had made an ill-chosen leap onto land.

I felt triumphant as I walked down the hall. Andrews spied me as she was walking to class and hurried over. For once, she had no interest in taking hold of my arm.

"You disgust me," she hissed. "I knew that you were depraved. To think that I almost gave myself to you!"

"At least there are some advantages to being accused of sexual harassment," I replied breezily. When people think you have molested a student, ordinary obnoxiousness isn't even worth a mention.

I closed my office door with a last, haughty look at Andrews. I decided the only course of action was to put on a stiff upper lip and go about my normal business, which is to say that I hid in my office most of the day. My stiff upper lip remained in place—except for some minor quivering due to a sciatica problem—until it was time for my Austen class. I collected my notes and walked to class. I opened the door, and all the students gave me shifty looks, except for Jacob, who was too busy holding Marcus in a headlock to notice me.

"Excuse me!"

Jacob studied me uncertainly, as if I might be a figment of his imagination. He continued to maintain a grip on Marcus, although he had loosened it to the point where he looked like a drunk clinging for support. He stared at me defiantly.

"Jacob, do you have feelings for Marcus?"

He gave me a blank stare.

"I only ask because you seem to have an irresistible urge to touch him. Freud suggests that aggressive action against someone of your own sex is often a sign of a repressed homosexual urge."

Jacob still looked confused.

"He thinks you may be gay because of the way you are touching Marcus," Laura explained helpfully.

Jacob jerked his arm away as if it had been scalded. Marcus returned his glasses to a reasonable position on his face and sat down. Jacob continued to stand.

"Are you going to take your seat?" I asked.

"What are you doing here?" Jacob demanded.

"I realize that you are not the most gifted student, but I would hope that after all of these weeks you would have at least realized that I am your teacher," I said.

"You were supposed to resign."

It was good to see that confidentiality in delicate matters such as this was being respected.

"As you can see, you were misinformed. So, I suggest that you sit down. We have a lot of material to cover."

Jacob gave me a sullen stare.

"But you're a . . . you're a . . ."

I could see the wheels slowly turning in his head as he tried to think of the word he had heard last night from his mother.

"A pedophile!" he finally blurted out.

The class sat in stunned silence. Jacob had a broad smile on his face.

"I'm glad those vocabulary flash cards are paying off," I said calmly, although I was seething inside. "Now, you have flunked virtually every assignment this semester. So, unless you sit down and do some work, I am afraid that you are going to find yourself back in school this summer. And what you have said is totally unacceptable. You need to apologize to me before we can continue."

Jacob remained silent.

"Jacob, if you are not prepared to apologize, I suggest that you leave class until you are ready."

"Fine," he said. He grabbed his bag and walked to the door. "You're not going to be around very long anyway!"

After he left, the other students all looked down at their books.

"Don't worry. I promise not to grope more than two of you this period," I said.

Ally and Rebecca exchanged a terrified look. Note to self: When under suspicion for molesting a student, avoid molestation jokes.

"Sorry. Bad joke," I said. "Let me try a different tack. I know that you've probably heard a lot of rumors about me. And I'm sure you are going to hear even more in the coming days. Just keep in mind that in this country people are supposed to be innocent until proven guilty."

At that moment, Caitlyn walked through the door. I hardly

206

recognized her. No bared midriff. No makeup. No tight clothes. A blouse and a long skirt. She looked like she had just walked off the set of *Happy Days*. Johns followed her through the door.

"What are you doing here?" I asked Johns.

"We've agreed that I need to monitor any interaction between you and Caitlyn as well as observe your general behavior," he said.

"We?"

"Yes," said Johns coyly.

"Fine." I sighed.

Johns simpered to himself in the corner. Caitlyn was completely self-possessed. Her expression was, if anything, beatific.

"Today, we are going to talk about Emma's relationship with Knightley," I said almost laughing at the irony of our topic. "So, what incidents do we need to focus on?"

"They talk so much about friendship," Rebecca complained. "There isn't a lot of passion."

"Yeah, what about sex?" Ally asked.

Johns smiled to himself.

"Mr. Johns," Caitlyn said. "This classroom has become a hostile environment where I no longer feel safe. May I leave?"

"Of course," Johns said as he wrote something down on a legal pad.

Caitlyn gathered her books and walked out.

"I think I've heard enough," he said following her out the door.

"Mr. Spencer," said Ally quietly.

I turned to look at her.

"I'm sorry," she said.

"That's all right," I said. "It's actually a good question."

The students felt so bad about what had happened that they worked hard, and we had our best class in a month. As they filed out of class, Marcus lingered by the door.

"Mr. Spencer?"

"Marcus, I'm sorry about Jacob. I'll try to make sure that doesn't happen again."

"Actually, I wanted to talk to you about something else. I was wondering if there was any way I could help."

I was touched. Marcus, the kid picked on more than any other at school, the butt of every joke, wanted to help. On the other hand, his offer was a fairly disturbing indication of how low I had fallen on the totem pole.

"That's kind of you, but I am about to become extremely unpopular. I think you will be better off keeping your distance from me."

"I'm used to being unpopular. So it doesn't make much difference to me."

I had to admire the kid's fortitude.

"If I think of anything, I will let you know, but until then, I don't want you sticking your neck out for me. I can take care of myself."

Actually, I had a noted track record for not being particularly good at taking care of anything, let alone myself. There were a slew of wilted plants, goldfish floating belly-up, and dogs who had heard the call of the wild in my past. Still, involving Marcus in my problems wasn't going to do either of us any good.

I retreated to my office and wondered whether I could avoid going to the bathroom for the remainder of the day when there was a knock at the door. I resisted the urge to hide under the desk.

"Come in," I said.

Samson entered the room. He sat down and stared at me mournfully.

"This is terrible," he said.

I breathed a sigh of relief. At least Samson was being sympathetic.

"I can't believe this is happening," he added. "Frankly, I don't know what to say."

"I know. I've been trying to think of a way out of this mess," I said.

"There is a very simple way out of this mess," he said. "You should resign."

"I thought you said this was terrible."

"Yes, for the reputation of the department. For my reputation! I've spent years establishing my good name, and you seem happy to destroy it. This is terrible for me! Think how this affects *me*!"

"But I didn't do anything."

"That hardly seems to matter at this point. I think it's pretty obvious you are going to lose the disciplinary appeal. Why don't you think about someone other than yourself? Just do the decent thing and resign."

"But I didn't do it!"

"What does that matter now? Just put an end to this. Don't drag it out. It's bad for everyone."

"It matters to me!"

"Always thinking about yourself. What about the department? What about me?"

"What about you? *What about you?*" I hesitated for a moment, but with nothing left to lose, I decided it was time to get a few things off my chest. "I'm faced with a sexual harassment charge, and you're worried about yourself. You know what? I'm glad I'm not going to be chair because it means that I can tell you what a pompous old windbag you are. Going on and on about what you've done as if you built the great wall of China or something. It's pathetic! Now leave me alone!"

"Well, I . . . I . . . I . . ."

He appeared to be having difficulty breathing. He stood up and left the office. As he walked out the door, Amy entered. I wanted to fall down on my knees and kiss her feet. Here! At last! My fair lady standing by her noble prince! Kate was wrong! Ron was wrong! I was wrong! Love would conquer all!

"John, I, uh, I . . . don't know what to say."

Say nothing, I thought to myself. What words can plumb the heart's hidden depths?

"I'm just glad that you're here."

"Oh, of course, this must be terrible for you. Really awful."

"I can't tell you how much . . ." My stiff upper lip trembled, perhaps even quivered. But I mastered myself. "Ron, Kate, and I are going to plan my defense later. We can use your help."

"That's what I came to talk to you about," she said, fingering her delicate wrist, a wrist that I suddenly wanted to devour with kisses. "Given everything that's going on, I think it would be better . . . Well, better for us not to see each other for a while."

I felt a stab of pain.

"You see," she rushed on, "I'm relatively new here. And my own position is not very secure. And I can't be seen with—well, I think it would be better if we didn't see each other."

"What if I just stop by the library?" I asked desperately.

"No, that would be worse. People would see us, and I just think it would be a bad idea. But good luck! I'm sure things will work themselves out," she said.

She turned to leave as Johns arrived at my door.

"Amy," he said, "I didn't expect to see you here."

She looked flustered.

"Don't worry, Johns. She won't be coming around anymore," I said.

"That's only appropriate, don't you think?" He sneered. "Given your, how shall I put it, proclivities. Amy, I'll see you tonight."

"Yes," she said, walking away quickly.

Tonight?

"My proclivities?" I exploded, angrier about his date with Amy than about my impending destruction.

"Yes," Johns said, "I'm here to inform you that Caitlyn will not attend your class until this disciplinary matter is settled. As you know, she found your class to be a hostile environment today."

"This whole thing is a load of crap."

"The administration has a duty to ensure the moral character and ethical conduct of its teachers."

"What are you, a policy manual in training?"

"No, I'm an acting department chair."

He paused and savored his new title.

"What happened to Samson?"

"The Head decided that the responsibilities of the job had become too much for him, so she appointed me in his place. She is telling him this afternoon. And my first act was to tell her to pursue you to the full extent possible. There is no place for this type of behavior in the school. I would also recommend that you reconsider resigning. Even if your appeal succeeds, I can make your life exceedingly difficult."

He turned to leave.

"Oh, by the way," he said from the doorway, "please don't make any effort to talk to Amy. You've already done enough to ruin your career. There is no need to drag her down with you, especially since I am planning on hiring her to take your place."

An hour later, I was still brooding about the latest miserable turn of events when Kate poked her head in.

"You don't look so good," she said.

"It hasn't been a banner day for John Spencer," I said.

"You can't expect the life of a child molester to be a bed of roses."

"Thanks," I said.

"Look, don't worry. It's always the hardest to get through the first day. I promise tomorrow will be easier."

"Easier? It's going to get worse. Johns is now my department chair. Caitlyn has been removed from my class. Amy told me not to talk to her. And I think she's dating Johns!"

"I warned you about her," she said.

"That makes me feel *much* better."

"I know this looks bad," said Kate, "but it's not as bad as you think."

I looked at her doubtfully.

"Really," she insisted.

It *was* as bad as I thought. I would be fired. And I would be disgraced. Maybe even sent to prison as some sort of pedophile, and I had heard what inmates did to pedophiles. I would serve my sentence and then work in some seedy, X-rated video store in Brooklyn—the greasy man behind the counter handing over videocassettes to other greasy men. I would obviously never date again. I would be reduced to lonely Saturday nights ordering takeout and downloading Internet porn.

Kate was giving me an annoyed look.

"I'm trying to explain how we're going to get you out of this! So, I would appreciate it if you would listen."

I tried to pay attention, but bad porn titles for my predicament kept scrolling through my mind: *You've Been Very Naughty!* (cover art: Caitlyn wearing a push-up bra and sucking on a lollipop). *I Need a Spanking!* (cover art: Caitlyn wearing short shorts and sticking out her butt). *Can I Sharpen Your Pencil?* (cover art: Caitlyn wearing a Catholic schoolgirl's uniform and straddling an oversized pencil).

"John! Are you listening?"

I tried to compose my face into the expression of someone who did not secretly imagine his life as a porn film.

"Sorry."

"I don't think we should get you a lawyer. It will make you look like you are trying to hide something. Besides, the faculty handbook says that you are only allowed to bring one other person to the hearing, and I want to be in that room with you."

"That's very kind, Kate, but I think ruining one career at a time is enough, don't you?"

"John, this is important."

"I know, but—"

"But nothing! Look, you obviously don't know what you're doing," she said crossly, "so I'm going to be in the room, and that's final."

She gave me a stern look.

"Now," she continued peremptorily, "what we really need is some evidence exonerating you."

I thought of the check in my apartment, but I dreaded using that. It would only disgrace me in a different way, although I would at least have the satisfaction of bringing Caitlyn down with me.

"Are you sure there isn't another copy of her paper somewhere?"

"Yes."

"Well, we'll keep working on it. If we make this whole process painful enough for the school, they might simply decide to sweep it under the rug."

My telephone rang—the Head's secretary to tell me that my hearing had been scheduled for tomorrow afternoon.

"That doesn't leave us much time," she said. "Get your things together. We've got to start working on this stuff."

She gave me a sympathetic look that sent my stiff upper lip all to hell again.

"John, it's going to be all right."

When she left, I packed up my things. O'Brien entered my office without knocking and sat down.

"Ah, well, the gig is up this time, I suppose," he said.

It was the most sympathy I had had from anyone other than Ron and Kate. I had to resist the urge to hug his gin-soaked body.

"Who can fight it?" he asked.

"It's going to be tough," I admitted, "but if I can—"

"I can't," he said, "I look at those young girls, and my mind goes crazy."

I began to feel a little uncomfortable.

"Especially that Caitlyn Brie," he said, licking his lips. "She's a tasty morsel, that's for sure. Why, if I had half a chance—"

"Listen, thanks for stopping by, but I have to get going," I said.

"What? Too good for my sympathy, are you? I'm not the one touching and fondling. At least I do what any decent person would do—buy some pornography, and enjoy it in the privacy of my home. But you—"

"Yes, me," I said, hauling him up by the arm and giving him a shove toward the door, "quite indecent. What would Yeats say?"

"Well, Yeats was a randy old bugger—"

I closed the door. When I arrived home, I tried to take solace from the fact that at least I still had a home. The phone rang.

"John?"

"Hi, Mom," I said wearily.

"What's the matter? You're not getting depressed again, are you?"

I took a deep breath.

"There's something I need to tell you. It's nothing to worry about. And it's completely untrue, but one of my students has accused me of sexual harassment."

"Oh, John, this is what happens when you're single! You don't have any natural outlets for your sexuality. And then you young men always watch all that porn. And—"

"I'm not watching porn—"

"—you make some lunge for some poor young woman—"

"—I didn't do it—"

"—if you would just let me set you up with a nice girl—"

"—are you listening?—"

"—already had to go to the neighbors to call the police when you were committing suicide . . ."

I held the phone away from my ear and let her talk herself out. Finally she stopped to catch her breath.

"Mom, will you put Dad on the phone?"

"Yes, but there's a lot we still need to talk about!"

"Hello, John, what's going on? Your mother is saying something about how you are a child molester."

"It's not true, Dad. But I am being charged with sexual harassment. I may lose my job."

"That's wonderful news! I just saw Ryan the other day. Things are really happening at his company. I know he would jump at a chance to hire a smart guy like you."

"I haven't lost my job yet."

"I know. I'm just saying that this may not be a bad thing. It may be a good thing. You could live with us until you got on your feet. And I know your mother has a number of nice girls she wants to introduce you to. I just think . . ."

After a few more minutes of this, I interrupted him and said good-bye.

The phone immediately rang.

"Dad, please . . ."

"John Spencer?"

"Yes?"

"This is Landmark Realty. We operate the building in which you currently reside," the voice said.

The word *currently* sounded ominous.

"Yes?"

"We wanted to give you notice that you are going to have to vacate your apartment within ninety days."

"What? You can't do that."

"As you know, you have no lease for that apartment. We have decided to make some renovations. You will receive the official paperwork in a couple of days. Good-bye."

BLEAK HOUSE

Ron, Kate, and I spent a grim night piecing together a defense that had all the sturdiness of a warm custard. After they left, I stayed up most of the night poring over the school's sexual harassment policy as if it were a passage from *Finnegans Wake*. Although I failed to find a loophole involving English teachers with good intentions, I did have the entire thing virtually memorized by morning. I stumbled through my classes and tried not to think about the hearing. Kate came to find me at the end of the day.

"Ron has plenty of students to testify on your behalf. Marcus is apparently chomping at the bit to say something," she said.

I attempted a smile and failed miserably.

"Don't worry. Everything is going to be okay," she said.

We walked in silence to the conference room. A group of trustees sat at the far end of the table looking grave. Caitlyn, her father, and two lawyers sat on one side. Johns was sitting near them. Caitlyn was dressed as if she had just come from a convent. Kate and I sat at the other end of the table. I had the crazy feeling that our chairs were slightly lower than the others, and I had to fight the urge to find a booster seat. The Head entered, called the meeting to order, and laid out the procedure for dismissal.

With very little left to lose, I felt surprisingly at ease. And when I noticed Johns nodding smugly to himself, I decided that it was time to begin putting my newfound knowledge to work.

"Ms. Van Huysen, I'm afraid you've failed to lay out the correct procedure for dismissal," I said, giving her my warmest smile.

"Really?" The Head drummed her fingers on the table.

"Yes, the policy explicitly includes the right to an appeal. Isn't that correct?"

"Well, yes, technically, there is the right to appeal," she said, clearly annoyed.

"I'm sure it was just an oversight on your part," I said. "Please continue."

The Head turned to Caitlyn.

"Caitlyn," she said.

"Yes," Caitlyn answered in a small voice.

"I know this must be extremely difficult, but can you tell us what happened?"

"I think so," said Caitlyn, taking a deep breath. "I was in Mr. Spencer's office when he just—well, he just attacked me. He grabbed my shirt and tore it, and I screamed. Then Mr. Johns opened the door, and I ran out."

The trustees looked even more grave.

"Do you have the shirt?" the Head asked.

"Yes," she said, reaching into her bag.

"Ms. Van Huysen," I interrupted, "we have no idea if this shirt is the actual shirt."

"This is not a police station. This is a school. And she could hardly have given us the shirt at the time because she was wearing it," the Head said sharply.

"There are no rules about how to collect physical evidence in the handbook," I said. "But you already know that."

"I hardly imagined having to collect physical evidence," the Head said. "And I'm sure you—"

"But what's even more interesting," I continued, "are the legal ramifications of that oversight. In their absence, one could argue that state statutes concerning the collection of evidence apply, and under those statutes, the shirt is clearly inadmissible."

It was amazing what you could find on the Internet.

"But I saw the shirt!" Johns cried.

"You got a good look at it?" I asked.

"Unfortunately," Johns replied.

"So, you wouldn't mind telling us what was on the front of the shirt?"

"What was on the front," he said with a slight hiccup. "Well . . . I . . . That is to say . . . What I mean is . . . No."

I smiled blandly at the Head.

"At least let her show people the shirt," said Johns.

"You might as well ask to see a pair of my socks," I replied.

But Caitlyn was already pulling it from a bag by her side. She held it up. There was a huge rip. Given that the shirt only covered about half of her upper body before the rip, it looked like a torn washcloth. Everyone turned back to me with renewed loathing.

"Ms. Van Huysen, I'm sorry. John is right. We have no idea if that is even the original shirt," Kate said.

"Do you really think she would fake evidence like that?" Johns demanded.

The Head looked uncertainly at the shirt and turned again to Caitlyn.

"I'm sorry I had to put you through that," she said. "You can go now."

I coughed softly.

"What is it now?"

"We have a few questions for her."

"Haven't you put her through enough already?" Johns asked.

"According to the procedure, we have the right to question any witnesses. It's in section ten under the—"

"I know the procedure," the Head said wearily. "Please continue."
Johns gave me a nasty look, which lifted my spirits immensely.

I nodded to Kate—we had decided last night that it would be better if she asked the questions. I was no legal mastermind, but it didn't seem like a promising strategy to have Caitlyn badgered by the man who was accused of molesting her.

"Caitlyn, this is your second year with Mr. Spencer as your teacher?" Kate asked.

"Yes," she said.

"So, you must like him, or you wouldn't have taken another class from him," said Kate.

"I guess," Caitlyn said more hesitantly.

Brie and Johns exchanged worried glances.

"I really don't see how this is relevant," said Johns, "let's not put this girl through anything else."

"Procedure," I reminded Johns breezily.

"You of all people!" Johns snapped.

"Yes, me of all people," I continued. "I am the one on trial here after all. And I am going to have to insist that my rights in this proceeding are not infringed."

"I would hardly call *your* rights infringed," Johns said.

"According to the faculty handbook, they already have been. If you will look on page—"

"I know the rules," Johns said.

"Of course you do." I smiled at him. "So, you won't mind allowing Kate to continue?"

"No," he replied through gritted teeth.

Kate squeezed my leg under the table, and I felt a warm glow spread through my body.

"Caitlyn, did Mr. Spencer write you a recommendation letter for college?" Kate asked.

"Yes," she answered.

"Why did you choose Mr. Spencer to write it?"

"Um, I think . . . Well . . ." She paused, staring down at her clasped hands. "I guess I thought he admired my work and liked me as a student."

"And did you find his behavior inappropriate?"

"No," she said.

"So, he liked you. You liked him. And over the previous two years, nothing inappropriate happened between the two of you," Kate said.

"That's right."

"Caitlyn," said Kate, "do you think it is possible that what happened in the office was all a big misunderstanding?"

Caitlyn paused.

"Yes," she said hesitantly, "I guess that's possible."

"That's enough for now," Johns interrupted. "This poor girl doesn't know what she is saying. We're going to take a break."

He shoved Caitlyn and her father out of the room as if they were trying to catch the last jitney to the Hamptons.

"Sylvester, this is quite irregular," the Head said. "I really don't think . . ."

"I hope you're happy," Johns said on his way out the door, "twisting the words of a young girl."

Kate and I looked at each other with resignation. I doubted we would ever get Caitlyn to admit as much again.

"This interruption," said Kate, "I have a bad feeling about it."

The Head walked over to us.

"John," she said in a low voice, "now would be the time to tell me anything that you have left out before."

Did she actually expect me to trust her? Now? Had she had a change of heart? Or was she just trying to get me to say something she could use against me? I thought of the many things that I could tell her, almost none of which would be to my credit. I looked at Kate, who seemed equally confused about what to do.

"I guess there are certain things . . ."

I stopped when I saw Caitlyn and the others file back into the room. Brie stared at the Head intently until she returned to her seat at the other end of the table.

"Caitlyn has some thing she would like to clarify," said Johns.

"All right," the Head said.

Caitlyn looked at her father, and he gave her a reassuring nod.

"Although Mr. Spencer never touched me before, he gave me a lot of strange looks."

"Strange in what way?" the Head asked.

"Like, sexual," she replied.

I wanted to stand up and denounce her. Caitlyn had made a pass at *me*—although it was difficult to imagine how I could work that into my defense without making myself look even more loathsome, especially after Caitlyn had transformed herself to look like Julie Andrews in *The Sound of Music.*

But before my indignation could work up a full head of steam, my conscience reminded me of all those times she had displayed her body like a piece of ripe fruit. Sure, I had tried not to look, staring at the Freud poster like some deranged idiot. But I couldn't help catching the odd glimpse. The tank top that stopped three inches above her belly button. The low-rider jeans that she wore without underwear. And the parade of thongs, as if she had a second job as a lingerie model. I wanted to crawl under the table before everyone saw the thoughts scrolling across my forehead.

"He looked at you in a sexual way?" Kate asked.

"I think it might have been sexual," said Caitlyn a little uncertainly.

"Anything else?" Johns asked quickly.

"Well, I think his classroom was a . . ." She paused as if she was trying to think of the right word. ". . . hostile environment for me as a woman."

"Caitlyn, are you sure?" the Head asked. She stared at Johns. "Your answer sounds . . . rehearsed."

Maybe the Head really did believe me. I felt a flicker of hope or, at least, a slight lifting of my despair.

"I . . . I don't know."

"This is very different from what you were saying a few moments ago," the Head said. "You realize that you hold a man's career in your hands. And if you think you may have been mistaken, there is no shame in admitting that."

Caitlyn looked down again at her hands.

"Well, maybe, um, maybe—"

"He even talks about sex in the classroom!" Johns shouted.

The Head gave me a stunned look.

"Is that true?"

"Of course not!"

"What about yesterday?" Johns sneered.

"Something happened yesterday," the Head asked in disbelief.

"One of my students asked a question about why Austen didn't write more about sex."

"You have turned a writer like Austen into a springboard for sexual inquiry?"

"Of course not! If anyone did, it was Caitlyn. She wrote a whole paper about Emma having sex."

The Head turned to her.

"Is that true?"

Caitlyn nodded.

"What did Mr. Spencer do?"

"He told me it was inappropriate and made me rewrite the paper."

I smiled the smile of the just until the Head gave me a dark look.

"Don't you think you should have reported this to one of the deans?"

"It was hard enough just talking to Caitlyn about it."

"So, you spoke to her about explicit sexual material? Does that seem like appropriate behavior?"

"I spoke to her about her paper!"

"Nonetheless, you seem to have created a highly sexualized atmosphere."

"That's preposterous," I said.

"Ms. Van Huysen, I really don't think we should subject this poor girl to any more of this," Johns said.

"But we have more questions," said Kate.

"Constance," Brie said firmly. "This has been a very trying time for my daughter. Very trying."

The Head's eyes flickered uncertainly between Brie and me.

"Yes," she said. "Of course. Well, then, it's time for us to make a decision."

I'd lost her. In the end, the choice between me and someone like Brie was really no choice at all.

"We have some other students who will vouch for John's character. I would like to bring them in," Kate said.

"I don't think that's relevant," the Head said.

"I think it is. It shows what other students—"

"I'm not interested in what happened with other students at the moment. I'm only concerned with what happened to Caitlyn," the Head said.

"But this is not the procedure," I said, although my complaint felt about as effective as asking Caligula to play nice right before he planned to feed you to the lions.

"I do not want to have to ask you to leave the room again."

Kate and I reluctantly stood up. Ron was waiting for us outside with a number of students, including Marcus and Laura. I gave them a halfhearted wave.

"When do the students testify?" Ron asked.

"They don't. The Head isn't going to let us bring them in," Kate said. "You might as well tell them all to go home."

"But they are pretty gung ho," said Ron.

Marcus was hopping from foot to foot.

"I'm sorry," Kate said.

223

Ron walked over to the group and spoke to them quietly. I could hear a few of them protesting. When he returned, his mustache seemed to be flying at half-mast.

"How did it go?" Ron asked.

"Kate was amazing," I said, trying to be upbeat. "I couldn't believe her in there. She practically got Caitlyn to admit that she was lying."

"That's great! Maybe we don't even need student testimony. I'm sure—"

He stopped when he saw our grim expressions.

"John never had a chance. This was decided before we entered the room."

"So, John appeals the decision," said Ron.

"It won't help. We'll be making the same case to the same people. We don't even have any proof that Caitlyn wavered. Did you see a court reporter in there? The next time this happens she is going to be so well rehearsed that we will never get that information out of her," said Kate, her optimism finally defeated. "We can drag this process out, but it's over."

The Head's secretary approached us.

"They're ready for you back in the conference room," she said.

Ron tried to look encouraging, but his general droopiness told a different story. They say that hanging juries always return verdicts the fastest, and we were clearly dealing with a hanging jury. As we entered the room, I saw that Johns had slithered back to his perch. He was trying to conceal a smile.

"We've discussed the case," the Head said after we sat down, "and we've decided that the preponderance of evidence is against you. Therefore, we have decided that you should be terminated, effective immediately."

She paused.

"You do have the right of appeal," she said, "but I would strongly urge you not to take that course. It is unlikely to change the outcome, and dragging this on will be bad for everyone involved, including yourself."

Kate looked at me sadly. The fight was over, and she knew it. I knew it, too. Then I saw Johns sneer at me. Before I knew what I was doing, I stood up and shouted out lines that O'Brien was always rattling off.

"Do not go gentle into that good night. Rage, rage against the dying of the light!" I yelled. I stopped abruptly. That was as far as O'Brien ever got.

"What are you saying?" The Head looked bewildered.

"I'm saying that I don't accept the verdict of this mock trial you conducted, and I am going to appeal," I said. "And if I lose that appeal, I'm going to take this case to court. I don't care if we drag this through the legal system for fifteen years. I'm an innocent man, and I am going to proclaim my innocence everywhere that I can for as long as I can to as many people as I can. And there's not a thing you can do about it!"

I stormed out of the room, unfortunately leaving Kate behind to collect our things under the evil glances of the Head, Johns, and the board members. She rushed out clutching everything to her bosom, which at that moment could only be described as heaving, a most intoxicating sight, especially given my emotional state.

"You were great. That was tremendous," she said breathily.

Before I knew what I was doing, I grabbed her and kissed her on the lips. She pulled away.

"What was that for?"

"That was my, I mean, our, uh . . . It was . . . a victory kiss."

I smiled weakly as Ron rushed up to us.

"What victory?" he asked hopefully.

"Symbolic," I said.

I felt triumphant—that is, until I returned to my office and sat alone for a few minutes to consider my prospects. I had insulted the disciplinary committee, the same people who would hear my appeal.

The only evidence I had would incriminate me as well. My sworn enemy was in charge of my department and was dating Amy. And I was about to be evicted from my apartment. Yes, all in all, things were clearly beginning to go my way.

AS I LAY DYING

I woke up the next day feeling as if my head was being squeezed between two hardback editions of the complete Shakespeare. Although
our emergency strategy session produced almost nothing in the way
of strategy, we did consume a fair amount of alcohol, and we de-
nounced "the man" and all he stood for in no uncertain terms. I
stood in front of the bathroom sink and ineffectually tried various re-
suscitative maneuvers.

I thought about calling in sick, but I realized that would only make
me look worse than I already did. I knew there was only one thing
left to do. I took the check from Brie and stuffed it in my bag.

I reached my office without seeing anyone—I had discovered an
alternate route that involved a dignified entry through a service door
and then a hard sprint down a basement corridor. But Günter was
waiting for me at my door.

"Günter, this is not the best time," I said.

"I've got my paper," he said, shoving it into my hand.

"That's great. I'll let you know . . ."

"Can I talk to you? It will only take a minute."

"All right."

We sat down I waited for Günter to begin, but he simply stared at
the floor.

"Günter?"

"My paper is about legal injustice in Dickens," he said without looking up.

He stopped and went back to studying the carpet.

"You see, things don't always work out the way that they should. Trials, I mean," he said.

You have no idea, I thought.

"But you can't just blame the individual. It's the system, you see. All these pressures," he said, shooting me a desperate look. "Don't you see?"

"Sure, Günter," I said soothingly, "sure."

He stood up abruptly and rushed out the door. I had no idea what was the matter with him, but I had my own problems to worry about. I set up an appointment with the Head and suffered through an endless day at school waiting for my meeting. The Austen class was unbearable. Everyone kept glancing at Caitlyn's empty seat, and a heavy pall hung over the room. I kept waiting for Banquo's ghost to appear and finger me as the guilty culprit.

Other than my classes, I avoided human contact almost entirely. By drinking very little water, I had cut down my bathroom visits to one per day. I had also given up going to the lunch room and was subsisting on soda and candy bars. At the end of the day, Kate hurried in.

"Listen," she said with excitement, "I've been doing some online research about sexual harassment, and I think we have a very good chance, if we end up going to court. There are a lot of different legal points in our favor."

"That's great," I said without enthusiasm.

"Don't you want to talk about this?"

"Maybe later."

She looked at me closely.

"What's the matter? Has Johns been harassing you again?"

"No."

"Students acting up?"

"No."

"So, what's wrong?"

I realized that the person I most dreaded telling all this to was Kate. It was almost worse than losing my job.

"I'd rather not say."

My phone rang.

"The Head is ready to see you," the Head's secretary said.

"I've got to go," I said to Kate. "I'm meeting with the Head."

"John, you're not going to resign, are you? I really think we can beat this. Don't give up now. What about not going gentle into that good night?"

"I'm not resigning," I said. "I have some . . . evidence."

"That's great news! What is it?"

I studied my fingernails with great interest.

"What's the matter?"

"Well . . ." I paused for a long moment. "It doesn't show me in the best light. Can we just leave it at that?"

"No, we can't just leave it at that. You know that you can tell me anything. It's not as if you haven't shared embarrassing details with me before."

I turned away from her. I couldn't bear the thought of her giving me a disappointed look.

"Brie tried to bribe me. He gave me a check for one hundred thousand dollars. He wanted me to sweep the plagiarism thing under the rug."

"But you didn't take it, right? That's why all of this happened," she said with excitement. "This is great news. This changes everything. The first thing that we need to do—"

"But I almost took it! I took the check home with me."

"But you didn't take it in the end," said Kate, although I was sure that, beneath her reassuring words, she was thinking something else.

"*Please,*" I said. "The way I handled the whole thing . . ."

"You're being too hard on yourself."

"No, that has been the problem all along. I haven't been hard enough on myself."

"But, John . . ."

I sighed and began my long trudge down the hallway to the Head's office.

"I hope you are here to tender your resignation," the Head said when I entered. "I really don't see what else we have to talk about."

"I have some additional evidence," I said.

"So do I," she said.

I looked at her in confusion.

"One of your students has come forward to confirm much of what Caitlyn has said. His name is Günter," she continued.

Et tu, Brute, I wanted to shout, but all I could manage to do was gulp for air, which suddenly seemed in short supply.

"So, what is this so-called evidence you are bringing me?"

"Uh, yes . . . Yes . . . Evidence . . ." I stammered.

She waited.

"A check. Brie tried to bribe me so I would drop the plagiarism case."

"Let me see it," she said.

I handed it to her.

"I already know about this," she said. "Frankly, I'm surprised that you would voluntarily bring this up."

Not quite the sun-breaking-through-the-clouds scenario that I had been hoping for.

"Mr. Brie told me about it when he called about the unfortunate incident in your office," she continued.

"Why would he tell you about it?"

"When a teacher tries to blackmail a student—"

"Blackmail!"

"Yes, apparently you threatened to cause a scandal that would ruin Caitlyn's chances of going to a good college."

"You can't honestly believe that."

"I'm afraid I do believe it. I have not brought it up before this because Brie asked me to keep it confidential."

"Oh please. Why would he do that, if not to protect himself?"

"He was protecting himself. He wanted to avoid the scandal for himself and the possible repercussions for his company of allowing himself to be blackmailed over something like this. He was quite broken up about it."

"So it's his word against mine."

"Actually, Mr. Brie's story has been confirmed by Mr. Snopes."

"What?"

The Head punched a button on her intercom.

"Will you please tell Mr. Snopes to come see me immediately?" She gave me a smile cold enough to keep fish fresh. "I hope this will make you change your mind about your resignation. Frankly, I think we are being generous by not pressing criminal charges."

I had a vision of myself as the girlfriend of an inmate named Mo with a tattoo of the Confederate flag on his forehead. Suddenly, losing my job seemed like the least of my problems. There was a knock on the door, and Snopes entered. He sat down beside me.

"Mr. Snopes," the Head said, "I think you know why you are here."

"Yes, I'm afraid I do."

He turned to me.

"John, I'm sorry that I had to do this, but when you approached me about blackmailing Brie, I had to say something. I know you were a little vague about the details, but your intentions were clear."

"I never said anything like that to you," I said through gritted teeth. I longed to reach out and throttle him on the spot.

"I wish you hadn't," said Snopes, "really I do."

"Thank you, Mr. Snopes," said the Head. "You can go."

"Before I go, I just to have say that I am saddened. Yes, saddened. Our children undergo so much stress in applying to colleges. And for someone to manipulate the system, well, I'm appalled. Appalled. I'm sorry, John, but you brought this on yourself," Snopes said.

"He's lying," I said after he left.

"John, I'm tired of your constant evasions. This meeting is over. I would suggest that you tender your resignation before your appeal tomorrow. If this comes out, it could be very bad for you, very bad."

She turned around and dropped the check into a paper shredder.

"What are you doing?" I cried.

"That could only cause trouble to innocent people. I'm not going to let you run some smear campaign against the Brie family."

My own stupidity staggered me. Would it have killed me to make a xerox of the check? What was I, the Pink Panther of crime?

"Don't you think I'm smart enough to make a copy of that check?" I spluttered.

Yes, brazen it out! Quite plucky of me actually, considering the circumstances. She would never think I was that dumb.

"Yes, well, I assumed you would do something like that, but let me give you a piece of advice. If you don't want to spend several hundred thousand dollars for legal expenses, you will make sure that no copies of that check ever see the light of day."

At least that is one piece of advice I won't have any trouble following, I thought. I limped back to my office and cheered myself with the reflection that since the false charge of blackmail could now be added to the false charge of sexual harassment, I seemed to be getting off relatively lightly.

There was a knock on the door, and Kate entered.

"How did it go?"

"They've added blackmail to my crimes."

"Blackmail!"

I explained to her my rapidly declining fortunes.

"What are you going to do?"

"Resign tomorrow."

She gave me a sad look.

"We can still fight this, you know," she said.

We sat in silence for a few moments.

232

"It's not worth it. Besides, I'm hardly blameless in all of this," I said.

"Don't say that," she said. "You're still one of the good guys."

If only, I thought.

"What happened to the teacher who talked me through my bad days in that first year by reminding me of all the good we are capable of doing?"

"Yeah, well . . ."

"I really liked that guy. I still do."

I smiled sadly.

"Me too. But I'm afraid it's too late for that," I said.

I was completely exhausted, and I wanted to be alone. I stood up and walked to the door.

"Thanks for all of your help."

We looked at each other, not knowing what to say. When I walked out the door, she was still sitting there. It was raining as I walked to the subway. For the second time in days, I fell into the pathetic fallacy. In my defense, I was really depressed.

METAMORPHOSIS

I unplugged my phone and disconnected my buzzer when I got home. I spent most of the night writing my resignation letter—or perhaps it would be more accurate to say letters. My first draft was five single-spaced pages. It included a number of quotations from poetry about lost innocence and a lament about the corrupting influence of money at private schools. It ended with a long, rambling account of how I became a teacher. My second draft cut back on the poetry, lamented the change in today's students, and ended with a long, rambling account of my time at Academy X. My third draft eliminated the poetry entirely but added a Vince Lombardi quotation, lamented the importance of college admissions, and ended with a long, rambling account of what this experience had taught me. My fourth draft inserted a Mother Teresa quotation in place of the Lombardi, lamented my own shortcomings as a teacher, and ended with an apology. My fifth draft cut the Mother Teresa quotation. My sixth draft cut the lament for my teaching. My seventh draft cut the apology. And my final draft read simply, "I hereby tender my resignation, effective immediately." I consoled myself with the thought that I wouldn't have to grade any final exams.

The next morning, I called in sick but told the office that I would come in for the hearing at the end of the day. If I was going to resign, I didn't see any point in putting myself through one more day of the proverbial slings and arrows. I watched Jerry Springer and Court TV. And I have to say that hearing about girlfriends who slept with their boyfriends' fathers and the boyfriends who beat them up put my own problems in perspective. On the subway ride to school, I stared listlessly out the windows at the walls of the dark tunnel.

I tried to work up some self-righteous indignation as I walked the last couple of blocks to school, but I couldn't manage anything more strenuous than quiet despair. I went to my office to drop off my things and found a piece of paper under my door. I picked it up, expecting some sort of death threat, but it was covered with gibberish.

Bigcheese72: It was LOL
Manhattangrrrl: Xlnt—r u clear?
Bigcheese72: ;)

It went on like that for a page. I had no idea what it meant and no time to decipher it, so I left it on the desk.

Most of the board members were already in the conference room looking bloody-minded when I crumpled into my seat. They stopped talking, and we sat in an uncomfortable silence as we waited for everyone else to arrive. Kate was supposed to be there, but I could hardly blame her for steering clear of me. Finally, the Head walked in, flanked by Johns and Snopes. Caitlyn, her father, and her father's two lawyers walked in behind her.

"Let's begin," the Head said. "As you all know, this meeting has been convened to consider John Spencer's appeal to our original decision to terminate him. Before we begin, is there anything you would like to say, John?"

I stood up.

"Yes, there is," I said. Johns stared at me with glittering eyes. "I've reconsidered my position."

I reached down for my resignation letter.

The door to the conference room flew open, and Kate burst in.

235

"Stop!"

"This is grossly inappropriate," said the Head.

"Kate, it's all right, really," I said. "This is for the best."

"I have new evidence," she said, flourishing a piece of paper that she pulled out of her purse.

"I don't think any of us are interested in more suspect tactics to drag this matter out," said Johns.

"If I could just have a few moments," Kate said, "I think I can prove to everyone's satisfaction that John is innocent."

The Head looked at Kate and realized that she was going to be as firm on this issue as the cafeteria's bread pudding.

"All right," the Head said grudgingly.

"First, I need to ask Caitlyn a couple of questions," she said. Caitlyn looked at her father, who shrugged.

"Caitlyn, do you use AOL's instant message service?"

"Of course," she said.

"What's your screen name?"

Caitlyn blushed.

"Big cheese 72."

A slight tingle ran down my spine.

"Thank you," said Kate, "I just wanted to confirm that."

She paused and picked up the piece of paper again.

"I have an instant messenger exchange between Big cheese 72 and another classmate discussing this case. Most of it is written using slang, so if you will allow me to translate the exchange—"

"No!" Caitlyn burst out. Everyone turned to look at her. She leaned over to her father and whispered something. He grimaced.

"Would you mind giving me a few moments to talk to Kate and John?" Brie asked the Head.

"It is highly irregular to carry on private conversations in matters such as these. I think—"

"Constance," Brie interrupted, looking at her sternly.

The Head nodded, and Brie left the room. Kate grabbed her purse, and we followed him out.

"You're brilliant," I whispered.

"Is there some place private we can talk?" Brie asked.

"Let's go to my office," I said.

We walked in silence. The room was so small that the three of us were nearly touching knees by the time we were all seated. Brie picked some lint off of his pants and gave us a bland smile.

"I think there has been a misunderstanding," he said.

"That's putting it mildly," said Kate. "I think I would call it a miscarriage of justice. A criminal conspiracy even."

Brie laughed.

"Criminal? I have a fair amount of legal experience, so I wouldn't start throwing around words you don't understand."

"What would you call it then?"

"Let's call this a negotiation," he said. "We can do certain things for one another. There's no reason that this can't have a happy outcome."

Kate gave him a dubious look.

"Of course Caitlyn will drop all of the charges," he said.

"That goes without saying," Kate said. "The question now is what charges John would like to bring against you?"

"Charges." He laughed again. "Do you know how much it would cost you even to try to bring a case like this to court? I'll bury you in legal bills before you ever set foot in the courthouse."

He smiled.

"But none of us want something like that. I prefer to focus on the positive. I can do a lot of things—for both of you."

"I know," she responded in a different tone. I gave her a confused look. "That's what I want to talk to you about."

"But, Kate . . ." I protested. She placed her hand on my knee and looked at me calmly.

"John," she said, "please trust me on this."

237

She had just single-handedly stayed my execution, so I shut up.

"Before we get to that, I want to know everything," she said.

"Is that really necessary?" Brie asked. "You know enough already. And I find that in these matters the less each party knows, the better."

"After seeing how you double-crossed John, I want as much protection as possible. If you have a problem with that, I'm happy to return to the hearing and read the rest of this," she said, waving the piece of paper.

Brie looked at her silently for a moment.

"All right," he sighed, "if you really think that will help. What do you want to know?"

"I want to know who else was a part of this."

"Johns organized most of it. He was planted outside your door in case anything went wrong. And he was the one who brought Snopes in."

I was burning to ask him what their payoff had been.

"Our own little deal is going to cost you," she said.

"That won't be a problem."

"Was the Head involved?"

"Constance?" He smiled. "No. She prefers not to know about these sorts of things. Don't ask, don't tell."

"All right, go back to the hearing. We'll be there in a couple of minutes. I need to work out a story with John."

"I would like to hear what you are going to say."

"You will soon enough." She smiled. "We still have a lot to negotiate."

He gave her an appraising look.

"All right."

"Kate, we can't do this," I protested after he left.

"Why not?"

"Because, well, first, look what happened to me," I said.

"That's not going to happen again."

"Okay, maybe not, but it's wrong! We don't want his money. We don't want to be one of those people."

At one time, I almost thought I did, but not anymore.

"It's just a little money," she said, "it's not going to change us."

"You're wrong," I said, "It does change you. You don't know what you're throwing away. You have to listen to me. You'll regret this the rest of your life."

She smiled.

"I know. I just wanted to make sure that you felt the same way."

I stared at her, dumbfounded.

"This was a test?"

"Yes," she said, "and you passed with flying colors."

"So, no deal with Brie?"

"No deal."

"What are we going to do?"

"We're going to go down there and tell the truth."

"You did all of this just to test me?" I asked again stupidly.

"Not just for that," she said laughing. "I wanted to find out who was involved."

"But he is never going to admit that," I said.

"He already did." She pulled a miniature tape recorder out of her purse. "I've got it all on tape. After our last hearing, I thought it would be a good idea to make sure that we recorded everything that happened."

I looked at her in amazement.

"Are there any other secret talents that you've been hiding from me?"

She laughed.

"Maybe someday you'll get a chance to find out." She stood up. "Come on. Let's go finish this."

We returned to the conference room—I had to stifle the urge to skip down the hallway. Kate grabbed my hand under the table and gave it a squeeze.

"Well," the Head said, looking more confused than ever, "Caitlyn has decided to drop her case against you, John, so all disciplinary proceedings are dismissed. I apologize for putting you through all of this. And I apologize to the board for taking up their time. I want to thank everyone for maintaining their professionalism during a difficult episode."

Everyone began to stand up. Brie was shaking Johns's hand, and Snopes put his arm around Caitlyn.

"Actually, there is still some unfinished business," said Kate.

The Head gave Kate a weary look.

"We've ended the sexual harassment case. That was the only business before the committee," the Head said.

"But in ending that case, some very serious issues have been raised, and I have to insist that we discuss them," said Kate firmly.

The Head reluctantly sat down. Brie gave us an angry look. Johns had a panicked expression on his face, and Snopes had tightened his grip on Caitlyn like a drowning man at sea.

"All right," said the Head, "what other matters would you like to address?"

"First, I think we need to discuss disciplinary proceedings against Caitlyn, who clearly manufactured this case. And that is on top of her plagiarism," Kate said.

"But I thought—" exploded Brie.

"You thought what?" Kate asked.

Brie muttered something to his lawyer.

"There is still no evidence of plagiarism," the Head said.

"Actually, a copy of Caitlyn's paper has been found," said Kate.

"We will, of course, look into that at a later date," said the Head. She started to get up again.

"And there's more," Kate said.

The Head sighed.

"We also have evidence that Johns and Snopes were part of this conspiracy," Kate said.

The Head stared intently at the two men. Johns staggered into a chair.

"That is a very serious charge," she said. "Do you have evidence?"

"Yes."

"After I've had a chance to review it, we will decide what action to take," she said.

She looked at Kate with grudging respect.

"Is that all?"

Kate nodded.

"This meeting is adjourned. And let me be the first to say, welcome back, John," she said with all the warmth of a February day in North Dakota.

Kate and I rushed back to my office. I didn't know what to say. I was on the verge of giving her my long-promised victory kiss when Brie opened the door.

"I thought we had a deal," he said angrily.

I stepped between Kate and Brie.

"No deal, I'm afraid, although we do have the entire conversation on tape," I said.

Brie turned pale.

"If you would like, we can tape this conversation as well," I added.

"I can pay you," he said.

"Oh, I know," I said. "Of course, I'll probably be able to get more in an actual court case against you, and the money would be so much sweeter."

"John, really, think about—"

"Look, Rob—it's all right if I call you that, isn't it?—we're busy here. Why don't you go have José fix you a mojito? I'm sure you'll feel much better."

I closed the door in his face and turned to look at Kate.

"Where did you learn to do all of that?" I asked. "Did you drop out of law school to become an artist?"

She laughed.

241

"It's good to see that years of watching *Law & Order* finally paid off," she said.

"I still have no idea how you pulled this off."

"It wasn't very hard. I was late coming to meet you this morning and found that piece of paper sitting on your desk."

"How did you know what that thing said?"

"*Please,*" she said, "how out of it are you?"

"What about Caitlyn's paper?"

"That's why I was late. I ran into Andrews, and we began arguing. I said a few choice things about Caitlyn, and while defending her, Andrews mentioned that she had kept a copy of the paper because she liked it so much."

I looked at her in wonder and realized that my victory kiss was long overdue. I stepped toward her and took her hand, rough and callused from working in the studio just as it was all those years ago. I paused for a moment, overwhelmed by the feeling that, for the first time in a long time, I was happy. It was like coming home after a long time away. I pulled her toward me, but there was another knock on the door.

"Brie," I yelled, "leave us alone!"

The door opened to reveal Marcus and, behind him, a sheepish-looking Günter.

"Marcus," I said, dropping Kate's hand. "What are you doing here?"

I decided to ignore Günter in the hope that he would slink away.

"We heard the good news, Mr. Spencer," he said, "and we just wanted to stop by to say how glad we are that everything worked out."

We, I thought indignantly.

"Thank you, Marcus. You stood by me when the entire school turned against me," I said, giving Günter a baleful glance.

"We heard that the case turned on a new piece of evidence," he said with a little smile.

"Yes, I found—"

I stopped and looked at him closely.

"Marcus?"

He seemed slightly embarrassed.

"I had better not say any more," he said, "I might have broken a few laws."

I put my arm around his shoulders.

"Marcus, I think this is the beginning of a beautiful friendship."

"It wasn't just me," he said. "I'm not the one who knew the nicknames for Caitlyn's IM buddies."

He nodded in Günter's direction.

"Günter?" I said in disbelief.

"I know," Günter said, looking miserable. "I'm sorry. I realized that I would rather be a character out of *Pickwick Papers* than Pip out of *Great Expectations*."

I smiled. Leave it to Günter to make the right decision using characters from Dickens. And I had assumed that we had all been playing roles in an Austen novel.

"I think they deserve a reward, don't you?" Kate said. "Let's all go out for dinner. John's treat."

Ron stuck his head in the door.

"John's treat," he said, "this is a historic occasion."

Dinner for everyone? It almost made me wish I'd kept the hundred thousand.

ALL'S WELL THAT ENDS WELL

In the end, Academy X took the scandal in stride and continued on, much as before. The school was too successful at getting students into Ivy League colleges for parents to care much about what had happened.

Caitlyn was suspended for a week, which she spent on her father's yacht in Barbados. She ended up going to the University of Pennsylvania. The admissions office was apparently willing to see what she had done as a youthful indiscretion, particularly after her father made a substantial donation to help build the new student center. And I decided not to bring a case against Brie. My part in the affair was hardly spotless, and dreams of riches had already led me astray once before. Besides, he was only doing it to protect his daughter, and as I had learned long ago, parents rarely behaved rationally when the well-being of their child was at risk. In my own mind, I thought he deserved to get off on a plea of temporary insanity.

With the Button Turbridge Student Essay Prize in tow, Laura headed off to Wellesley in the fall. She loves it and, no longer overshadowed by girls like Caitlyn, has decided to run for class president. Marcus is happily ensconced at MIT and is dating a woman who enjoys both Dungeons & Dragons and Jane Austen, incredible as that sounds. Günter has already founded a new literary society at Harvard. He claims that the existing ones are too bourgeois for his taste. And he is dating a German woman who, he tells me, is disciplining him in the ways he always needed. I'm supposed to have lunch with all of them over the holidays.

Johns was fired and had to return all of the money he had received from Brie. Out of sympathy Brie gave him some sort of low-level editorial job at his publishing company. The last I heard, he was fact-checking celebrity cookbooks. Snopes was too important to the school to be fired, so the board chose to blame everything on Johns. Snopes also denied ever receiving anything from Brie, although he bought a summer house in the Hamptons the following year.

The Head was so impressed with Kate that she promoted her to the new position of Dean of Faculty. I am a little worried that the job is going to her head. At the very least, it has reinforced a tendency toward a somewhat high-handed manner. I wish I could tell you that things between us have changed. Instead, we seem to have fallen back into our familiar friendship, although I'm still looking for the right opportunity to show her how I feel—as you can imagine, the cafeteria hardly seems like the right romantic backdrop. And there is always the hope that Gay Dan will come out of the closet. For her birthday, he bought her tickets to a Barbra Streisand concert, so I'm optimistic that a full confession can't be far behind. My own hopes can weather the delay, particularly since it has led to a modern-day miracle—Ron has started dating one of Dan's colleagues. She even persuaded him to shave off his mustache.

As for me, life goes on pretty much as it did before. In the end, I didn't become chair, but I also didn't end up in jail as a pedophile, so all in all I came out better than I expected. Amy has gone back to giving me the cold shoulder, and I have momentary pangs when I see her—well, to be honest, I complain about her to Ron and Kate constantly. I'm now the adviser to the computer club. I thought it was the least I could do for Marcus. It's not the most glamorous position, but I do feel incredibly hip when I hang out with them. And I'm acting in the school play, a minor character in *The Crucible*. My mother is relieved that her son is not a pervert, although she insisted on signing me up for a dating service. My father is disappointed that I kept my job. He continues to call Ryan regularly to let him know I am still interested. I did get to keep my apartment. My eviction was unsurprisingly the work of yet another division of Brie's conglomerate. It took a couple of phone calls and some unseemly begging. But there is no dignity when it comes to New York real estate. I'm also enjoying teaching more than I have in a long time. It's funny how you don't appreciate something until you almost lose it. There is even some talk that I might make a good dean, but I try not to think too much about that. Best of all, I have recovered a part of myself that I had lost through the years. All along, I had been trying to teach Caitlyn to be more like Emma. But it turned out that I was the one who had something to learn.

I hope that some day I will persuade a close and trusted friend to join me in a happy union and so end my own story much as Austen ended *Emma*. Even without that, though, only a few small words need to be changed to make the two endings match and allow me to write that the wishes, the hopes, the confidence, the predictions of the small band of true friends were fully answered in the perfect happiness of the outcome.

ACKNOWLEDGMENTS

I would like to thank Judith Riven, my agent, who guided me through every step in the process, and Gillian Blake, my editor, whose deft touch improved the book in countless ways. I am grateful to my family for all of their support. Many thanks also to Peter Sheehy, Barry Bienstock, and Christina Lowris for their help and to Heesun Choi for too many things to list. And a special thanks to all of my friends at the lunch table.

A NOTE ON THE AUTHOR

The author currently teaches at a private high school in New York City. This is his first novel.